We've still got time, Mike thoug~~~
effective rifle range for another few minutes—as~~~ ~
they really did intend to open fire rather than just playing tit
for tat. Then the boats were visible—hopping around in the
choppy seas.

It also soon became clear that his assumptions were all
wrong. Ibrihim Hassan had changed the rules again.

Mike realized his error the instant six flashes of light
flared partway up the side of Ras Xaafuun and then continued to burn as they arced out toward the other boat. For a
split second he watched in horror, then opened his mouth to
order evasive action.

"This is Trident One..Incoming!" reported Alex before
Mike could say a thing.

"Roger, Trident One." There was a brief pause while the
entire team concluded from the way the missile tracks
seemed to be curving toward Alex's boat that they were heat-
seekers.

An eventuality for which they were totally unprepared. . . .

Titles by Michael Howe

TRIDENT FORCE
SEA HAWK
THREAT LEVEL

THREAT LEVEL

MICHAEL HOWE

BERKLEY BOOKS, NEW YORK

THE BERKLEY PUBLISHING GROUP
Published by the Penguin Group
Penguin Group (USA) Inc.
375 Hudson Street, New York, New York 10014, USA
Penguin Group (Canada), 90 Eglinton Avenue East, Suite 700, Toronto, Ontario M4P 2Y3, Canada
(a division of Pearson Penguin Canada Inc.)
Penguin Books Ltd., 80 Strand, London WC2R 0RL, England
Penguin Group Ireland, 25 St. Stephen's Green, Dublin 2, Ireland (a division of Penguin Books Ltd.)
Penguin Group (Australia), 250 Camberwell Road, Camberwell, Victoria 3124, Australia
(a division of Pearson Australia Group Pty. Ltd.)
Penguin Books India Pvt. Ltd., 11 Community Centre, Panchsheel Park, New Delhi—110 017, India
Penguin Group (NZ), 67 Apollo Drive, Rosedale, North Shore 0632, New Zealand
(a division of Pearson New Zealand Ltd.)
Penguin Books (South Africa) (Pty.) Ltd., 24 Sturdee Avenue, Rosebank, Johannesburg 2196,
South Africa

Penguin Books Ltd., Registered Offices: 80 Strand, London WC2R 0RL, England

This is a work of fiction. Names, characters, places, and incidents either are the product of the author's imagination or are used fictitiously, and any resemblance to actual persons, living or dead, business establishments, events, or locales is entirely coincidental. The publisher does not have any control over and does not assume any responsibility for author or third-party websites or their content.

THREAT LEVEL

A Berkley Book / published by arrangement with the author

PRINTING HISTORY
Berkley edition / July 2010

Copyright © 2010 by Penguin Group (USA) Inc.
Cover illustration by Craig White.
Cover design by Judith Lagerman.
Interior text design by Laura K. Corless.

ISBN: 978-0-425-23542-3

BERKLEY®
Berkley Books are published by The Berkley Publishing Group,
a division of Penguin Group (USA) Inc.,
375 Hudson Street, New York, New York 10014.
BERKLEY® is a registered trademark of Penguin Group (USA) Inc.
The "B" design is a trademark of Penguin Group (USA) Inc.

PRINTED IN THE UNITED STATES OF AMERICA

10 9 8 7 6 5 4 3 2 1

1

Early February 2009

With her high white sides and four rows of picture windows all sparkling and glinting in the intense sun, *Summer Skies* looked more like a large iceberg than a ship. She seemed totally out of place as she steamed south through the Red Sea with the brown, utterly barren Arabian coast still visible to port and the Suez Canal almost eight hundred miles astern. Although she might look like a cruise liner—and had once been one—*Summer Skies* was now a school ship. She sailed around the world once every eighteen months, stopping at culturally significant places and conducting college-level classes while at sea. Students could join for one semester or the entire year—with time off in December and July to fly home for a vacation. The room and board were, of course, considerable and the scholarships few.

Carol Rogers, blond, perky and almost eighteen, watched the distant coast with little interest as she leaned on a railing eighty feet above the water, a frown on her face. To her intense irritation, Eddy and Tom, her two teenaged companions, both seemed totally unaware of her presence. She glanced to her left. "Tommy . . ."

"Hm? Hey, Eddy, I was right, wasn't I? Those dudes in Arabia really do wear those hats and robes around on the streets. They don't just dress up in them when the TV cameras are around."

"There were a lot in normal clothes. Except for the women, but I didn't see many of them."

"Yeah. I'm talking about the others."

Damn him, she thought. The pyramids had been kind of interesting, but Jeddah had been an absolute nothing. Just another city filled with skyscrapers surrounded by hovels. As far as she could tell, the whole damn Middle East was nothing more than dirt, flies and beggars who wouldn't keep their faces out of yours.

She hadn't even wanted to come on this trip. She'd wanted to stay home, with her friends, her clothes, her little doggie Gladys, the cheerleading squad and her new BMW, but Dad had insisted—said she had to learn about the world around her.

She already knew as much about the world as she wished to know.

Carol might possess very little interest in the big, wide world around her, but she was very much a focused realist. She knew the only thing on the whole boat that did interest her at the moment was Tommy—smart, funny Tommy with the crazy smile—and it was on Tommy that she was totally focused. And last night he'd been totally, cosmically focused on her. For at least an hour, anyway. Today, he was back to cars, baseball and Frisbees, and swapping stupid jokes with his new best bud, Eddy. It was as if, for him, last night had never happened. Yet it had and she would never forget it. Now that it was over, done, she didn't know what to make of it. She was beginning to suspect, however, that she did know where she stood. Nowhere! It was history, and no more. Be real! Stuff happens. That was yesterday. This is today. We must move on.

Uncertain whether to laugh or cry, she rested her chin on her hands, which were resting on the warm, varnished wooden rail, and stared down glumly into the crystalline blue so far below. How, she asked herself, could the water be so pretty and the land so ugly?

On the bridge, Captain Gustav Johansson, *Summer Skies*'s master, stood silently, his hands clasped behind his back. Johansson was a short man of almost sixty. He had quick eyes and naturally dark hair and looked very trim, and much younger than he really was, in his summer uniform—blue trousers and a white shirt with four gold stripes on each shoulder.

Johansson wasn't looking at the sun-scarred, oil-soaked land baking to port. Nor was he admiring the clear blue water through which his ship was slicing. He was looking forward, over the bow and beyond, to the future. He was certain he was not going to enjoy the next few days.

* * *

The afternoon of the second day after leaving Jeddah, *Summer Skies* was approaching Bab el Mandeb, the narrow strait where the Red Sea joins the Gulf of Aden and the Indian Ocean beyond. The sky remained clear and the sun hot.

Gustav Johansson stood on the wing of his bridge and looked at the flotilla of ships converging on the strait. Tankers, containerships and more tankers, with an American destroyer cruising its beat, keeping the peace. But it wasn't the mass of ships all trying to fit through one narrow strait that bothered him. It was the Gulf of Aden that lay a few hours ahead. During the past two years pirates had attacked countless ships of all sizes, shapes and nationalities there. They'd either robbed or captured and ransomed a hundred of them.

Maybe it shouldn't surprise him, he thought. Piracy had been a well-established occupation in this part of the world for millennia. Indeed, if it weren't for the piracy practiced in the region, there would have been no reason for the merchants of Europe to struggle with the long, dangerous Silk Route across Central Asia to the mystifying and tantalizing Orient.

Still, in this day and age—in a time of instant communication and satellite surveillance—the situation was totally improbable. And yet, for various totally improbable reasons, it was all too real. Political reasons. Diplomatic reasons. Economic reasons. Reasons traceable to the most basic elements of human nature.

Down on C Deck, Carol, Tom and Eddy—their classes long over for the day—were laughing and splashing in one of the ship's pools as they debated whether to go to the casino or a movie that evening. If Carol continued to feel any dismay or confusion about the night before she didn't show it.

Two hours later, after the three teenagers had returned to their rooms to prepare for the night's pleasures, *Summer Skies* passed through Bab el Mandeb. Captain Johansson laid out a track that tended more or less down the center of the Gulf of Aden and ordered turns for twenty knots. He then looked around the bridge, at the two men attending to the control panels, at the mate of the watch and the two lookouts. All seemed awake and alert. He walked over to the aft bulkhead and called the head of the security group the owners had finally agreed to provide. "Ahern, this is the captain. I want two of your men armed and ready at all times. And the others ready to be on station in five minutes or less."

"You've got it, Skipper."

Johansson didn't like Ahern personally. And he disliked being addressed as "Skipper." He always felt uncomfortable among men who eagerly made it their business to kill other people. Men who seemed to live for the pleasure of inflicting death. He didn't like the idea of private armies, either. The difference between them and pirates was often difficult to distinguish. Finally, he didn't like men who worked at making the tattoos on their arms dance in an effort to impress little girl coeds.

But Gustav Johansson was even more of a realist than Carol Rogers. And he was a proud man too. He was not about to surrender his command to a few half-naked, seagoing muggers. Not when he commanded a ship the size of *Summer Skies*. If he wasn't going to surrender, then he was going to need armed men. Men like Ahern.

Crossing his fingers mentally Johansson lay down fully dressed in his sea cabin behind the bridge, to rest his far-from-young eyes. As he tried to doze off, lulled by the very slight vibration that a seaman can sense aboard any living ship, he thought about his passengers. He'd been forced to conclude, after two trips around the world, that most were nothing more than pampered princes and princesses. Many were just as irritating as their parents undoubtedly were. There were exceptions, of course. Every semester there were a few who stood out, who struck him as destined for great things. He had to hope so. He liked to think these expeditions served a purpose greater than just to provide an extended holiday for kids bored by the ease of twenty-first-century life.

As Captain Johansson dozed, the weather around his

ship began to change. The season of the Northeast Monsoon was coming to an end. In time the winds would lessen, as would the overcast and the rain. But on that particular night, the monsoon was not finished with its tricks.

* * *

Fifteen-year-old Ali Yusuf sat on the packed dirt floor of the one-room hovel he shared with six other scrawny, occasionally employed young fishermen and stared into the pot of muddy water boiling on the fire. Outside, a warm, thick night had settled over the northeast coast of Somalia.

The concrete block structure had once been a house—albeit a simple one—but one wall was now gone and half the roof had collapsed—all the legacy of a minor battle between clans many years ago. This monument to Somali politics was located in the port town of Basalilays, perched on the dry, rocky, almost featureless shore facing the Indian Ocean. Behind the town stretched hundreds of thousands of square miles of equally featureless, sand-covered gray brown limestone, its sterility leavened here and there by sparse, struggling communities of low, gray green vegetation.. About a hundred miles to the north, Cape Gwardafuy, the tip of the great triangle that is known as the Horn of Africa, jutted out between the Indian Ocean and the Gulf of Aden. To the south stretched another thousand miles of endless beaches. Barren beaches indistinguishable from those that stretched to the north.

Basalilays is a dusty, impoverished place that might seem, at first glance, to have little reason for continued existence. Except for its small harbor and the presence there of one of Somalia's powerful clan chiefs, Ibrihim Hassan. Ibrihim's family had always lived on the land side of the town, near the mosque—a tired, whitewashed structure that until recently was the most noticeable building for many miles. And the senior Hassan, the head of the family, had always been chief of the local clan, since time immemorial.

The port—the true source of what wealth Basalilays could call its own—is created by a quarter-mile-long, curving spit of sand and rock that encloses a shallow haven. Much of this seawall is natural—sand and stone placed there by the geologic forces that shape the world. In some places the wall has been reinforced over the centuries by crudely placed riprap. Thanks to this occasionally water-swept, reeflike defense against the fury of the Indian Ocean, Basalilays has survived the centuries as a home for fishermen and pirates. Survived without necessarily prospering.

Ali and his friends knew that someplace within that pot of muddy water were the bones and offal of a scrawny chicken, what remained after most of the meat had been stripped by someone significantly more prosperous than they.

"Did you talk with him?" asked Salem as he stirred the stew. Like the others, he was dressed in a dirty shirt and ragged, and equally grimy, trousers. This wardrobe, along with a second shirt and pair of pants, a knife, a tattered Koran and a small collection of lengths of line and other knickknacks, represented the total wealth of each of the young fishermen.

"Yes, I spoke with Ibrihim Hassan," replied Ali. "He asked me if I can shoot a rifle."

"What did you say?"

"Yes. Then he handed me a rifle and told me to prove it by hitting a jar he ordered placed on the top of his garden wall, about fifty feet away."

"And?"

"It was a big jar. I hit it with my second shot. I won-dered where the bullets went but then decided that was Allah's business, not mine." As he spoke Ali watched a pair of flies buzz around each other, performing a dance of sorts in the air.

"Where did you learn to shoot a gun?"

"My father showed me. He was a soldier for Hassan during the last civil war." Ali cringed inwardly as he spoke. His father was dead now. He'd died right before Ali's eyes, blown into almost unrecognizable body parts by a grenade during one of Somalia's frequent civil brawls.

"So what did he say?"

"He said he had many people who want to join in the business and he would think about it. He said he will send for me if he decides to use me."

Salem continued to stir the pot while he wondered if he should even bother to believe Ali. He damn well knew his roommate didn't always tell the truth. But then who in Somalia did? In Somalia you did and said what you had to do to survive. Talk of honor was a luxury of the wealthy. Obedience—or deceit—was the lot of the rank and file.

As he described his audience with the clan chief, Ali's thoughts drifted from the boiling chicken parts to the huge sums of money it was said some men made from piracy along the Somali coast. He knew that much of the money was taken back by the political and religious chieftains like Ibrihim Hassan—or the chieftain's "soldiers" if they felt strong enough that particular day. Still, it was said that many pirates, if they were clever, still managed to hang on to a fortune. And the proof was right around him, even in this miserable little town. Two pirates—who had once been impoverished fishermen—lived not far away. Each was now building a big new house and buying an automobile and throwing money around in all directions. And taking the prettiest girls for themselves, although it was said they were now spending most of their time at least a hundred miles from the nearest salt water, in Garowe, the capital of the semiautonomous Puntland region, where they were strutting around, being big men.

And their new houses were nothing compared to the one Suleiman Hassan—Ibrihim's eldest son and chief lieutenant—was building. And that couldn't compare with the magnificent new mansion Ibrihim himself was putting up right next to the mosque, totally overshadowing the tired old structure with its slightly tilted minaret.

"Inshallah," mumbled Salem as he looked into the pot, thinking that if Ali could do it maybe he could too. Except that he didn't even know who his father was, let alone whether he'd ever fought for Ibrihim. The others just nodded, more interested in the night's meal—and on keeping an eye on one another, especially Ali—than in future careers, no matter how glittering those careers might be.

They all crowded a little more closely to the fire. Perhaps because the temperature was beginning to drop, perhaps to better defend their interest in the pot's contents, perhaps as protection from the darkness closing in around them.

* * *

"I hear what sounds like an outboard, sir, running fast. Someplace to port," reported one of the lookouts to the mate of the watch. Although the stars remained clearly visible overhead, the monsoon had started blowing again and the Gulf of Aden had developed a very noticeable chop. Not enough of a sea to make any difference to a ship the size of *Summer Skies*, but enough of one to make handling a small boat both wet and challenging.

"Stop!" The voice that emerged from the bridge-to-bridge radio was accented but still understandable. "You are ordered to stop immediately. If not, we will open fire and kill all your passengers."

The mate ran to the port bridge wing and looked out into the windy night, a look of intense concentration on his face.

There! He thought he could see something. The slight glow of the phosphorescence generated by a turning propeller. A blob of enhanced darkness rising and falling a hundred yards away. He grabbed the phone and called Captain Johansson. Then, as the captain's standing orders directed, he called Ahern and told him to get his people armed and up on deck.

Four decks below, and fifty yards aft, Carol Rogers lay on a deck chair located on a small balcony along the ship's side. She was tired, dizzy from too much drink and supremely happy now that Tommy was lying on the chair next to her and Eddy was nowhere in sight—sound asleep in his cabin or maybe passed out in one of the ship's two bars.

"What's that!" said Tommy, suddenly sitting up, thereby dragging Carol out of her daze.

"Wha . . . ?"

"Dunno . . . Sounds like there's a boat out there." The boy dragged himself out of the deck chair and over to the rail. Not to be left out, Carol followed.

"There *is* something down there," remarked Tommy as he and Carol sagged over the rail, high above the dark sea. Almost immediately, the predawn dark around the two teens was ripped apart by a horrible, yellow red flash followed by a thunderous boom that made the whole ship shudder. A ball of super-hot gas blossomed, snapping the teens' heads back and throwing them against the bulkhead behind them. A dense, billowing cloud of acrid smoke then rolled out from the balcony and disappeared into the dark sky.

Stunned, the mate on the bridge paused in midstep. Should he immediately sound the general alarm and close the watertight doors? That would undoubtedly panic half the passengers. Before he could reach a decision, Captain Johansson was standing beside him.

"We're under attack, Captain. There's a boat of some sort off to port, and they've fired some sort of missile that hit the superstructure about amidships."

Johansson, now hatless, leaned out over the edge of the wing and looked aft. He could see what looked like the flickering of a fire well above the waterline. A flickering reinforced by an occasional thin tongue of flame that spurted out into the night.

"Come right ninety degrees, Mr. Perkins, and call for emergency speed."

"Yes, sir."

Johansson then raced over to the radar display. Which ships were in the area? Not many, as it turned out. "Are any of these warships?" he asked the mate.

"No, sir, but there's an Italian destroyer about eighty miles to the east, I think."

"Very well." He then studied the radar again and could detect nothing that resembled an attacking small boat. It—or they—must be lost among the waves, he thought. He then called the radio room and ordered them to transmit an SOS giving their position and reporting that they were under attack.

The phone buzzed. "This is the duty steward supervisor. There's been an explosion is cabin C 103. I have four men fighting the fire and the purser is on her way now."

"Thank you," said Johansson. He picked up the microphone of the public-address system and spoke into it: "Ladies and gentlemen, this is Captain Johansson. *Summer Skies* has been attacked by what we believe to be pirates in a small boat. There has been an explosion and fire on C Deck. We have called for assistance and are maneuvering to escape our attackers. As of this time I do not know if there have been any injuries. Please remain in your cabins until further notice. I should be able to tell you more within the hour."

"Bridge," barked the walkie-talkie, "this is Ahern. There's one boat off our starboard quarter and another off the port bow."

"Left full rudder, Mr. Perkins," snapped Johansson, wondering where the boat that had fired the missile was and hoping it was well astern by now.

"Ahern, have your people forward open fire on that boat near the bow. Do the same to the boat on our quarter—as long as you can. And don't let them get any grapnels over."

"You've got it, Skipper."

Even as the security chief acknowledged the order and the first cracks of automatic rifles could be heard faintly from fore and aft, *Summer Skies*'s bow turned to the left and her massive, overhanging stern skidded ponderously to the right, riding over and crushing the boat off the quarter, then forcing the wreckage down into the ship's sharp, spinning screws.

"Bridge," reported the radio room, "three ships including the Italian destroyer have acknowledged our SOS. The destroyer is headed our way."

"There's another boat out there, sir," reported the starboard lookout, "but I don't think it's trying to approach us."

"This is Ahern. Either we've sunk this boat forward or it's turned and run."

"Captain," said the mate a few minutes later, "I think you surprised the shit out of them."

"Let's hope so, Mr. Perkins, but we still have another three hours before that Italian ship can reach us." He turned and studied the radar a moment. He still couldn't see anything that looked like a small boat. Either they'd managed to ram or swamp them all or they were so small that they blended in with the breaking waves. How, he wondered, could they even operate this far offshore in these conditions? Shaking his head, he then drafted a follow-up message to the commander of the international antipiracy force operating in the area along with one to *Summer Skies*'s owners.

Twenty minutes later Johansson was standing outside the still-smoldering cabin looking at the mangled, charred bodies that had once been two teenagers. He gave himself forty-five seconds to wallow in the anger, disgust and sadness. He then returned to the single-minded performance of his duty and sent a second follow-up message.

* * *

"How's the weather up there in The District, Alan?" asked Alex Mahan as she looked into the teleconferencing screen at Alan Parker, the secretary of defense's liaison with SecResGru2, also known as the Trident Force.

"That's not even funny, Alex," snapped the deputy secretary of defense. "It's a goddamn mess. Snow and ice everywhere."

"Why don't you come on down and visit us here in Tampa," continued Alex. She'd already known about the meteorological mess in the northeast—and about Alan's aversion to anything that inconvenienced him—and enjoyed irritating Parker every now and then. "It's seasonably cool but there's not a cloud in the sky. It's no trick at all to get a sunburn today"

"Is your executive officer always this flippant, Mike?" snapped Parker to the tall, middle-aged naval officer sitting next to the willowy young woman.

"She's a little worse than usual today, Alan. I'm sure she'll control herself from now on," replied Captain Michael Chambers, U.S.N.

Chambers, who had started his career as a SEAL and then returned to the fleet, having decided he really did like boats—big and small—was the commanding officer of the Trident Force. The unit had been created several years before to handle especially tricky maritime situations, primarily involving terrorism but not always—situations in which imagination, cleverness and even a little tact and finesse were as important as brute force. Chambers reported directly to SECDEF, much to Parker's frequent annoyance. The deputy secretary tended to act as if he exercised some sort of operational control over the Tridents, but even he knew he didn't. His job was to forward SECDEF's personal orders and, on occasion, data from other sources.

Parker, sitting at his big, polished desk with the flags of the United States and the Department of Defense standing at attention behind him, glowered briefly, then cleared his throat. "It's time for you people to get to work, earn your pay. SECDEF has a project for you. One, quite frankly, that's filled with even more land mines than usual."

As he said it, a slight smile crossed Parker's face—as if he were anticipating Chambers and his gang screwing up in some utterly embarrassing way.

"We're ready, Alan," replied Mike, who was already sitting so straight that he couldn't sit up any straighter.

"A cruise ship—*Summer Skies*, filled with eight hundred American college students—was attacked a few hours ago in the Gulf of Aden by pirates, and the daughter of one of the President's most generous supporters was killed, along with another student."

"Did the ship escape?"

"Yes. It has an escort now and is headed back to Djibouti for repairs," explained Parker, referring to the modern, strategically and commercially important port in the small country of the same name located on the southern shore of the gulf just to the west of Somalia.

"I'm sorry to hear about the kids," said Mike, thinking they were probably about the same age as Kenny, his only son. Most were probably a little older, he decided after a moment.

"So's everybody. And it's not just the kids. The whole shipping industry's been in an uproar for some time about this piracy crap. They've taken something like a hundred ships this past year alone in the Gulf and in the Indian Ocean along the Somali coast and informed opinion has it that when the monsoons stop blowing, they'll start moving farther offshore into the Indian Ocean. Merchant ships carrying cargoes belonging to the United States government have been attacked, and insurance rates have gone through the roof. The President wants something done about it and so does SECDEF. He feels enough is enough."

"Isn't there already a multinational task force there working on it?"

"Of course, CTF 151. Every now and then we catch some of those damn Somalis in the act, but that's not going to be enough. It still won't be even after we send more ships, which we're in the process of doing. Between the political situation—the pirates are coming from Somalia and landing their booty there, and Somalia has nothing that even resembles a government at the moment—and the current wording of the various UN resolutions, our options for meaningful action are limited."

"Makes me think of the Barbary Pirates."

"Yes. But we can't just put the marines ashore. Not in the current international climate."

"And what would they do if we did? Arrest a few people and leave or stay and try to run the country?"

"Precisely."

"What's the Agency doing?"

"They're trying to get what intelligence they can—who's running it, where the money is going—but it's difficult for them to work there. And it's even more difficult to do anything with the intel once we do have it. Every time we get caught messing around inside that damned country, somebody of ours gets hurt and all the Africans and all the Arabs jump on our backs. And it doesn't do any good to remind the Arabs that some of the ships being taken are theirs. They just go ahead and let their insurance companies pay the ransom."

"What does SECDEF want us to do?"

"He wants you to stir the pot a little. He feels there's some wiggle room that you and your personal crew of pirates can maneuver in. I think he wants a three-pronged approach—the Agency doing what it can ashore, CTF 151 working offshore and you operating inshore."

"Does he have anything specific in mind?"

"Not that he told me. I'm not sure he really knows himself. He says you're to come up with something in the next week or so then head out and execute it. I do know the new President wants something done. Pronto. He's already having enough trouble with the conservatives as it is. So get over there and kick some ass without getting us in more trouble with our 'allies.' I'll let ComCTF 151 know you're on your way. Your XO is best equipped to establish liaison with her old friends at Langley and with anybody else you may feel you want."

"Anything else, Alan?"

"No. Get to work." The screen went blank. That's how Alan Parker liked to sign off. Dramatically making clear that he was ending the conversation, not you. And before you got a chance to ask any questions he didn't want to answer.

Mike glanced at Alex. "Get everybody in here at 0800 tomorrow. We'll brainstorm a little."

Alex was the only member of the team who wasn't a full-blooded naval person. Mike had recruited her from the CIA, where she had a reputation for having a Rolodex jammed with people who would do favors for her even if not for anybody else. She was also an administrative genius who, one way or another, seemed able to leap tall bureaucratic buildings without even thinking about it. She was equally accomplished at jumping out of airplanes, diving and employing practically any personal weapon with lethal effect. "I'm on it, Boss."

At least, she thought, he doesn't want everybody in at eight tonight. She probably had Jill Chambers, Mike's wife, to thank for that. And thank her she would because Alex had a date that night with a guy she was really getting to like.

2

The advertisement for a wonder drug used by many real Americans to enhance their declining virility came to an end and the scene returned to the studio. There, prominent cable TV personality Mort Cornish—dressed in a three-piece business suit and rep tie—was sitting at a round table with Al Savage, a widely recognized political media operative who had opted for a black turtleneck with black blazer.

"Al," said Mort, leaning across the table as he spoke, "you were saying about the new administration?"

"They're dropping the ball, Mort. It's amazing how quickly they've managed to make all the wrong moves. We've already discussed their economic blunders—their war on capitalism—but they've also managed to lay the foundations for disaster in the War on Terror. I mean, three months ago it was all but won—it was just a matter of a little mopping up—and now it's exploded again. Just a few days ago, for example, they attacked an innocent ship and killed two young Americans. This sort of thing is intolerable, but the administration has yet to announce a plan to end it. The fact is that the patience of the American people is fast running out."

"You refer, of course, to the attack on the school ship by Somali pirates?"

"Right, but don't let that 'pirates' business confuse you. They're not just a bunch of common thugs, they're all dedicated radical Islamists who are determined to destroy the West. Remember, while most of them look like Africans, they're also Moslems."

"I take your point, but is it feasible to free up enough resources from Iraq, Afghanistan and Pakistan to operate effectively in that part of Africa?"

"We've got the technology, Mort, to do it all quite painlessly. First we blockade the coast and sink any boat of theirs that's more than two miles out to sea. Then we use our drones—Predators and Raptors. We use them to keep a close eye on these people, and when we think we see the slightest hint of terrorist action, we send more drones to strike hard. Dead terrorists can't kill innocent Americans."

"Has anybody explained all this to the new administration?"

"Yes, there are still a few patriots left in Congress and the media, but the administration just babbles about treaties and conventions. The last administration never let that sort of thing stand in the way of their exercising our national power."

"And keeping America great."

"And keeping America great, Mort."

* * *

It was almost midnight. A norther had blown up and a chop had developed on Tampa Bay. Mike watched Ted

Anderson, driving a powerful tractor borrowed from the air force, move the oversized trailer carrying the second of the power catamarans across the dimly lit "backyard" of the Trident Force's headquarters at MacDill Air Force Base. Anderson was a black SEAL petty officer—originally a ship fitter—whose cleverness, self-control and physical abilities enabled the team to carry out the most fast-moving and hard-hitting of maneuvers.

"This little ramp of ours is too damn small, Captain," called out the SEAL in a low voice as he guided the trailer toward the Tridents' own private launching ramp.

"I'm not worried. You got the first one in without even scratching the gel coat," replied Mike.

Ted grunted something quietly, something lost in the subdued rumble of the tractor engine. As he did, the tractor pushed the trailer to and down the ramp and the cat glided out into Tampa Bay.

Even before the twin-hulled boat started to slide clear of the trailer, Chief Boatswain's Mate (DV) Jerry Andrews lit off one of its three outboards, and the instant it was afloat he backed it carefully into deeper water. There, about fifty yards offshore, he anchored and started working through the same checklist that Alex and captain of marines Ramon Fuentes were using aboard the first cat, which was anchored twenty yards to starboard.

Fuentes was not only a marine to the core but also a very, very gifted linguist. Just to confuse matters, and to prove that life is more complex than some are willing to admit, Ray was also an ardent Puerto Rican patriot. It was his contention that, in time, his island home would get its act together and, building on its two—or maybe three—cultural traditions, create the society of tomorrow.

Mike knew that Ray made a few people nervous—including Alan Parker—but he and the other members of the Trident Force found his complexity both endearing and very, very useful.

After Ted had pulled the trailer back out of the water and chocked its wheels, he and Mike climbed into a small rubber boat and motored out to the second cat. While Ted and Jerry went through the checklist, Mike thought just how frantic the past week had been for the whole team, and especially for Andrews. Jerry, Chief Boatswains Mate (DV) Gerald Andrews, had spent most of his career as a naval salvage diver. When the vast majority of the navy's salvage capability was outsourced, Jerry had drifted to the Trident Force, where his diving skills and matchless ability to both handle and maintain just about anything that floated had proved invaluable on any number of occasions.

Once Mike had decided what he wanted for Alan's little war on piracy—although his plan for using them remained somewhat fuzzy—Alex had little trouble rounding up the two thirty-five-foot-long power catamarans. Each was already equipped with three 275-horsepower outboards that could drive them at forty knots under even halfway reasonable conditions. Thanks to the economic conditions, the U.S. boatbuilding industry was almost flat on its back and the cat's builder—whose plant was located within a hundred miles of Tampa—was ecstatic to get rid of some of his bloated inventory at list price. He was also more than eager to arrange for their delivery to the team's building, which contained a large storage room for all their toys. It was just one more example of the power of Alex's magic wand.

Acquiring the boats was the easy part. The real challenge had been to convert them from yachts to mini-warships; to reinforce, arm and install lightweight, ceramic armor, along with a small suite of basic but effective electronics, in a very short period of time. And to paint them an ugly, flat gray. It had been an all-hands evolution for the team since Mike had preferred not to bring in technicians from beyond his own command. That the alterations had been accomplished as quickly as they had was thanks to Jerry's having worked out a plan in no time, then having worked twenty-two-hour days to turn those plans into reality. Days about one hour longer than those worked by everybody else.

"Checklist complete," whispered Ray's voice over the radio.

"Roger," responded Mike. He would have liked to schedule several shakedown runs in the cats, but time was pressing, so he hoped one night's voyage up and down the bay would shake loose whatever wasn't properly mounted and give them at least some feel as to how the boats handled.

"Our checklist is complete, Captain," reported Jerry a few minutes later.

Mike looked around at the lights winking along the surrounding shores and the relative dark in which the boats floated. There were probably fifty people who might be vaguely aware that SecResGru2—the Trident Force's formal name—possessed two large catamarans. Of them, only a half dozen knew how the cats had been modified and what they were for. Mike wanted to keep it that way.

"Headsets, everybody," he said over the radio and loud enough for Jerry and Ted to hear him. Each team member's headset was connected to a walkie-talkie circuit. Mike's and Alex's were also on the radio circuit.

"Alex, you get under way and proceed down the bay and out the Southwest Channel. Conduct the drills we've discussed, report any problems and avoid as much as possible anybody's seeing you clearly."

"Roger."

Mike watched as Alex lit off the three engines, throttled them back while Ray recovered the anchor, and then headed off into the night. A floodlight from the air base reflected briefly and feebly on the boat's flat gray side. The reflection then winked out and the boat all but disappeared from sight. Five minutes later Mike directed Jerry to follow them.

Once well clear of the shore, Jerry shoved the throttles forward and the cat surged up on the plane. He and Mike both settled their butts on the padded leaning post that ran athwart ships just aft of the control console.

At first, with the wind's blowing from the north, the bay was almost smooth, but they soon found themselves skipping over a growing chop with the wind behind their backs.

Separated by a mile or two, the boats ran south through the night, gliding and occasionally pounding over the chop. As they went, they practiced accelerating and decelerating, turning, stopping and traversing the fifty-caliber gun mounted forward of the control console. To starboard the lights of St. Petersburg flashed by and to port those of Ruskin and a string of other, smaller towns. Up ahead, the towering Skyway Bridge soon came into view. Because the bridge's span was relatively dimly lit, the brightly illuminated yellow triangles formed by the two central pylons and the cables that stretched from their tops seemed to float magically over the dark bay, glittering in the thin night air. Both boats passed under the bridge, slowing as they did, and continued on out to open water, where each then commenced a sequence of high-speed maneuvers.

"This is one hell of a test we're giving these vessels, Captain," commented Jerry as the cat leapt totally out of the water only to crash back down on the next wave. "Almost qualifies as abuse."

"I know it pains you, Chief. I guess they're your babies now, but we both know it has to be done."

Jerry nodded in agreement.

So far, so good, thought Mike as the cat's twin bows sliced through and bounced over the Gulf of Mexico, the waves funneling between the two hulls and slapping them as they went.

There was a solid *thunk* forward. "Shit!" grumbled Jerry. "One of the ready ammo boxes broke loose."

"I'll secure it for now," said Mike as he worked his way around the console.

All in all, the shakedown was working out well. Alex had reported no problems in her cat, and the loose locker could be easily corrected. Equally satisfying was the fact that there hadn't been another soul on the bay. Except for a Coast Guard helo. Their privacy was understandable, Mike thought, since it was the middle of the night in the middle of the winter, and anyway people didn't seem to be using their boats as much as they used to. As for the helo, it had hovered a moment, shined a light on them and then wandered off. Clearly they'd read the classified notification Mike had issued concerning their activities. Otherwise, at the first sight of the fifty the helo would have gone to General Quarters and caused all sorts of confusion.

After an hour of bruising exercises, Mike signaled for both boats to return home with Alex once again in the lead. The trip back up the bay was the final test for the cats and their crews. The stiff norther combined with the boats' high speed created a near-hurricane force, a bitterly cold wind.

"Haven't had that much fun in years," remarked Jerry, tongue in cheek, as he throttled back and approached the Tridents' private ramp.

"Yes," agreed Mike as he massaged his windburned, numb face. "We ought to do these things more often."

By four A.M. the cats were back ashore and under cover

and the Tridents were gathered in their conference room drinking coffee and attempting to defrost.

"Jerry and I will re-secure this locker while it's still on our minds," said Mike. "The rest of you head home. I want everybody back at noon to dismantle the boats and prepare them for shipping. Then we'll take forty-eight hours to try to make peace with our families and friends. After that we hit the road."

The next afternoon was spent disassembling the weapons and center consoles and stowing them on the cats' decks, well below the gunnels, along with various other odds and ends the team thought it might find a use for. Each boat was then wrapped and packed in a way that its true nature was not totally obvious

* * *

"You willingly agreed to let this man use your little truck?" asked Ibrihim Hassan. The clan chief was a small, desiccated man with a face that might be described as angry or harsh or just set—a face that reflected decades of struggle in an unforgiving land among an unforgiving people.

"Yes, Excellency, for the afternoon," replied the plaintiff.

"Did you charge him to use it?"

"Yes, Excellency. A reasonable sum. Plus the cost of the petrol he used."

Ibrihim, who was seated in the shade of an awning in the new garden of his wonderful new house, right next to an orange tree that was in fragrant bloom, looked at the man and listened out of habit, although his mind was on other things.

"And then?"

"He drove it over the edge of a ravine and beat it all up."

Ibrihim was old. Almost eighty, which made him very old in a land where the average life expectancy is in the mid forties. But Ibrihim's longevity wasn't surprising since he was a hereditary clan chief. Clan chiefs were expected to live long so they could lead their people against their more hostile neighbors and adjudicate their internal disputes wisely so they did not have to kill one another. Coincidently, the chiefs ate better than most of their clansmen.

"Do you deny this?" demanded the clan chief of the defendant.

"I did not intentionally drive it over the edge of the ravine, Excellency. And I was not careless. One of the front tires exploded."

"So you refuse to pay this man for the repairs?"

"I paid him for the use of the truck. It is not my fault that the tires were bad. The machine almost killed me!"

Ibrihim looked at one of the two fountains that graced his new garden. The Arab masters of long ago had possessed many sparkling fountains. So had the English and the Italians. But his father, who had been clan chief before him, had not. Now Ibrihim had not one but two fountains, thanks to the revitalization of the maritime trade. Perhaps, he thought as he glanced over the garden wall at the shabby, weather-stained minaret that poked tiredly into the sky, it was time to do something about the mosque. Some badly needed repairs. An expansion, maybe, and new tile work. All to celebrate the glory of God and the growing prosperity He was bringing to Hassan and all of Basalilays.

Turning his mind back to the matter at hand, he reminded himself that the law was straightforward. But he was not only a judge. He was also a politician and leader. Then he thought about what he'd heard concerning the attack on the cruise ship. It had been a disaster! A dozen

Somalis had been killed—fortunately none of his clansmen, and especially Suleiman—since the expedition was the work of another clan a hundred miles up the coast. How many times had he reminded his son that it was folly to attack large, fast passenger steamers. Yes, the ransom might be great if such a ship was taken, but that so rarely happened. Only old fools or ignorant young men ever even tried.

"Does the truck still run so that you can use it for your business?"

"Yes, Excellency," replied the plaintiff, "but it looks terrible. People think I am a fool."

"Before this happened you were friends?"

"Yes, in a way."

These men are both fools, thought Hassan with a strong sense of irritation, but I suppose I must put up with them.

"Very well. You"—Ibrihim nodded at the defendant—"will pay for repairs to the truck, but you do not have to pay for the new tire. And you can take six months to pay the full sum, one sixth each month. And I wish to hear no more of this matter."

* * *

The mid-February sun beat down with surprising fury on the tarmac, filling the air with the faint perfume of jet fuel and abused rubber. Mike and Alex stood and watched as the two large, shoe box–like packages were rolled into the nose of an air force C-5 Galaxy. The huge plane—almost two hundred and fifty feet long and weighing almost four hundred tons—was the size of a small ship. Yet, despite the great size of the plane's belly, the boxes were a tight fit, with only a foot or two of clearance on each side.

As the second of the boxes disappeared into the plane's gaping mouth, Mike's cell phone buzzed. "Chambers."

"Mike. This is Alan. How close are you to getting off?"

"We should be airborne in an hour."

"I damn well hope so. A ULLC—a supertanker—was captured a few hours ago, and the owners have already agreed to pay a ransom of fifty million. The ship's still under way, for Christ's sake. The pirates haven't even anchored it, and the owners are already collecting up the cash and having it delivered by helo."

"Alan, this won't be the first time you've sent us on a mission where, when we turned and looked back, nobody was following us."

"Yeah, well, that's what we pay you for, although I still think your plan is pretty feeble. We want closure on this business, not research and experimentation. We want them closed down and on trial. Or even better, dead."

"This is the best I can do until I get there and get a feel for the situation and the area. The Agency hasn't been very forthcoming with intel, and nobody else has come up with any ideas that can be executed the way things now stand."

"We've all got our problems, pal. Don't worry, there've been suggestions, but they've been shot down as inappropriate. Now, you get over there and kick ass." Predictably, the phone went dead.

"Where are Ray and Ted?" asked Mike.

"Right behind you, Boss."

Mike turned to find the missing members of the team standing behind him.

"Were you able to make peace with Jamie about missing her birthday party?" he asked Ray.

"I hope so. I just hope I don't miss her first communion. If I do, Sandy might just collect up Jamie and move out."

"I certainly hope this thing isn't going to drag on that

long. Now, let's get aboard that winged monster and help Jerry secure the cargo. Alan wants us the hell out of his country."

A small chorus of "rogers" and "aye, ayes" erupted.

A half hour later, after the Tridents had settled into the Spartan seating and living accommodations forward of the cargo bay, the huge plane rumbled down the runway and into the air, its jet-powered propellers making a whirring hiss. It was on the first leg of its nine-thousand-mile flight to the American facility at the Djibouti airport with refueling stops at Bermuda, the Azores, and Sicily. At Djibouti a Chinook helicopter to be borrowed from the Africa Command would airlift the two eight-ton boxes—one at a time—out to the amphibious assault ship U.S.S. *Wake Island*, which would be waiting twenty-five miles offshore in the Gulf of Aden.

Mike glanced at Alex, expecting to see her banging away on her computer. But she wasn't. She was reading a copy of *Cosmopolitan* and laughing. She must have sensed his gaze, because she looked up at him, rolled her eyes while continuing to laugh and then went back to the magazine.

This mystery man she was going out with must really be something, he thought, to get her thinking about glamour.

* * *

Prince Saeed stood in the bitter, driving sleet on the exposed pier in Vladivostok. He watched as one of the dark red, rust-streaked containers was hoisted into the barely transparent air and then allowed to settle onto one of the stacks of containers already in place on the deck of the containership *Eastern Trader*. The ship, which was Greek-flagged but controlled by a Saudi investment trust, was relatively small and totally unremarkable for her type. Just under six hundred feet long and with a beam of a hundred feet, she had a carrying capacity of 1700 TEU, roughly 850 forty-foot standard containers.

For the past several years the ship had been making a scheduled run between Sydney, Australia, and Vladivostok—with stops at Manila, Hong Kong, Shanghai and Pusan, depending on cargo availability—but that was now all over. She'd been called back to the Mediterranean by her owners. After leaving Vladivostok, she would stop at Colombo to bunker and then go on to Mumbai to load farm machinery. From Mumbai she would head east to the Gulf of Aden, then into the Red Sea. There she would make a quick stop at Jeddah and then steam on through Suez to Cairo, where she would deliver the tractors and combines.

The prince, whose thin, tanned face and prominent, hawklike nose was largely hidden between his upturned topcoat collar and the hat jammed down on his head, looked around through the dense, gray afternoon air, at the pockmarked gray green water and the other ships—most barely visible—spread around the harbor, which struck him as an exceptionally dismal one. He shuffled one foot slightly and felt the slick, hard ice pellets slide beneath his soles. Saeed hated Vladivostok and he hated the weather. He hated all of Siberia, all of Russia. Although he would have considered it pretentious to describe himself as such, the prince thought of himself as a man of the desert. He wouldn't have tolerated the sleet even if he were in San Moritz, skiing. Of course it wouldn't have been sleeting on him there. But, he reassured himself, what he was doing had to be done. It was beyond essential. The world was changing and The Kingdom was now in greater danger than it ever had been since its creation almost a century ago.

Up until now The Kingdom's oil, and its great wealth,

had served to protect it from its many external enemies. But it was beginning to look as if the West might eventually get its act together and reduce its dependence on The Kingdom's oil. Not swear off it, of course, but become less pitifully addicted to it. And as the West's addiction lessened, the likelihood of its turning on its former pusher would only increase.

"This must be a great day for you," remarked Gregor, the short, skinny, pasty-faced Russian standing beside the tall Arab prince. "Your king will be pleased with you."

The prince turned and looked at him, his neutral expression concealing the frown he felt. Gregor was the "broker," the private businessman who had put together the deal with a cabal of renegade, underpaid army officers. Modern Russia, he thought. The land where men like Gregor might be working for their own accounts but were working so closely with the government that it was impossible to think of them as businessmen. Without Putin's approval, the deal never would have happened, yet the president (in fact if not on paper) would be totally able to deny it all. And the fact that business wasn't all that different in The Kingdom or anywhere else didn't make the prince dislike Russia, and especially Gregor, any less.

Despite the size and importance of this one particular transaction, Saeed found the arrangement almost embarrassing. He was accustomed to associating with kings and presidents and world-class businessmen. Men of power and importance. The worm shivering next to him was no more than a crafty small-time operator wrapped in an expensive camel hair coat that was too big for him and with a diamond stuck in his earlobe. "Yes, I'm sure he will be."

"Okay," said Gregor a chilly eternity later, clapping his half-frozen, gloved hands together, "that's the last of ours."

Prince Saeed watched as a puff of smoke burst out of the ship's funnel.

"We can go now," offered the Russian.

"No," said Saeed, realizing the nasty, doughy little "broker" was even colder than he was and deriving grim pleasure from further tormenting him. "We will wait until the last containers are loaded above ours and the ship leaves."

The Saudis' need for their own nuclear program and defenses had been recognized for some time, thought the prince. The Israelis already had their own. As did many others. Half measures had been tried. The Kingdom had attempted to work through Iran, but that had never come to much and he'd never liked that approach. He was convinced that the first Persian nuclear missile would be aimed at Tel Aviv and the second at Riyadh, even if the Saudis had financed the whole project. Recently they'd tried to work through the Pakistanis, who also had their own program and bombs—a reality that Saeed found embarrassing. Who were the Pakistanis to have a bomb when The Kingdom didn't? But again, the arrangement was just costing them money. The Americans were all over the Pakistanis and the Americans didn't want the Saudis—or anybody else—to elbow their way into their exclusive little nuclear club.

The only possible path was clear. The Kingdom had to go on its own. There could be no doubt that what he was doing had to be done, even though it was little more than a stopgap until their own program was up and running. It was a matter of survival.

Almost an hour later the last of the containers had been loaded and secured aboard the ship. Within minutes two tugs emerged from the cold, gray evening and put lines over to *Eastern Trader*. Then, with much tooting of steam whistles, they pulled her away from the dock. After casting off the grimy tugs, the ship turned and headed south, down the channel, toward the Sea of Japan, the first leg of her fourteen-thousand-mile voyage to Jeddah and beyond.

Saeed turned and walked to the waiting car, thinking how amusing it might be if he reached it before Gregor. It would be a pleasure to slam the door in his face and drive off, leaving the nasty little Russian standing in the icy night. He quickly dismissed the thought. It was childish. Totally beneath him.

* * *

Mike, seated in one of the spare seats on the flight deck of the C-5, looked out the window as the flying monster rumbled into its final approach to the Djibouti airport. Below was the white-specked blue Indian Ocean and ahead lay the airport itself along with the fast-growing Camp LeMonier, the home of the U.S Africa Command, of the Joint Task Force and of a regiment of the French Foreign Legion. To the right, in the distance, he could see the city and the port. They were the same dusty mixture of the new and the old that characterizes so much of the Near and Middle East. Everywhere else he looked was hard, sunbaked rock and barren soil with a low wall of equally spiritless-looking hills rising to the north. It was a harsh, tightfisted land, he thought, although it must have some beauty somewhere. It was also said to be the cradle of the human race. Someplace around here the first Homo sapiens was supposedly born. Hard to believe, although it was also said that in the distant past the climate was damper and more suitable for human life.

"Here we go, Captain," said the pilot. Mike gave him a thumbs-up, and the big bird floated down through the clear, hot air with surprising grace, then landed with nary a jolt. The pilot, thought Mike, had the hands of a gifted dentist. A half hour later the plane was parked in the military section of the airport with its nose open, ready to discharge Mike, his team and their toys.

"Very well," said Mike straightening up and taking a deep breath as he walked out of the plane, "I have to make some courtesy calls, Alex. I want you to supervise unloading the luggage and then get it off to *Wake Island*. I should be done in two hours or so—I hope. If I'm not back when the last cat leaves, jump in the Chinook and go yourselves."

"You want me to go with you, Boss?"

"No, thanks. The four of you will have a lot to do here."

"Roger."

"Welcome, Captain Chambers."

Mike turned to find an American naval lieutenant standing behind him. The young officer, like most of the other personnel at the facility, was dressed in desert camouflage, and it was for this reason that Mike had dressed his own people in the same uniform, rather than the blue jumpsuits that he preferred for both practical and sentimental reasons. He wanted them to stand out as little as possible.

"Thank you, Lieutenant," replied Mike, returning the salute.

"By some miracle I was able to get the two people who feel they have to talk to you, and who I understand you want to talk to, to agree to be in the same room together. In fact, they're waiting."

"Lead on."

After a brief jeep ride under a sun even hotter than that at Tampa, Mike was led to a conference room in one of the camp's admin buildings. Waiting for him were Preston Olbrig, the CIA chief in Djibouti, and Commander

Robert Patterson, the head of intelligence for the Joint Task Force.

"How was your flight?" asked Patterson as he signaled to a Djibouti in a white shirt and trousers for coffee all around.

"What can I say? At least the air force serves pretty good meals. Unlike some other airlines."

The three men laughed.

"Captain," continued Patterson, "the information we have on you and your mission is a little sketchy. I understand you report directly to SECDEF, but is there anything you can tell us to facilitate liaison?"

"Commander, the awful truth is that our orders *are* sketchy. We're supposed to stir the pot and see if we can come up with some new ideas—something short of launching World War Three—for dealing with these pirates. We've got two armed power catamarans that we're going to operate from *Wake Island*, and we're going to start by trying a little delicate harassment, just to see what happens. I fully intend to keep you both posted."

"Umm," the two responded almost in unison as three cups of coffee appeared on the table.

"I wonder, Commander, if you could give me a brief update on what the JTF's been able to achieve so far."

"As things now stand we've got five or six ships to cover millions of square miles. Every now and then we stumble on an attack and are able to stop it. Helos are some help, but it's still a matter of catch as catch can. We're never sure where they're going to come from and when. I sometimes think half the country is pirates."

"And the Agency can't come up with anything ashore?"

"This isn't Europe." Olbrig grunted. "We stand out here like sore thumbs. Even our black officers. We have a number of local stringers—some in the government, one or another of them—but most of what they report is garbage. Everybody in Somalia has his own agenda."

"And Somali intelligence?"

"Which one? There are at least three. The so-called national government looks okay on paper, but they're trying to govern from Kenya because the security in Mogadishu is so awful they're sure they'll get killed there. The northwestern provinces have declared independence and call themselves the Republic of Somaliland and the area around the Horn calls itself Puntland. Puntland claims to be a semiautonomous part of Somalia. They pay lip service to the central government but little else. All these entities are controlled by constantly squabbling gangs of clan chiefs and clerics, many of whom have their own private intelligence groups. We've tried to talk to some of the identifiable intelligence officials, but, well, many of the more powerful clan leaders are up to their ears in the piracy business, as far as we can tell."

"What do they do with the money?" asked Mike. "Can we get at them through that?"

"You'd think so, but it's not easy. The minor pirates spend it here, right in country. The bigger guys spend some here and ship some out, but there's no real banking system, just a thousand tight-knit and impenetrable money exchange operations. Most are oriented around families or clans."

Mike sighed in sympathy. "For a start I think we'll operate along the Puntland coast. There appear to be a number of harbors that are very active—based on the reports I've seen."

"That's as good a place as any to start. Who knows where it'll lead you."

Mike's cell phone rang. "Captain, this is Alex. The second toy is all rigged and ready to go. Should we leave with it now or wait for you?"

"I think I've learned as much as I can here. I'll be along in twenty minutes. No reason to waste the people's money on an extra flight"

"Roger. We'll be here."

"Is there anything more you'd like to know about us?" asked Mike.

"No, thank you," said Olbrig. "It's going to be damn interesting to see what you manage to come up with."

"Just please remember," added Commander Patterson, "to follow the rules of engagement. Either that or, if you have to break them, do it in a way that nobody notices. Good luck."

"You *do* know," added Olbrig as all were standing and shaking hands, "that our new 'pirate czar' is due to arrive anytime now. I'll be reporting to her and so will the other Agency personnel from Mombasa to Aden. I'm sure she'll want to talk to you."

"Pleased to. Ask her to give me a call at her convenience."

* * *

A little more than an hour later Mike was gazing down at the massive gray form of the amphibious assault ship U.S.S. *Wake Island*, which was steaming slowly through the blue waters of the Gulf of Aden. It felt almost like a homecoming, he thought idly, since he had commanded a very similar ship a few years before.

During the later years of the twentieth century, ships like *Wake Island*—some displacing forty thousand tons and stretching over eight hundred feet from bow to stern— had developed into one of the navy's most useful tools for projecting controlled force onto land and dealing with the small, yet increasingly tangled, conflicts of today and to-morrow. Their full-length flight decks provided a home for a small fleet of helicopters and short-takeoff-and-landing airplanes. Their boat well aft—with its opening gate across the stern—provided a home for a variety of landing craft—everything from traditional boats to hovercraft. And the ship herself provided a home for up to two thousand marines and their supplies.

Mike continued to watch as the pilot deposited the cat—which was hanging below the Chinook—precisely in the center of one of the aircraft elevators on the ship's deck. The pilot hovered while the lifting wires were tripped and then drifted toward the bow and settled the Chinook gently on the steel deck.

When Mike stepped out onto the flight deck, he was greeted by a lieutenant commander. "Captain Browning's respects, sir, and apologies," said the officer after saluting. "He wasn't sure precisely when you'd be arriving and got involved in a meeting with the department heads. He should be right here soon."

Mike nodded. He sympathized totally with Browning. Running a ship this size meant having to work through others who then had to work through still others. It was the captain's job to make sure everybody understood the big picture. It was also his job to make sure everybody was right on top of even the smallest details. It was a mat-ter of continuous communication, continuous evaluation and continuous attempts to keep one step ahead of what-ever was happening at the moment.

Anyway, he knew Pat Browning and liked him.

With the lieutenant commander leading, they headed for the nearest door into the superstructure. Just as they reached it, Captain Browning emerged.

"Welcome, Mike, welcome," he said as he saluted.

"Thanks, Pat."

"Sorry I'm late, but Mr. Sherman here is one of my best. Be an admiral in no time."

Sherman seemed pleased to receive the compliment.

"Why don't we have him help your people get settled in with all their stuff while you and I go up to my quarters so you can tell me as much as you're willing to about what you're really here to do. That way *Wake Island* can contribute as much as we can to whatever felonies you're here to commit."

Over the years Mike had come to the conclusion that once an officer had made full captain, he was either very serious all of the time or more than a little mellow. Pat was one of the mellow ones, which was good, since Mike remained less than sure where the whole operation was going to lead.

* * *

Shortly after the Tridents left Djibouti, Amanda Cochran was staring out the window of a CIA jet transport as it glided down toward the same runway Mike and his team had arrived on. She looked at the military facility growing out of the arid, seemingly limitless plain of hard, lifeless, sunbaked rock and soil. She could have been landing practically anywhere, including Iraq or Afghanistan. But she wasn't landing in Iraq or Afghanistan, she was landing in Djibouti, and she wasn't sure she really wanted to be.

Once she might have been pleased to have been named the Agency's "pirate czar." Pirates were, after all, in the news—but generally on the bottom of the front page if not on the second. There was no way of getting around it. Iraq, Afghanistan, Pakistan, Al Qaeda and the Taliban still occupied the attention of the American people, and she wanted to be on the projects that got the big headlines, because that's how careers were made. The pirates might be nasty, but they weren't number one. Osama remained the media king.

The job she was about to start was so close to being desirable without actually being so that she suspected she might have been set up. She did have enemies, there was no doubt about it.

But all was not lost, she reminded herself. If she could break the pirates, or even establish a strong Al Qaeda or Taliban connection, she might very well end up on top in the end. And the way to do that was to hit the ground running. She'd already notified Olbrig, the local Agency chief, that she wanted to meet with him just as soon as she landed. Aden, Mombasa and Mogadishu—assuming there was anybody in Mogadishu at the moment—would quickly follow. She was going to kick some ass and light some fires.

One way or another she was going to turn the pirates into career-enhancing gold.

3

"Trident, this is Trident One. Alpha Station," reported Alex, her voice squawking quietly on the radio as she reported that her cat was on station.

The two cats were gliding and bouncing across the choppy waters of the Indian Ocean. Twenty-five miles to the north lay the bone-dry coast of the Horn of Africa, the northeast corner of Somalia. Seventeen hundred miles to the east the Indian subcontinent jutted out into the ocean named after it.

"Roger," replied Mike as he looked at the small radar screen mounted on his cat's control console. He could see a total of five blips on the screen. The other power cat was about four miles away, and the four small Somali fishing boats, which the team was shadowing and which he assumed were maybe thirty feet in length and probably open, were located between the two cats. *Wake Island*, their mother ship, was twenty-five miles farther out at sea and beyond the range of the cats' radar.

"Alpha Station?" remarked Ray. "When did she start using navy talk?"

"It's just to keep the rest of us off balance," explained Jerry. "Next time she'll say 'Yoohoo, guys, I'm here.'"

The night was black, and the Northeast Monsoon was blowing in from the open ocean at over twenty knots and carrying the smell of rain. It was a chill wind—chill enough to make the chest and back armor the Tridents were wearing over their jumpsuits seem almost comfortable. It was the sort of night during which more than one seaman had seen things—things that might or might not really be there. It was the sort of night that made Mike feel tense and on edge, even when he wasn't chasing pirates.

"Trident One, this is Trident. Remember to avoid visual contact. Their night vision gear may be just as good as ours so we're going to have to rely on our radar. We want them to hear us, to know that we're here, but we don't want them to know exactly what we are."

"Roger, Trident. We'll be just like hobgoblins. What if we're too far for them to hear us?"

"Show a light every now and then. That won't tell them anything more than that you're there."

"Hobgoblins?" remarked Jerry Andrews, who was on the helm.

"Yes, make-believe goblins," offered Ray Fuentes.

"I like it," replied Chambers. "How does the Hobgoblin Force sound?"

"Alan will never go for it. Especially if he knows it was Alex's idea."

"I suppose not."

The three stood in silence a few minutes, listening to the rumble of the three 275-horsepower outboards and flexing their legs slightly as the cat, now moving at a moderate speed, bounded over, and sometimes through, the long, increasingly sharp waves. Jerry thought he detected a slight pulsing from the engines—as if they were out of sync. He tinkered with the throttles a little and the throbbing seemed to fade away. Mike then spoke into his radio. "Mamacita, this is Trident."

"Roger, Trident," replied Radarman First Class Arnold Reynolds in the combat information center aboard *Wake Island*.

"Have any of those three vessels we identified as possible targets of our suspects changed course or speed?"

"Negative, Trident. They're continuing as before."

"Roger."

"We're not going to warn them, Captain?" asked Jerry, ducking as a sheet of spray flew aft at him.

"No. If we do and if they're sane, they'll change course to evade these fellows. We want the pirates to deploy into an attack formation. Then we can act against them. And the possibility remains that they're not pirates, just fishermen. We don't want to cry wolf too many times."

"Four open boats heading out to sea together, sir? On a night like this? Where I come from there aren't no fish worth that sort of misery."

"Yes, I think they're pirates. That's why we're here."

"These guys really do come out of nowhere," mused Ray as he stared out into the wet dark. "As far as I can tell there are maybe a half dozen real harbors along this coast. And a few other little indentations. Yet, from what the reports say, these guys seem to pop up everywhere. Sometimes in big boats, sometimes in ridiculously small ones."

"I assume the big ones, those decrepit trawlers they sometimes use, have to come out of some sort of harbor. My guess is that many of the small ones are launched off beaches."

"I guess we're lucky to have latched on to these guys."

"I guess so."

"And if we end up with prisoners?" asked Jerry.

"Chances are we end up letting them go. Or somebody else up the line does. That's what those who pass for authority in Somalia will do, and nobody else wants them, especially not as prisoners."

"I thought the Kenyan government has agreed to try them," said Ray.

"We'll see what comes of that. They're having their own problems at the moment, and there seems to be some question of how well their courts are working these days."

Andrews sighed. "This really is a half-assed mission, Captain."

"Don't let it bother you, Boats."

"That's why they gave it to us," interjected Ray. "Alan Parker probably thought it up himself after a few too many martinis and is undoubtedly already working up a list of nasty thing to say next time he calls."

"Along with a ration of useless advice."

"Just concentrate on the job at hand," said Mike as the cat dove into another wave, shuddering and tossing back another sheet of spray as it did. "Right now we're trying to harass them, learn more about them and increase their cost of doing business. And maybe stop an attack or two."

"I understand that, Captain," said Jerry, not taking his eyes off the compass, "but please remember that I'm just a simple deck ape at heart and all this political stuff is sometimes a little unclear to me."

"And to everybody else," added Ray Fuentes quietly.

"Trident, this is Trident One." It was the voice of Ted Anderson, who was with Alex in the other cat.

"Roger, Trident One."

"It looks to us as if this little fleet is splitting in half."

Chambers looked down at the radar display. "Damn," he mumbled, "that's just what they're doing. Two are turning north and two south." He felt a tightness beginning to form across the back of his head, just above his neck.

Why were they splitting up? he wondered. Was it part of their original plan? Were they going after two different targets or planning to attack from two sides? Or were they reacting to the team's presence? He paused, figuring he had a minute or two in this case to make a decision. Prudence suggested that he maintain his force intact. Even though each of the cats was heavily armed, things did happen. Bad things. At the same time, he had to assume the boats were responding to their presence and he wanted to keep the pressure on.

"Trident One, this is Trident. Continue to shadow the two boats headed north. We will do the same with those headed south."

"Roger, Trident."

"Mamacita, do you copy?"

"Roger, Trident."

"This is Trident. Request you put a second helo gunship on alert. Just in case."

"Roger, Trident."

"It looks like they've speeded up, Captain," reported Ray.

"Very well. Jerry, keep up with them."

Ray stared out into the darkness, unable to overcome the sensation that they were just blundering around. And, he suspected, everybody including Mike felt the same way. It was typical, he decided, of most of the jobs they got.

* * *

Ibrihim Hassan sat at the desk in the second-floor room he used as a private office and felt every one of his almost eighty years—seventy of those years spent fighting and killing his clan's enemies—his enemies—when not trying to keep peace within the clan.

For most of his life his primary reward had been the respect and fear of those around him and a somewhat higher standard of living than that enjoyed by most of his people. Then, fifteen or so years ago, he'd focused on the growing profits being made through piracy. What had started as attacks on foreigners poaching fish in Somali waters had become a business. A return to the practices of long-ago times. A strange business for men of such a bitterly dry land, he'd thought, but not all that different from traditional, land-bound brigandage, and much too lucrative to be overlooked. With a minimum of effort he'd reminded the leaders of the various pirate gangs in the area who was chief. It had been necessary for one or two of the gang leaders to die for him to make his point, but he had. And the profits had grown and grown, especially after they'd hit on the idea of collecting ransom rather than just stealing the silverware.

Hassan looked around his office and liked what he saw. The eight-bedroom house, which he had just finished having built, was not only very much to his taste but also provided a good reflection of his power and prestige. Sturdy concrete-block walls with handsome arches were stuccoed inside and out. The extensive—and intricate— tile work was well done and the new—but thoroughly traditional—furniture was very satisfying. Whatever the state of Somalia, he, as a clan chief, was prospering. And thanks to his rapidly growing maritime business, he was prospering on a scale his father could never have imagined. With any luck he could send his grandsons to school in Europe.

There was a knock at the door and one of his serving girls entered, carrying a cup of tea. It was Jasmine, the pretty one, the one of whom his wife was jealous—and with good reason. Although, of course, it was none of his wife's business. She should just be happy that he hadn't cast her aside, as was his right.

The girl placed the cup on the desk and looked at him, questioning.

"Yes," he said. "In a while. Go to my bedroom and prepare yourself. I will be along."

Jasmine backed out the door and closed it. After sipping the tea, Hassan stood and walked over to the window. Looking out over the servants' quarters and his new garden with its fountains and high wall, he watched as two of his guards patrolled the entrance to the compound. Even in Puntland attacks were always possible. Rival clans. Random gangs. Foreigners and outsiders.

Some years ago Ibrihim and the other chiefs in northeastern Somalia had worked together to drive away the forces of men even they considered religious fanatics. Not to mention threats to their own power. Out of that effort Puntland had emerged, an autonomous but loyal part of the Somali nation. They had then used their own resources to impose some order over the region. By doing so they'd avoided the near total chaos that plagued the southern half of the country, the portion said to be under the control of the transitional government. They had also avoided having the Ethiopian, then the African Union, "peacekeepers" forced on them. They were all thieves and thugs. Especially the Ethiopians, who had always lusted after Somalia for her access to the Indian Ocean. Worst of all, many were Christians, or Marxists—or something—and clearly hoped to stay on forever as conquerors.

Puntland, he thought. The Land of Punt. A proud land, one that had been wealthy and powerful 4500 years ago when it exported gold, frankincense, myrrh, ebony, ivory and slaves to the north. A land sacred to the ancient Egyptians—those who built the pyramids, not the Arabs of today. Sacred because the Egyptians claimed it was their original, ancestral homeland.

Ibrihim was a Moslem but he was not an Arab. He was of Punt, the land that had given the world the titans of the Nile, and it was more than natural that he should have a strong pride not only of place but also of race.

Hassan returned to his desk. He would have liked to know how Suleiman and his four boats were doing, but he wasn't worried. His eldest son was smart, tough and experienced, and the odds were very much on his side. He turned his attention to the statement he'd just received from his bank in Dubai. Yes, he must do something about the mosque. If he allowed it to continue as it was, he would be doing a disservice to Allah. It was also an eyesore that irritated him.

He placed the statement in a drawer of the desk and stood. He would go to the girl now and have his pleasure.

* * *

Ali sat on the dark beach, listening to the almost invisible surf as it broke on the shore. He was exhausted, so exhausted that he couldn't sleep. And he was bitter. Because he didn't have his own boat, the only work he could find was working for Osman in his small skiff and he hated it. Osman was old and lazy and stupid. He made Ali do all the work—rowing, pulling in all the fishing lines, dragging the boat up on the beach at night. And then the old crook kept almost everything they managed to catch for himself. And he said vicious things about Ali, accusing him of being a bastard simply because he had never personally met Ali's father.

How could the old pig have met Ali's father? Ali's family had lived in a town ten miles away from Basalilays until eight years ago, when Ali's father had been killed in one of the inter-clan brawls that erupted from time to time. Now more destitute than ever, Ali and his mother had moved to Basalilays, throwing themselves on the mercy of one of his father's distant relatives.

In Basalilays Ali had attended the government madrassa for almost four years—until it had closed because the government had forgotten to pay the teacher. During that time he'd learned to read and write Arabic and Somali. More or less. Although the school was run by the government, the written vocabulary he acquired was largely composed of words that occurred in the Koran and his handwriting was a horror. Ironically, the teacher's efforts to impress his students with the evil to be found in the outside world had just inspired a faint dream in Ali to learn more about life beyond Somalia's dust, heat and grinding poverty.

Ali's mother had died two months after the madrassa closed, and the distant relative lost all interest in Ali's welfare. The boy was on his own. For a while he roamed the streets with others in his position. Stealing what they could, occasionally coming across an odd job for which they were paid table scraps. Then he had come across Osman. Nobody else would work for him, so Ali ended up doing so.

Ali worked and Ali struggled and Ali enjoyed an occasional bitter laugh with the other anchorless youths with whom he lived. He would have liked to have a girl, but that would have to wait. Girls cost money.

But now, *inshallah*, his life was about to change. It was just a matter of time. Ibrihim would send for him and he would soon be richer than he could even dream.

He tried to reassure himself that it would really happen, but even now, only a few days after meeting the clan chief, his faith in the future was beginning to weaken.

But, he reminded himself, to lose hope was to die.

He threw a rock out into the dark sea then turned and headed back toward the miserable hovel he called home.

* * *

"Mamacita, this is Trident."

"Roger, Trident."

"Request you reanalyze your radar and satellite data to identify all vessels within one hundred miles of my position that may be likely targets for our targets."

"Roger. Wait."

Mike waited while Ray, who had relieved Jerry at the helm, periodically changed course from one side to the other to reduce the enervating head-on pounding to which the chop was subjecting the catamaran. What, he wondered, was it like in the Somalis' boats? They must be getting pretty badly beaten up in these seas.

"Trident, this is Mamacita."

"Roger, Mamacita."

"To the south there are six vessels, ranging from a good-sized tanker, on ballast, to several small coastal freighters. All headed north. Some within a few miles of the coast, some offshore. To the north there are eleven, including at least three big tankers and a cruise ship. All headed either toward or away from Bab el Mandeb. Do you desire more details?"

"How many friendlies?"

"To the south, only Mamacita. To the north, two. The Italian and Chinese destroyers, but they're up near the Yemani coast."

"Where's the flagship?"

"The *Nassau*? She's around in the Gulf of Aden with the Spanish destroyer."

"Roger, Mamacita. Out."

"We're in no position at this point to identify these guys' objective or objectives, are we, Captain?" remarked Ray.

"No, we're going to have to continue the flea strategy, attach ourselves to them and ride along."

"What happened to the hobgoblins?"

"They're closely related."

A few minutes later the radio hissed to life. "Trident, this is Trident One."

"Roger, Trident One."

"Do you want us to close in on these guys and see if they're carrying weapons? If so, maybe we can stop them."

"Our XO is getting a little impatient," remarked Mike.

"It's unlike her," opined Ray. "Normally she's the most self-controlled person on earth."

"Trident One, this is Trident. For the time being we will continue to shadow without giving away our true nature."

"Roger, Trident."

The two Trident cats, which were now well out of each other's radar range, continued to pound through the night, their courses and speeds dictated by the vessels they were following, the dark waves banging against the two hulls and loudly slapping the belly of the bridge deck—the structure that ran from one hull to the other.

"Captain," announced Ray shortly after midnight, "they're turning again. In fact, they seem to be counter-marching. They're headed back toward us."

"Now what?" said Mike, who was back on the helm. Should he man the gun? No, not yet. "I'm going to turn north to get out of their way."

"And if they try to follow us?"

"I'm sure we can outrun them. If not we'll find out how well armed they are."

"Trident, this is Trident One," announced the radio a minute or two later. "These guys seem to be turning around and heading back for shore."

"Are you sure they're not trying to close with you?" Mike had full confidence in Alex and Ted's ability to fight their way out of just about any situation, but at the same time, he wondered briefly if his decision to divide his forces really had been the best one.

"Negative."

"Very well. Our group appears to be doing the same. Continue to follow them from the distance."

"Roger."

"Trident, this is Mamacita." Reynolds must still be on duty, thought Mike as he recognized the radarman's voice.

"This is Trident."

"Based on our plots, neither of those groups you're following is headed back toward where they came from. The northern group seems to be headed toward a tiny in-dentation in the coast and your group is headed toward nothing, as far as we can see. The coastline is as smooth as a baby's bottom."

"Roger, Mamacita."

"Up, over the beach," remarked Ray.

"Why not?" added Jerry, who'd been napping. "These guys are real seagoing guerillas."

"Then they must have some means of moving the boats overland."

"Or maybe they just leave them there," offered Mike. "As things now stand we can't chase them ashore. But we'll follow them until they disappear from the screen."

"And into the desert," mumbled Ray to himself, "just like an Arab sheikh on his stallion."

"Did you copy Mamacita's last?" Mike then asked the radio.

"Roger. We'll keep an eye on them until they seem well into that inlet. Or whatever it is."

"Then get back to Mamacita before the sun comes up."

"You make us sound like vampires."

"Hobgoblins, vampires," said Ray. "Alex's fertile mind is hard at work."

"I suppose so, even if her circuit discipline is a little weak."

Ray continued chuckling. Good days, bad days. Great victories, utter fiascos. They all counted on the thirty years you needed to get full retirement benefits.

* * *

The morning sun had just risen above the roofs of the surrounding one- and two-story buildings, turning them and the surrounding, desolate countryside a gleaming, although transitory, gold, as Ibrihim Hassan sat behind his desk and glowered at his middle-aged son. "So you never saw who they were or what kind of boats?"

"No, Father," replied Suleiman.

"Tell it to me again."

Suleiman sighed. He was a grown man now, had been

for years. More than old enough to be a clan chief, not that he resented Ibrihim's longevity in the slightest. But his father knew little of the sea. In sum, he resented being interrogated by the chief even though he knew that he must submit to it.

"We first became aware of them when we were about five miles out. We could hear, from time to time, the pulsing of what sounded like very big outboard motors. We looked and could, at first, see nothing, although I felt certain there were two, one on each side."

"Are you sure it wasn't helicopters?"

"Yes, the sound was very different. Also, after a while we spotted lights flashing from time to time."

"They didn't approach you or fire anything?"

"No, they just continued along beside us, several miles away I would guess."

"And then?"

"By about one in the morning I was convinced they must have been some sort of coalition force and that they were waiting for us to attack our target. I assumed they were stronger than we were, so, to make absolutely certain they were following us and to try to lose them, I sent two boats north and took two south. It now appears there were at least two of them, because one followed me to shore and Mohamed says one followed his two boats also. Perhaps it is all just as well. The seas were much bigger than I had expected and several men were almost thrown overboard."

"Where are the boats now?"

"Two are back at Basalilays and the other two are pulled up on the beach several miles to the north."

Hassan continued to stare at Suleiman for several minutes. "I don't like receiving bad news, Suleiman, but in this case I find no fault in your actions. In fact, you did the

right thing. I am proud of you. It's now clear that the coalition is changing its tactics. This was inevitable. We
must, therefore, change our tactics, and the first step is to
install those yacht radars on the small boats."

"What about power for them?"

"We can use car batteries and only turn on the radar
when we have use for it."

"It will be of considerable help in finding our targets.
But it must be kept out of the water."

"It will be of much greater use in the hunt for those who
hunt us. If they change the rules, we change the rules."

* * *

"Having you and your men with us has been a great relief
for me, Colonel," remarked the *Eastern Trader*'s captain,
Andreas Papadis, as he studied the navigational plot,
which showed the ship to be within fifty miles of the tip
of the Malay Peninsula and close to the southern entrance
to the Strait of Malacca.

"Yes," replied Colonel Rasheed bin Sharif as he also
studied the plot. "To have neglected to send a party such
as mine would have been utterly foolhardy. Especially in
view of the decision to not replace your usual crew with
carefully selected Saudis."

"I can see that you view the crew as a risk—Filipinos,
Latins, Africans—but it would have been noticed if they'd
all suddenly been replaced."

"Yes. That was what my superiors concluded," answered the colonel a little sourly.

Colonel bin Sharif was a Saudi special forces officer
although, like the rest of his party, he was dressed in
slacks and a polo shirt. He was also a minor prince. Sufficiently minor that he discouraged the use of the title in

all but the most formal settings. He felt he had earned his military title and was proud of it. And he would be even prouder when it was General.

The colonel and his party of eighteen Saudi commandos had filtered almost unnoticed aboard the ship while she was still in Vladivostok. Ever since, armed with a wide selection of detection devices and an immense amount of firepower, they had been on continuous watch. One section of six men was always alert, awake, armed and patrolling the decks. The other two sections could reach their combat stations in two minutes.

Then, once they'd entered the southern end of the South China Sea—a soup of islands large and small, many of whose heavily overgrown shores were rarely visited by twenty-first-century men—the colonel had reorganized his force into two sections. Nine men on duty at all times. For, despite the efforts of the Somali pirates to make a name for themselves, the waters *Eastern Trader* was now passing through were still considered the most pirate-infested on earth. And both Captain Papadis and Colonel bin Sharif had the same stark orders. Under no circumstances was the ship to be taken. There was to be no surrender, no agreement to ransom. The ship was not to be taken. The ship was not to be taken by anybody. The fact that Papadis had never been told precisely what was in the containers was of little importance. He could guess, of course, and it didn't particularly bother him. He was being paid very well.

Two hours later the shimmering, distorted images of the glittering office towers of Singapore were visible far ahead and to the right. Soon the towers themselves appeared above the horizon, growing out of the surrounding green, and the waters around them were crowded with boats, ships and islands.

The colonel's head suddenly snapped to the right as a voice whispered in his ear. It was one of his three lieutenants, reporting that a boat off to starboard was behaving strangely. He grabbed a pair of binoculars and hurried out to the bridge wing with Captain Papadis following close behind.

"Yes, I see it," said bin Sharif into the small microphone mounted on his shoulder after scanning the surrounding waters. He then turned to Papadis. "You see that boat out there? What do you think?"

Papadis studied the boat for a moment through his own glasses. "Anything is possible, Colonel, even during the day, within sight of Singapore."

The colonel studied the boat some more. Under no circumstances was the ship to be taken. At the same time, he was to avoid doing anything that might bring the ship to the attention of the authorities. "Call the other section, Lieutenant. They are to take their stations and remain undercover. They are to do absolutely nothing else unless I say so."

"I understand, Colonel."

4

The gray and blue U.S. Navy Sea Dragon helicopter—
uncomfortably large for the landing pad below it—hovered,
hissing and roaring, in the hot, humid air over the fantail
of the Dutch destroyer *Nassau*. Mike Chambers, wearing
a helmet and life vest, stood at the helo's big, opened door
and looked down on the gray ship rolling slightly in the
blue sea. After a slight pause he stepped out the door and
started to descend, swaying a bit on the hoist wire. It was
an act he'd performed hundreds of times, and each time he
did, he gave it his full attention. Simple though it may have
seemed, it was easy to damage yourself through carelessness. And, in the past, he'd done just that. This time, however, he was able to make a landing that was not only safe
but also graceful, and to unsnap his harness before he was
dragged off over the side.

"Welcome, Captain Chambers," said one of the two
Dutch officers that greeted him.

"Thank you," replied Chambers as he saluted what

proved to be the ship's commanding officer. With him was the flag lieutenant of Commodore van Rijn, the commander of Joint Task Force 151.

After some brief chitchat, Mike was led forward to the commodore's office. Van Rijn was standing at the door to the office, looking out over the windblown waters of the Gulf of Aden.

"Come, sit," said the commodore after being introduced to Mike. "Thank you for coming to introduce yourself. May I offer you something to drink?"

"A cup of coffee would go down well, sir."

After nodding at the waiting steward, van Rijn turned back to Chambers. "Tell me about your activities since you arrived here."

Mike described the past few nights spent attempting to, at the least, harass likely pirates.

"And your conclusion as to the effectiveness of this program?"

"We've learned a little, we think we've prevented one, maybe two attacks, and I like to think we've put a little pressure on the pirates. I can't claim any great naval victory, I'm afraid."

Van Rijn chuckled, then turned serious again. "Captain, we both know this situation is absurd. Two hundred years ago, fifty years ago, the procedure for dealing with pirates was straightforward. Warships were expected to capture them and deliver them to the nearest—or most practical—admiralty court. Here, now, we walk a slack tightrope. We have to take great care to not injure innocent parties, and even when we do capture these brigands, we have trouble finding a court willing to deal with them. To complicate it even further, they seem to have developed a very effective strategy of generally not harming their victims physically. They even have 'spokespersons' who appear on television. The result is that the victims tend to not fight back as much as they might otherwise. They just wait for the ships' owners—or their insurance underwriters to be more precise—to pay the criminals off.

"But," continued the commodore before Mike could respond, "innocent people are being killed—those two young Americans a few weeks ago, for example. This is not a game and we are not dealing with Robin Hood and his band of merry men. We are dealing with murderers."

"Yes, Commodore."

"I know you know all this. I repeat it to emphasize why I'm going to tell you that you are involved in a very dangerous enterprise. Personally, I like the idea of going after them. Of hunting them and harassing them. But one unfortunate incident can be disastrous for both of us. There are a number of governments in this region who are looking for any opportunity to embarrass the West. And especially to embarrass your country. I also like your idea of identifying and tracking one or several likely pirate vessels at a time. It won't solve the problem—we can't possibly track every potential pirate—just as we can't protect every likely victim, but as you say, it will help put the pressure on them. The only other alternative at this point is to try to organize a convoy system, but we both know that nobody would like that."

The commodore paused and looked out a porthole for a minute, then continued. "I sometimes feel like the British naval commander during your War of Independence. He had fifteen or twenty ships to patrol a thousand miles of coast, and he was further hindered by the desire not to antagonize the colonists any more than absolutely necessary. And the situation will just get worse when the monsoon season ends and the weather improves. Then they will go even farther out to sea, farther to the east."

Once again the commodore paused, then continued.

"I understand that you're not under my operational control, but I must make a request—continue your experiments and let me know if you find anything especially effective. I will do my best to cover your back, but you must give me the earliest possible notice if something goes seriously wrong, something I may have trouble explaining."

"If something does go wrong, Commodore, I hope I will be the only person you hear it from."

"That would be very desirable."

* * *

At four forty-two in the morning a powerful monsoon squall exploded over *Eastern Trader*, inundating her with a solid mass of hissing, pounding rain, furiously flashing lightning and gale force winds. Thanks to the rain, the nearly impenetrable darkness surrounding the ship was made totally so, the heavenly fireworks creating little more than an imprecise glow in the all-encompassing wet.

Since entering the Strait of Malacca the previous afternoon, the ship had made good time. She was now over halfway through. With the heavily forested shores of Indonesia more than fifty miles to port and the equally heavily wooded shores of Malaysia an equal distance to starboard, there would have been little to see except other ships.

"Colonel," said Captain Papadis to bin-Sharif, who was dozing on the bridge, "this rain is causing trouble for the radar. There is a great deal of sea return, and I'm not sure a small boat would be identifiable at the moment."

The colonel was on his feet instantly. They were in one of the most dangerous parts of the strait and he was very much aware of it. It was a section in which operated several of the exceptionally vicious and ruthless pirate gangs that plagued the region—gangs reputed to be greatly more bloodthirsty than the Somalis were believed to be. He'd considered ordering his entire detachment to be on the alert but had resisted the temptation. They'd been in the danger zone for many hours and would be for another day. It would be folly to exhaust his men in that way. He wanted them alert if needed. So he'd kept nine men on watch at all times and then decided to follow Captain Papadis's example by dozing in a chair on the bridge.

After wiping his hand quickly across his face, the colonel walked over to the radar display, which the captain was still attempting to adjust. As advertised, the screen was a mass of little glowing spots. "How long do you anticipate this will continue?" he asked.

"Perhaps a half hour," replied the captain. "Then the screen will clear. These storms are not unlike those of the desert. They scream and torment, then move on."

Bin-Sharif smiled at the captain's analogy, then whispered into his collar microphone. His earpiece whispered back. The captain looked at him questioningly.

"My lieutenant reports that both his radar and optical sensors appear undependable at the moment, but his men are on station and alert. Not to mention wet."

With that, the colonel looked around the darkened bridge, at the shadowy figures of the mate of the watch and the two hands standing behind the consoles that monitored and controlled almost every aspect of *Eastern Trader*'s life. Everything seemed in order, so he returned to his chair to save his own energy, totally confident in the ability of his commandos to deal with anything the local trash might try.

The attack started three minutes later when one of bin-Sharif's sergeants noticed a faint glow in the water right alongside the ship. He recognized it as the phosphorescent wake of a boat. Grabbing a corporal, he ran forward, skidding slightly on the water-covered deck and reporting the situation to the lieutenant as he did. By the time the grapnel from that first boat had caught on the midships lifeline, the off-duty section was already on the way to their stations.

The sergeant and his companion had immediately hit the deck and crawled to the rail, a shallow river of rainwater flowing over their hands and knees. When they reached the rail, they peeked quickly over the side. The lightning flashed again, faintly illuminating a speedboat filled with armed men some twenty feet below them. After exchanging a half-seen nod, each grabbed a grenade and tossed it almost directly down into the boat.

There was a double flash, then a combined roar. The sergeant looked down again at the roiled water slipping along the ship's side. The boat was gone, although the grapnel and its line remained tangled in the lifeline. He also noticed that the rain was already beginning to slack off, while the wind continued to scream.

On the bridge, Captain Papadis called for maximum speed while bin-Sharif walked from wing to wing, bouncing slightly on his toes, scanning the night and using his communicator to ask his officers and sergeants questions or issue orders.

Then, on the fantail, another grapnel appeared.

"The lights!" snapped the colonel. Two sixty-inch searchlights, one mounted on each side of the superstructure's second level, snapped on and nailed the boat astern with their burning blue white light. So powerful were the lights that the drizzle landing on their housings began to sizzle almost immediately. The pirates had no time to

shield their eyes, and before they could recover sufficiently to shoot the lights out, they were all dead, chopped
to pieces by a fifty-caliber machine gun and four automatic rifles.

The attack ended as quickly as it had begun. One of
the Saudi lieutenants was crouched on the forecastle when
he became aware that another boat was alongside, riding
the bow wave just under the anchor. He turned slightly
and found himself looking into the mustache of a pirate
who had evidently reached the anchor and was now pulling himself up over the rail. The lieutenant raised his sidearm and shot the boarder in the face, just above the
mustache. The now-faceless body remained where it was
for an instant then toppled backward and disappeared, as
did the boat.

Neither Captain Papadis nor Colonel bin-Sharif ever
had any idea whether or not there were more than three
boats involved, and neither really cared. Within another
few minutes the deluge completely died and the radar
once again became useful. The nearest blip was a large
tanker, about a mile ahead and to starboard.

"I'm afraid we'd better report this to the local authorities," said the captain.

"No. That will just lead to further questions."

"Despite the storm, Colonel, I think we have to assume
that somebody else saw that attack. That tanker over there
was undoubtedly aware of it. They will report it, and
there will be questions about why we didn't report it."

"If we do report it?"

"I will send a message giving them all the details. We
have nothing to hide."

"Will they want to board us or tell us to return to Singapore?"

"No. For what reason? We suffered no casualties, and

they understand better than anybody the cost of diverting a ship from her schedule."

"Very well."

The colonel then headed aft to commend his men for their excellent work, while Papadis leaned on the control console and took a deep breath. He was very much looking forward to returning to the Mediterranean and the Atlantic. He was getting too old to put up with all the shit that went on in the eastern seas.

Eastern Trader continued to race north through the unsettled night.

* * *

"Okay, Jerry, let's get down to basics. How do you say 'boat'?"

Jerry looked at Ray across the stainless-steel table in the quarters Mike had arranged for them aboard *Wake Island*. The space, one of many aboard the ship intended to house twenty embarked marines, was Spartan. Bunks along the bulkheads, two tables and fifteen not-very-comfortable chairs, all secured to the deck. Three opened cans of soda on the table. The visible surfaces were all painted steel or stainless, with occasional highlights of fireproof laminates. The light was from harsh, blue white fluorescent tubes. Jerry listened to the faint hum of fresh air being forced in and felt the faint vibrations of the ship's main engines. Then he glanced to the side at Ted, whose expression showed that the SEAL thought Jerry would blow it. "*Dooni*. Did I pronounce that right?"

A look of disgust flashed across Ted's face as Jerry mouthed "Gotcha!" at him.

"Yes," said Ray, "I think you have it pretty right. But remember, Somali isn't one of my strongest languages. I've learned the little I know the past three weeks from a

CD. And don't forget they've got a mess of very different dialects. Supposedly a lot of Somalis can't understand each other very well."

"Thank you, sir."

"Always a pleasure, Chief. Now, Ted, how do you say 'ocean'?"

Ted smiled. "*Bad-weyn*. Sounds kind of Arab to me."

"It may have started there. They use a lot of Arabic words."

"How's our little language school going?" asked Mike as he appeared at the watertight door.

"Between Somali, Arabic, Italian, English and a lot of waving and shouting, we may be able to communicate, Captain."

"Good. Where's Alex? She allowed to skip class?"

"She's in the comm center, sir. Networking with her old buddies at that other organization."

"I'm back now," said Alex as she stepped through the door, a frown on her face.

"Bad news?"

"Not terribly important but potentially very irritating."

"And?" asked Ted.

"It seems the Agency's new Indian Ocean pirate czar arrived at Djibouti right after we left and immediately started kicking butts. It's somebody I know slightly— Amanda Cochran."

"I've heard of pirate kings," observed Ray, "but never of pirate czars."

"Where have you been the past two hundred fifty years, Ray? We don't have kings in the United States. Just czars. Or czarinas, in this case."

"What's the problem with all this?" asked Mike, trying not to smile too much at Alex and Ray's exchange.

Alex took a deep breath. "Mandy's young—younger

than I am—and very hard-charging. The consensus is that she's bound and determined to become the first woman director of the Agency. One way or another, which means that she'll always end up on the winning side, no matter which side she started out on."

"But we don't work for her," said Jerry.

"That's what you and I think, but I'm not sure that's what she thinks. Everybody says her management style is very hands-on. We're going to have to be careful with this chick."

"Maybe she'll get some good intel for us," said Jerry, a hopeful tone to his voice.

"Maybe," answered Alex, her skepticism obvious.

* * *

Ali was sitting in the shade of a dilapidated lean-to on the beach, repairing some of old Osman's fishing gear, while the old man dozed in the shade of his beached boat. Hearing a mechanical growling, Ali looked up and spotted a rust-splotched jeep grinding its way through the rocky sand toward him. Desperate for any distraction, he continued to watch as it seemed to be headed directly for him. It slowed as it reached the beach but didn't stop until it had pulled up beside him, almost hitting him. "Get in," directed the driver. "Suleiman wants to see you."

An hour later Ali was standing, with two other young men—neither of whom he'd ever seen before and both of whom, based on the scars on their faces and arms, were experienced fighters—in the large, walled garden behind Suleiman Hassan's partially completed new house, located not far from his father Ibrihim's.

"You have been chosen to join our brotherhood," said the pirate captain with a stern look on his face. Left to his own devices he would not have selected Ali—he was too young and inexperienced—but Ibrihim had insisted. He seemed to feel some obligation to the boy's dead father. "You will be doing men's work," he said, looking directly at Ali, "and you will be expected to act like a man. The work is hard and it is dangerous and we have no time for boys. If you serve your brothers well, you will become rich men. If not, you will die. If it is necessary, it will be me who will kill you. Do you understand?"

"Yes, sir," replied Ali, ecstatic at the thought of escaping Osman and not totally appreciating the truth behind Suleiman's words.

* * *

Mike Chambers walked out one of the steel piers in *Wake Island*'s flooded boat well and stopped next to Jerry, who was looking at the middle outboard on one of the cats. Standing with him was Chief Engineman Richard Clarke, the senior engineering petty officer assigned to care for the team's six monster engines. Despite the overhead deck, which protected them from the sun, the air was hot. And salty. With the gate closed, the water in the well was calm, but the cat was rising and falling slowly because the ship herself was rolling slightly, thanks to the long swell from the east, the spawn of a wind blowing steadily over thousands of miles of fetch, all the way from India and beyond.

"What's the conclusion, Chief?" asked Mike, looking at the chief engineman. As he spoke, his voice echoed slightly in the football field–sized well. "Is it Anderson's overactive imagination or is there a problem?"

"There was a problem, Captain, but we've fixed it. A bracket came loose and was tapping. You've been working these boats damned hard the past week, and they weren't built to MilSpec. I mean, Chief Andrews did an excellent job of beefing them up, but still. You going out again tonight?"

"Plan to."

"Captain Chambers?"

Mike turned to find a junior petty officer standing behind him. "Yes?"

"You're wanted in the comm center, sir. A deputy secretary of defense wants to speak with you."

Mike groaned inwardly. "Very well. Thank you." He turned back. "Chief, please do what you can so we'll be in top shape tonight."

"Absolutely, Captain," said Clarke.

"I know better than to pry, Chief," said the senior engineman to Jerry after Mike had left, "but you guys certainly do seem well connected. You seem to get anything you want, including your own nine-hundred-foot-long ship to play with."

Jerry pondered his answer. Captain Chambers had always made it very clear that on missions like these, security was a top priority. The fewer people who knew who they were and exactly what they were doing the better. Especially on a ship the size of *Wake Island*, where almost three thousand people were all busy e-mailing home at all hours of the day and night, unhindered by the careful censorship that was so difficult to impose in any but the most obvious combat situations.

How much should he tell Clarke? Clearly, the engineman, like everybody else aboard, knew they were there to do something about the pirates. Did he need to know more? Jerry doubted it. Not at the moment.

"Don't sound so envious, Chief," he finally replied. "These connections are a real pain in the ass. We spend half our time tangled up in politics. There are more people in D.C. who want to get us—or at least don't like us—

than there are bad guys floating around the rest of the world. And it's not just Captain Chambers who has to fight the gators. Somehow we all get dragged in, and sometimes it makes me damn nervous."

"I'll take your word for it, Boats."

When Mike reached the secure teleconferencing room, Alan Parker was on the screen in his usual position. Seated behind his desk with his suit coat on and his tie precisely positioned.

"How're we doing, Mike?"

"Working hard, Alan. Every night. All night."

"So what's the score?"

"We've made contact with likely vessels twice, and we think we've prevented either two or three attacks."

"No heads to hang over the mantel?"

"Not yet. As I've already told you, our plan at the moment is to move up and down the coast and try to spot them and put pressure on them. If we can catch them in the act, all the better. I'd hoped the Agency would've told us a little more about their organization and who's in charge, but so far all we've had to work from are a few faint patterns we think we've come up with. Is SECDEF getting impatient?" As he said it, Mike thought of a remark Alex had once made—that as far as Parker was concerned, everybody who gave the United States the slightest heartburn should be nuked back to the Stone Age.

"I suspect he is, though he hasn't said anything specific. But a lot of other people have. The new administration is settling in, and they want something to point at to prove they're able to handle their new jobs. More important, they want to prove they're not soft on terrorism. And they want it right away. Action, Mike, action! They're especially eager, I might add, for evidence that either Al

Qaeda or the Taliban is part of all this. Something they can give to the media. If you would produce that, a lot of people will be very happy and you'll be a hero."

"A lot of people, Alan? How many people know about what we're doing? How many, besides the crew of this ship, even know we're here?"

"Only people who have a need to know, Mike. Don't get upset. Actually, it's the Agency, and they're not even totally sure what you're doing, but they seem to feel you're about to trample on their turf."

"What! Has SECDEF put us under Agency control?"

"No, of course not. But you're getting in and up close with the pirates. They think it's kind of like flirting—one thing leads to another. And they worry about their turf even more than the rest of us do."

"Alan, please. If SECDEF is concerned, let me know. Otherwise, I've got a long night ahead of me."

"Mike, I'm trying to do you a favor, to give you a heads-up. Amanda Cochran, the Agency's pirate czar, is headed for you right now in a helicopter. She's decided to go out with you tonight."

"She hasn't even bothered to contact us yet."

"She's a very boots on the ground person and she's on her way to visit you. Now you know."

"Do I have to take her?"

"It would be the polite thing to do. And the diplomatic one too."

Damn it, thought Mike. Tonight of all nights! He'd planned to try a new tactic to see if he could get the ball rolling. Push the envelope a little. It was a tactic Commodore van Rijn probably wouldn't object to. Not much, anyway, unless somebody complained to him. But he knew from long experience that the Agency sometimes had its own worldview and its own agenda, and he was uncomfortable with their having invited themselves for a boat ride.

"Okay."

"Remember, pal. The pressure's building here. We need action. I'm pushing to send in some Raptors to plaster the raggies, but there's a lot of unconstructive chatter about collateral damage. No matter what the *New York Times* may say, these people are all Al Qaeda. For proof, just look at all the terrorists we've got detained around the world. Some of them are Somalis. They're out to destroy our homeland."

"We'll do our best, Alan."

* * *

Ali was as excited as he was nervous as, chewing a mouthful of khat, he walked down the dusty road to the beach with the other new pirates, who were bragging about their feats of valor in a recent skirmish between two sub-clans. It had been a minor affair—a dispute over a few cattle—and had involved no more than twenty men on each side, but two had died. According to his companions, the dead had been pigs over whose death no tears were warranted.

At last, thought Ali, he was really free of Osman. He was a man, now. And he would soon be rich. Good food, money, clothes, girls, a house of his own. Maybe even a car. He'd be important, respected and even feared.

"Halt!"

The pirates halted and turned to look at two of Ibrihim Hassan's heavily armed "policemen" standing beside one of the plaster-and-block buildings along the road. From the faded writing across its front, it seemed it had once been a food store. It was now clearly long abandoned.

"Come here," continued one of the thugs, pointing at Ali.

The boy walked over to them.

"Give us khat," said the one who'd spoken before.

A bolt of fury cursed through the boy. The bastards were pigs. Pigs, rapists and thieves. He and his new shipmates would make short work of them. Except his new shipmates weren't showing any sign of offense. They were sniggering.

When he saw the barrel of one of the thug's rifles start to rise, he regained control. "I work for Ibrihim Hassan," said Ali, hoping to impress the thug. Or, at the very least, appeal to his team spirit. "Just like you."

"Everybody around here works for him and he wants you to obey my orders."

Ali slowly pulled a plastic bag containing what was left of his supply of the mildly narcotic leaves out of his pants pocket and held it out. If he had been carrying the Kalashnikov rifle that Suleiman said he would soon be given, he wouldn't have hesitated to kill both the bastards. That's what a man did in a situation like this. But he was unarmed at the moment. The world was filled with rapists and thieves, he thought with bitter resignation. That was the way of life. In time he would be wealthy and powerful enough to be at the other end of the business, but for now he'd have to go along with it.

The thug took the bag and opened it.

"Garbage!" he snarled. "This is garbage khat." He then emptied the leaves from the bag, ground them into the dust and glowered at Ali, challenging him to respond.

"May we go?" asked Ali through gritted teeth. They hadn't even wanted the khat. All they'd wanted to do was humiliate him. Force him to do their will.

The thugs looked at each other a moment. "Go," snarled the more talkative of the two soldiers.

The thought occurred to Ali that even after he was rich, he'd still have to avoid situations where others could take his newfound wealth from him. He already knew well that there were few rules in Somalia, the principal one being that a man must do whatever he had to do to protect what was his. And he couldn't count on anybody. Not his clan chief, not his shipmates.

Steaming, Ali continued down the road with the other new pirates, who continued to make jokes about him. They were met on the beach by a small fishing boat with an outboard, which carried them out to the old, wooden dhow anchored in the tiny, beach-lined harbor. Long before they reached it, Ali could smell it. Long-dead fish, rot and diesel. The ancient fifty-foot vessel, which hadn't been painted in a lifetime and would have been considered a relic just about anywhere else in the world except on the Indian Ocean, was to be his home for almost two weeks. As they approached the dhow, Ali saw a flash in the sky over the ocean. Then he heard the faint rumble and recognized it as a helicopter. He'd never been in one, but like practically everybody else in the world, he knew what one was. It was the enemy, and if he'd had his Kalashnikov he would have shot it down without hesitation.

* * *

"Ray," said Alex over the helo intercom, "you realize just how insane this whole situation is, don't you?"

"You mean because the pirates are hiding right in front of us?" replied the marine as he stared out the window at the barren coastline and the indentation that passed for a local harbor.

"They're not even hiding at the moment. That brown thing down there, is that a dhow?"

Ray studied the boat through his binoculars. It had a bow that swept up and forward and a high, square stern. It was, indeed, a dhow, a relic of the Middle Ages. Except that thousands were still in use, and this one undoubtedly had an engine. It also had a boat of some sort stowed on deck, across its low waist. Not that a big fishing boat carrying a small one proved anything. "Looks like one to me."

"Fishing boat or pirate?"

"I'm not sure there's a difference around here. We won't know until they actually attack somebody, and then it'll be too late."

"We do get the damndest jobs!"

"I have a feeling Commodore van Rijn feels the same way. That's what the boss seems to think."

"Maybe we'll be able to change the rules a little tonight."

* * *

Ali had come to think of himself as a fisherman, but he could hardly have been considered an experienced seaman. He'd always fished from a small boat, close inshore, and never gone out in truly rough weather, an activity which Osman had considered not only too much work but also a waste of time. The boy's real nautical education, therefore, started within twenty minutes of the ancient dhow's getting under way, shortly after dark.

The instant the dhow plodded out from behind the breakwater, it slammed into the first of an infinite number of monsoon seas and its motion became terrifying. It pitched its bow high up and over one monstrous, barely visible wave, only to dive into the next with a bone-jarring shudder. Then it rolled, a long, slow, sickening roll with a stomach-wrenching snap at the end followed by another long, slow, sickening roll in the other direction.

Nothing he'd ever experienced had prepared Ali for any of this motion, and the acrid stench of the antique diesel—which was impossible to escape—made it infinitely worse. He felt as if the low, thick monsoon clouds had trapped the nauseating fumes and wrapped them tightly around his head. He knew he was going to be sick, and he resented Ibrihim's thugs even more because he'd been told that khat was able to help ward off seasickness. He sat on the deck amidships, next to the boat stowed there, fighting against the inevitable. Yet, despite the foreknowledge and the pain in his gut, he was surprised, even shocked, when it actually happened, when his stomach spasmed and it's watery, acid contents burned their way up his throat and out his mouth.

"No, not here. Not on the deck," shouted Suleiman. Then he laughed.

What did Suleiman or anybody else care if he was sick on the deck? thought Ali. The boat already stank, and the waves that were occasionally washing over it would wipe the mess away. Clutching anything he could find, he crawled aft and toward the side. There he joined the other newcomers—who were already lying with their faces pressed against the rough, stinking deck planking, their heads inches from the rail, struggling fruitlessly to prevent the next eruption, oblivious to everything but their own misery. They were real tough guys, thought Ali with faint satisfaction, but they were not seamen any more than he was.

So great was Ali's suffering, so great the knife-like, bitter-sour ache in his stomach and so great the headache that came with it, that he found it impossible to dream of the wealth and pleasure that lay ahead. He even found himself wishing he was back in the hovel. Or out with the old bastard Osman, fishing in calmer waters.

"Up, all of you!" shouted Suleiman. "There is work to do and I'm not going to let you lie around while your brothers are working.

"Up!" he shouted again as he kicked Ali in the ribs. He still didn't like the boy, but Ibrihim had insisted.

5

"You have anything good for us, Reynolds?" asked Mike, walking into *Wake Island*'s semidarkened CIC shortly after dusk. As he passed the several other operators on watch, each staring into his or her own glowing display, he was aware that they were all trying not to see him. The whole ship had been told that their five passengers and the two muscle boats they raced around in didn't really exist.

"Between radar and helo reports, two likelies, Captain. Three small boats headed north from this cove and a larger, slower boat—probably the dhow your people reported seeing—headed south," replied the petty officer, pointing at the display in front of him as he did.

"Very well. We'll go after the three small boats tonight." The dhow was probably too big for tonight's experiment, he thought as he stepped out of the CIC, headed down a series of ladders and walked aft through the cavernous helo hangar to the boat well.

Mike was very much aware of the activity that surrounded him, the continuous, round-the-clock internal
motion of a large warship. Officers and sailors going here
and there. Cleaning, fixing, looking, sometimes arguing.
The sights, the sounds, the smells were totally familiar to
him, yet for the first time in many years he didn't really
feel part of it. On this job, as on most others, he'd intentionally kept his team apart from both the ship's company
and the embarked marines. The Tridents operated on their
own schedule, and there was no reason for any of the details of their activities to be known except to a few. It
made perfect sense, yet it was also beginning to give him
a sense of isolation, one he knew the rest of the team
shared. And, from a personal standpoint, that isolation,
combined with some of the enemies he'd made the past
couple years, might develop into a barrier to his receiving
his admiral's flag. He'd be in the promotion zone soon,
and SECDEF had assured him that taking this job would
not cause him problems, but the reality was that it just
might. Promotion to flag rank involved a lot more than
driving boats around. It involved the most exquisite politics, and on that front he suspected he was not winning.

He was brooding too much, he told himself as he ducked
through a watertight door and onto the pier in the well.
Jerry, Ted and Ray were already in the cats, stowing gear
and checking them out. Alex was standing on the pier talking to a small, almost frail-looking young woman dressed
in brown-splotched desert camouflage trousers and blouse.
That, he concluded, was the new pirate czar. She must have
arrived while he was working with Reynolds in the CIC.
As he walked toward them, Alex looked up. "Captain, this
is Amanda Cochran. Amanda, Captain Chambers."

As they shook hands, Mike reassessed the czar. Physically she looked frail, but her eyes certainly were not.

They could flay you in a moment. "I'm glad you could join us."

"I've already heard rumors about your activities, Captain, so I figured I'd better get a handle on them right away. So tell me, in your own words, what have you been doing since you arrived and what do you plan for the future? Give it to me verbally tonight then in writing within the next two days."

"Ms. Cochran," rumbled Mike, momentarily disconcerted by the woman's totally unanticipated frontal assault—he hadn't even had time to say the wrong thing—"we're taking you with us tonight as a courtesy to facilitate coordination and liaison. If you're concerned with command and control, you're going to have to take that up with the secretary of defense. Now, please either hop in that boat or go back to Djibouti."

"Let's hit it," said Mandy, changing course one hundred and eighty degrees. Clearly she was trying to maintain the illusion that she was in control. Alex was right, thought Mike. She's able to flip at an amazing speed and can undoubtedly play on both sides of the net at the same time.

Alex handed Mandy a set of chest armor along with a life vest, headset and lightweight helmet, while Mike put on his own. The three then stepped into the cat, and Mike lit off the three big outboards.

A few minutes later the two cats edged out of the well into the dark, blustery night, the rumble of their powerful engines echoing off the surrounding steel bulkheads. Mike, Alex and Amanda were sharing one boat while Ray, Ted and Jerry manned the other.

"Mamacita, this is Trident," said Mike into his headset microphone, speaking very carefully and clearly so he could be understood above the growl of the three big out-boards.

"Roger, Trident. Your targets are maintaining course and speed. Your intercept at two zero knots is three four seven degrees. You should pick them up on your radar in about forty-five minutes."

"Roger, Mamacita. Keep us advised of any changes."

"Roger."

Mike turned to three four seven degrees, noting out of the side of his eye that Ray was doing the same.

"Ms. Cochran," said Mike a few minutes later in an effort to clear the air, "we have always worked well with the Agency and certainly hope to continue doing so. In fact, we are almost desperate for the sort of intel you can probably provide—like who's in charge and how do they know where to intercept their targets—some don't appear to me to be random encounters."

Mandy hesitated a moment before answering, as if calculating or at the least considering her words carefully.

"We haven't been able to learn as much as we'd like. We think some of the gangs have centralized control. Others seem little more than some local thugs getting their hands on a few rifles and heading out to sea. We haven't had a great deal of luck yet in infiltrating any of them to any depth." That was all she felt like giving him. It was almost all she knew, for that matter, although she did know where some of the money was going. Not that the knowledge had proved particularly valuable up to now.

"Fair enough. If you'll do what you can, we'll do what we can."

"Sounds like a good plan." What else could she say at the moment? she asked herself.

"Okay, Boss, we've got them now," said Alex a few

minutes later, breaking the silence that had descended beneath the roaring of the engines and the slap of the waves on the hulls.

"Trident One, this is Trident."

"Roger. We have the target on radar."

"Roger. We'll follow the same procedure as before. You run around and behind them and take station to the west."

"Roger."

"Ms. Cochran," shouted Mike a few minutes later, "this is what we've been doing so far. Making sure they know we're here without letting them know exactly what we are. Tonight, we're going to ratchet the action up a little. We're going to buzz them to see if we can get them to open fire."

"What! I wasn't told anything about this sort of entrapment action. I'm not sure this is in compliance with the Agency's protocols. Has this been authorized? What happens if they're really just fishermen?" Mandy's almost-cooperative tone had disappeared, replaced with one of sincere hostility.

"If they're really just fishermen, then they'll curse us but not open fire."

"I'm not going to order you to stop, but if this blows up . . ."

"We were counting on you for that. Are you armed?"

"I have an automatic."

"Grab one of those M-16s while Alex makes herself comfortable behind the fifty."

"Trident One, this is Trident. Stand by to execute provocation. You will pass astern of the target first then stand clear while we pass ahead of them. If you are fired upon, return fire if you have a clear field."

"Roger, Trident."

"Stand by. . . . Execute."

As he gave the order, Mike turned his cat toward the three boats and increased speed until the outboards were screaming. Now that they were making almost thirty-five knots, the cat's pounding became intense—bone-rattling—and the wind's scream moved up the scale. He glanced at the radar again and could see the blip that was the other cat zooming toward the targets. A cascade of cold sweat raced down his spine as he wondered if they had shoulder-fired rockets. A fast-moving target was hard to hit on a dark night with an RPG, but missiles could be dangerous, especially if they knew how to use them.

Then he wondered if the cats could take the new level of abuse he was about to inflict on them.

Too late now to worry about that. And far too late to worry about what might happen if he ended up killing three boatloads of innocent and impoverished fishermen. It was all a matter of discipline. He knew he wouldn't open fire unless he was absolutely certain he was being fired on, and he was equally certain about Ray. He took a deep breath and concentrated on the maneuver. He studied the radar again. He was going to cross before Ray, so he slowed, taking care to prevent the churning, breaking seas from taking control of the boat away from him.

Five minutes or less to go.

The targets were in sight now and so was the other cat, roaring past them, creating a towering, cresting wake. Mike tensed. His objective was not to swamp any of the boats, but it was a possibility. If Ray ended up capsizing any of them, Mike would have to back off, to give the Somalis a chance to pick up any swimmers. He could almost hear Mandy Cochran's mind working, practicing her version of the affair, just in case it turned out to be the sort of incident that would drive Alan Parker into a sarcastic tirade. Then he didn't have time to think about anything but driving the cat, because he was about to cross ahead of the boats at a range of maybe thirty yards.

The cat screamed forward, its wake erupting volcanically and rolling toward the Somali boats. At this range, with his night vision goggles, he could see the boats. And their crews. Most were hanging on for dear life as the boats were pounded and rolled. A few were shaking their fists.

They were past them now. A hundred yards at least. He noted on the radar that Ray, who was also now well past, had slowed to an idle, waiting for further instructions. Mike slowed and turned to continue watching.

"I think they have a pretty good idea who and what we are now, Captain," remarked Alex. "Even if we're not sure what they are."

"Yes, let's see how they react." He then directed Ray to take station fifty yards abeam of the boats.

Almost as soon as the maelstrom created by the two cats' wakes had subsided, the Somalis turned and headed back to shore. Not a shot had been fired. No weapons had even been displayed.

"Captain," said Alex as they approached within a few miles of the coast, "did you notice that little mushroom growing on that one boat's mast?"

"No." He studied the boat. "I'll be damned. They're changing the rules as fast as we are. They're putting radar on their small boats now."

"I guess we're not the only ones who can raise the ante."

Mandy said nothing but listened intently. She was in the intelligence business. Her role, at the moment, was to listen and look and determine how what she was learning might best be put to use. Why express an opinion, why say anything, when it might just be used against her later?

* * *

Ibrihim Hassan was not a fisherman and never had been. Neither had been his father or grandfather or any other direct ancestor. All had been clan chiefs and would have been offended if it were suggested that any of them were fishermen. Hassan was also old, his thin body worn by decades of military and political brawling. Ibrihim Hassan was the last person in the world one might expect to find in a thirty-foot open boat pounding through a stormy night in the Indian Ocean. Yet, there he was—seemingly oblivious to the pounding and the spray that occasionally soaked him—staring in delight at the radar screen. He could now see his enemy and confirm that they were two fast boats. Even better, it looked as if they were going to close in, so that he could see exactly what they were. Exactly what he was dealing with. The confirmation was well worth the pain in his arms and back. "Mohamed," he said to his second son, "do you see them? Here and here." As the old clan leader spoke, he pointed at the small radar display.

"Yes, Father. Should I tell the men to prepare to fire?"

"No! I told you that before. Only if they fire at us. We are here tonight to learn, not to attack. That will come."

"As you wish."

Hassan continued to watch, fascinated, as the two cats approached. He could now hear the roar of their engines very clearly. Then he could see the white glow of their bow waves in the distance. He found himself tensing. They were probably heavily armed. And armored. Were they preparing to open fire? What exactly did they have in mind?

And then the first was roaring out of the night and past. Astern. "Tell the men to hang on hard, Mohamed," he shouted. He adjusted his night vision goggles and turned, grabbing the thwart with both hands as he did.

He could see it now. Big and gray, with a big machine gun mounted forward. And what else might it carry? He also recognized that it was a catamaran and appreciated the fact that the two hulls provided an extra portion of stability.

"Father!" The anger in Mohamed's voice was clear, even above the roar of the engines.

"Control yourself, Mohamed. Discipline is called for. Do not fire unless they do. We are not in a position to win at the moment."

The first cat screamed past, its wake rolling in on them and starting to crest like a tsunami just beginning to feel the seafloor.

Even as the first waves were hitting them from astern, the second cat thundered in from the other side and crossed their bows. Again Ibrihim studied it with great care and almost delight. It was gone in an instant, leaving behind another mass of rolling, breaking waves that slammed into the first, multiplying the confusion to produce what was, for a few minutes, a truly threatening mass of boiling water.

"Good," said Ibrihim after the waves had partly subsided. "We now know what we are dealing with. We can also assume that since they have not been seen near the shore, they are operating from that big American ship we've spotted offshore. We will go home now and see how far they follow us."

"What if they do that again?"

"If they do, they do, but I don't think they will open fire on us. Not now."

Mohamed was not happy, but there was nothing he could do. It was all very well that Ibrihim thought he knew more about the enemy, but as far as Mohamed was concerned, enemies were for killing, not studying.

* * *

The dhow continued to pitch and roll through the night, hobbyhorsing as it went. By dawn it was almost a hundred miles offshore. Suleiman consulted his handheld GPS again, then had the tired, stinking engine slowed. "We're here. Four men will be on watch with binoculars at all times. The rest of you hang on—we'll be rolling. And keep the Kenyan flag handy."

Ali, who had been cleaning the hold and hating it, groaned as he stuck his head out the door and scanned the empty horizon. "There's nothing here!"

"But there will be," explained one of his more experienced shipmates. "Many ships pass this way."

Ali stared blankly as the gray dawn grew lighter in the east. He was empty and exhausted from the rigors of seasickness. If somebody had tried to tell him that he'd slept fitfully, he would have denied it. And yet, when not working he *had* slept on and off, and now that the wind had decreased, calming the Indian Ocean, he was on the verge of returning to the living.

"Here, take some of this," said the boatswain, handing him a plastic bowl filled with beans and a large cup of water. Ali stared at it. "Eat it. You'll feel better and we'll need every man today."

* * *

"Colonel bin-Sharif has already proved himself to be a good choice, Your Excellency," remarked Abdul ibn-Abdullah to his boss, Prince Saeed.

Saeed looked at his assistant, who was sitting across the aisle from him in the small business jet. He was young, of good—although not royal—blood and extremely useful. "So far he has handled himself, and the situation, very well. We must hope he continues to do so. When are they to arrive at Colombo?"

"In three days."

"Is everything arranged there?"

"Yes, there will be minimal formalities."

"Remind bin-Sharif to be alert."

"Yes, Your Excellency."

Saeed looked out the window of the plane. Ahead, although still not yet visible, lay the holy city of Medina. Ten miles to the east of it was a small airport. Two miles from that was a new petrochemical facility that had just started operations. As might be expected with such a plant, the facility had an extensive security system to protect against terrorists of all kind. And within the petrochemical facility was the new home for the Topol missiles, a large, garage-like building in which the weapons would be reassembled and stored until the king found it convenient to tell the rest of the world about them.

* * *

Mandy Cochran stared glumly out the window of her office at the utter nothingness that surrounded the joint facility. Thousands of square miles of dry, hard dirt, mud hovels and goats. If Djibouti weren't one of the very few countries in the region that even pretended to like the United States, and if Somalia weren't only a few miles to the south, she'd never have been there. And Somalia was even worse.

She took a deep breath. She *had* fallen into a trap, a

trap laid by some of her enemies back at Langley. She'd allowed herself to be ushered into oblivion.

She'd known the risk, of course, and had hit the ground running, but the ground was proving too mushy, too slippery, to provide much traction. Many of the sources she'd been told were in place weren't worth shit, and it was going to be incredibly difficult to recruit and control more.

And she found the command-and-control situation totally confusing. On one level there was Combined Joint Task Force 151, which had recently been formed to chase pirates, replacing CTF 150, which had been in charge of chasing pirates but was now supposed to be chasing druggies. Then there were the U.S. Fifth Fleet, the Africa Command, the French, Italians, Spanish, Chinese and Saudis—and the governments—Somaliland, Puntland, the transitional government that supposedly ran the whole country—were even more elusive and jelly-like than she'd imagined they might be.

And that damn naval group—the one Alex Mahan was involved with—was going to be a serious problem for her. If they screwed up, they could take her down with them, but she now appreciated that she had no control whatsoever over what they did or didn't do.

There was a knock at her door.

"Yes?"

The door opened, and Preston Olbrig walked in with his deputy, Abdul Jones—a tall, slightly stooped young black man—immediately behind him.

"How was your boat ride?" asked Olbrig as he sat down at Mandy's beat-up conference table.

"That's ancient history. Have you come up with a plan yet to develop more resources within these pirate gangs? It's something you should have done long ago."

Gets right to the point, doesn't she? thought Olbrig.

"Since we discussed this yesterday, we've actually lost one. He was in one of the big gangs, but he's disappeared now. As far as we can tell, he got his cut of that big ransom from that supertanker and decided he didn't need us."

"And now? How do you plan to replace him?"

"It's a matter of luck. It's damn hard for Americans to fit into Somalia, to swim with the fishes, as Chairman Mao used to say."

"They like money, don't they?"

"Too much. Like the guy we just lost."

"How about guys with a grudge against individual pirate leaders?"

"We keep looking."

"I consider that answer nonresponsive."

Olbrig glowered.

"Maybe I should go in myself and see what I can come up with."

Abdul burst into laughter. "Some of these people have very bad attitudes about women who don't know their place. Worse than just about anywhere else I can think of."

Now it was Mandy's turn to glower. She already didn't like Jones, and she was sure that in time she would like him even less. "I want to explore the question of working more closely with the local security people. The Somalis. See if we can get them to work more with us."

"Which one?" asked Olbrig.

"What about this Sheikh al-Abbas you mentioned in your summary. Isn't he the head of Puntland security and aren't a lot of the pirates coming from Puntland?"

"You can try," agreed Olbrig, "although Abdul thinks the sheikh gets a cut of the action. Even if he doesn't, a number of the clan leaders whose support is necessary to keep the government in power do."

"Maybe we can find a way to make it worth his while."

"Bribe him? Why not? What do you say, Abdul?"

"It's worth a try."

"Set it up. Does he speak English?"

"Of course. But he won't. At least he never does when he's dealing with me."

"Then Abdul comes with me to translate in case I have trouble with whatever dialect he prefers."

And if you manage to offend him, I die at your side, thought Abdul glumly.

"And Preston," continued Mandy, "I want some serious action—pronto—on the money side. By next Friday I want a transparent, actionable and supportable Power-Point presentation of exactly how the pirates' profits support terrorism. I want the precise route the money follows from here to Baghdad or Kandahar or Damascus."

Obrig sighed. "I know I told you we think much of it goes to banks in the Emirates and in Europe, but it's very hard to get the details with no government to speak of in Somalia and no real banks."

"If the Treasury Department can trace American tax evaders, we can certainly lean on the foreign banks for information like this."

"The banks in question don't see any reason to cooperate. No Americans are involved, and we really can't threaten them much since we owe them so much money."

"They hate terrorism as much as we do."

"Maybe."

"Anyway, there is a nexus. No Americans may be involved, but U.S. currency is. Just take my word for it, that gives us the authority to act any time, any place."

Obrig nodded. While he wasn't sure he totally agreed with her logic, he suspected the powers in Washington did. And he didn't want to spend the rest of his life in Djibouti.

"I don't really care whether the trail you put together leads to Al Qaeda or the Taliban or Hamas, but it has to lead to one of them. And it has to be clear and simple enough for the average congressman to understand."

* * *

Shortly before midnight the two cats—guided by their GPS—crept in toward Basalilays, the little indentation in the coast to which the pirates had returned the night before, each boat running only its center outboard at slow speed. The sky was heavily overcast, with occasional drizzle, and the darkness ashore was broken by no more than an occasional, very feeble light. When they were two miles offshore, they launched three ocean kayaks, gray with a layer of fabric armor built into them.

While Jerry and Alex remained at the cats' helms, the other three members of the team slid over the side of the cats, tied themselves into the kayak spray skirts and shoved off.

"Remember," said Mike, "we're only going in to look around. We don't want them to know we were there. We don't even want to be in their dreams. Now paddle like hell. We've got a long trip, and this chop is just going to make it longer."

The kayaks, each fourteen feet long, sliced through and over the Indian Ocean as each team member worked his paddle smoothly and vigorously, dipping the blade in one side then the other, hindered as much as aided by the waves that attacked them from astern. Within minutes they were all sweating heavily.

Following more than an hour of very hard work, Mike spotted the low breakwater that turned the nick in the coastline into a small fishing harbor. He paused and scanned the breakwater, alert for a sentry. Seeing none, he scanned ashore for any sign of life and detected none. He did, however, see three boats pulled up on the rocky beach fifty yards in front of a jumble of shadowy hovels.

"How much water do we have?" he said quietly to Ray, who was now alongside him. The marine pulled out a small depth sounder and stuck it in the water.

"Eight feet, Captain," he reported as the two other kayaks pulled up alongside and hovered.

Mike studied the shore. He wanted to take a look at the boats, if for no other reason than to confirm they were being used for more than fishing. But he didn't want to be caught. If they botched it, especially if somebody got killed, it would be an international incident of the worst sort.

It was time to move, he reminded himself. If they were going to do anything about the pirates without nuking the entire country, then they had to know more about them. A few nitty-gritty details. That's why SECDEF had sent them.

He scanned the shore again through his night vision device. Was there a sentry there? Asleep between the boats? Awake among the boats, watching the three faint shadows floating out in the middle of the harbor? He could see nothing. Would some guy really sit out there in the drizzle? Why not? He, Ted and Ray were doing it. Who would he be guarding against? Them? Other pirates?

What about dogs? There were bound to be some, but he didn't hear them. Maybe these people were too poor to be able to support them.

"We're going in," he whispered hoarsely, his stomach slightly knotted with tension. "Ray, keep taking soundings every few strokes. When we reach the beach, I want you to stay with the kayaks while Ted and I look around. And remember, if we see anybody who might see us, make like a shadow and disappear."

"Aye, aye, Captain," responded Ted and Ray.

"Let's move."

Paddling with the greatest care and pausing every now and then to let Ray catch up, the three faint shadows drifted toward the beach, their nerves tuned to detect the slightest motion—or glimmer—ashore.

Making less noise than the waves breaking on the shore, they beached the kayaks and waited, scanning around them for any sign of life. Seeing nothing, Mike and Ted crept up the beach to the nearest boat, which proved to be an incredibly ancient and decrepit fiberglass skiff with an equally ancient seventy-five-horsepower outboard. The boat itself stank of long-dead fish, as did the air around it. While Ted kept an eye on the neighborhood, Mike leaned over the side of the boat to examine its contents. Three rusty metal gas cans and one plastic one. Several oars and a tangle of lines. A thin layer of oily-feeling water in the bilges. Just a typical, third world fishing boat, thought Mike.

How the Somalis could operate as far offshore as they did without drowning themselves continued to amaze him. They must really be desperate—both the pirates and the fishermen. But then they were the same people for the most part. He touched Ted's shoulder and shook his head, then pointed at the next boat.

Trying to blend into the darkness of the night, the two crept to the other boat, which turned out to be almost identical with the first. Then Mike felt Ted's hand on his shoulder. He looked first at the SEAL, then in the direction his shadowy arm was pointing. At an insubstantial shadow that was flowing out the doorless opening into one of the hovels that existed along the edge of the beach.

The two Tridents crouched behind the boat, hoping to blend into the surrounding wet dark, and watched as the shadow disappeared into the darkness.

Where was he going? thought Mike. Would he be back? How soon?

He didn't have to wonder long. The shadow returned in no more time than it takes to take a piss and, without pausing, slipped back through the opening.

The Tridents gave the shadow time to return to whatever dreams he might have been having, then edged over to the third boat. Mike didn't really expect much this time and was pleasantly surprised when he immediately discovered a thwart, a plank secured across the boat from side to side, with a four-inch hole in the middle of it. He crawled over the lower of the boat's two sides and reached down into the wet bilge. As he'd expected, there was a wood bracket secured to the boat's bottom. He felt around to see if the mast that he assumed went with the thwart and bracket was there. It was not. But there was a shell casing lying in the water. It was a big casing, probably for an assault rifle. He pocketed it for later examination. Then he heard a soft gnawing sound, followed by a scratching and scuttling. He froze. A rat. It must be a rat. It sounded as if it was in the boat with him.

Disregarding his fellow passenger, Mike felt around for more evidence of the mast and the radar but found none. All, including the battery that must have powered the radar, had been removed.

He looked over the side of the boat and slipped carefully from the gunnel. He waved at Ted then started to creep toward the hovels to see if there were any weapons lying around and to try to get an idea of how many men lived in the structures. He remained uncertain what they would do if another shadow appeared to go relieve himself. He didn't want to be spotted, and he didn't want to leave a dead body lying around, and he especially didn't want to be captured. The Somalis weren't always nice to captured Americans. He was damned if he did and damned if he didn't, and he'd been in the same situation before. It had always worked out, one way or another.

Suddenly the night was shattered by a dog's bark. There was one, initial, tentative bark then a furious, almost hysterical barrage.

"We've had enough fun for one night," he whispered to Ted. "We're leaving."

Before Ted could nod, both were scuttling back toward the boats as the dog's barks became louder and nearer.

By the time they reached the water's edge the scrawny little mongrel was twenty feet behind him. Ray was crouching with the painters from the three kayaks in his hand.

"Quick!" hissed Mike unnecessarily as all three, now standing in knee-deep water, rolled into the kayaks and started paddling like hell, with the dog continuing to rage at the water's edge.

Mike led the way across the little harbor to the low, curving seawall and followed along it to the entrance. It only rose a few feet above the water and seemed to be composed of rocks piled along a fringing reef or shoal of some sort. As he paddled, Mike worried what they might have left behind them as remembrances of their visit. Hopefully, no gear. But there were bound to be footprints. Since they were wearing sneakers, their prints might be indistinguishable from those of the locals. Hopefully.

"We learn anything there, Captain?" asked Ray when they were almost a mile offshore.

"I think so. One of the boats has a mast that they take home with them—along with the radar I'm certain they're now using. And there was an automatic rifle shell casing lying in the bilge. There are probably more, but I didn't want to spend time looking for them."

"Not many fishermen use automatic rifles," offered Ted.

"And," added Mike, "we're going to have a nice little chart of that place just as soon as Ray sits down and draws it."

Sonya looked out over the main room of the Club Bestial. Outside, a heavy snowfall was repaving Moscow's darkened streets. Inside, strobes were pulsing and two bands were playing as a hundred of Russia's moguls and power brokers—former KGB functionaries, children of former Party chieftains, hereditary thugs—danced and drank with women as sharply dressed as they were.

She's not at all different from me, thought the tall, fair B-girl as she studied a buxom redhead in a dress that must have cost as much as Sonya earned in six months and with a fortune's worth of jewelry dangling from her ears. Some guy gives her nice clothes and jewels to sleep with him. The club gives me better clothes than I could afford on my own—but no jewels to speak of—to amuse and sometimes sleep with its members. And why not? Every girl in Moscow needs money these days.

Of course, one of the main reason's she'd taken the job was the hope that one of the big guys might decide he liked her and move her into his big penthouse apartment and give her a ton of jewels. Just as long as he was good-looking and smart enough to keep somebody else from taking all his money.

But, she added to herself, there is a difference. I get money from the club, and I get money from the guys who take me to bed, and every now and then I get money from Jacob. And working for Jacob, she thought with a modest sense of pleasure, *did* make her different, because she had a secret that none of the glitzy women around her would ever even guess.

But maybe not. How many of those slick chicks were getting money from the government or somebody else to spy on their husbands or boyfriends or whatever they were?

"Hey, Blondie. Come over here!"

Sonya turned and looked at the small, pasty-faced man leaning against the wall a few feet from her. "Hi," she said as she stepped over to him, "are you a new member? I don't remember seeing you here before."

Ugly little bastard, she thought. But she was paid to be nice to all the members, ugly or not.

"I like you," said Pasty Face as he grabbed her arm and dragged her to a table. "Yeah, I'm a new member and you're going to see a lot of me here, so you'd better be nice to me. I'm what they call 'obscenely wealthy,' you little whore. I just finished doing a deal with the richest people in the world and there'll be more to come. Some-day I'll be the richest man in the world and I won't have to come to this club, because I'll have my own in the base-ment of my house.

"Now, sit!" he commanded with all the grace of a newly made merchant as he forced her down into the chair.

Sonya sat, a smile pasted on her face. The little grub

was obviously drunk. Very drunk. Most of the people in the room were drunk. Only the B-girls, the bartenders and waiters, the bouncers and the cashiers were sober. They had to stay that way or they would be out on the street with their noses broken. In the snow with no money to help support whoever it was they were helping to support—parents, brothers, sisters, all the people the state was supposed to support but somehow couldn't. Club Bestial's management was very serious when it told its employees not to drink on the job.

"And let me tell you something else," ranted Pasty Face. "Those fucking Jews are going to get the surprise of their miserable little lives very soon."

Sonya was far from well educated, but she did know enough to latch on to the phrase "richest people in the world" and the bit about the Jews. Which Jews did he mean? she wondered. Russian Jews? American Jews? Israeli Jews? She didn't know, and she wasn't totally certain who the "richest people in the world" were. Could it be the Americans? Whoever it was, it sounded like something Jacob might pay to hear. "Please get me a drink," she said to the drunk, smiling as invitingly as she could.

"Of course. I know how these things are done. I'm not a fool from the country."

"I'm Sonya. What do I call you?"

"Gregor."

"You don't sound as if you're from Moscow, Gregor," observed Sonya while they waited for her ginger ale. "What do you think of the city?"

"I've been here many times," said Gregor as he reached with one hand toward her breast.

"What is it that you buy and sell?" asked Sonya. "What is this wonderful thing that has made you obscenely wealthy?"

Gregor's eyes, which had seemed a little drifty, suddenly snapped into focus. She'd just made a serious mistake, she thought. She'd pushed too hard. Asking what people do, what they buy and sell, can be a very dangerous thing anywhere in the world. And especially in Russia.

Gregor stared at her a moment, almost as if his lust was battling with his better judgment. Drunk though he was, he realized he might have already said more than he wished to. "We'll dance—close—then we go. Who do I see to get you out of here?"

"That guy over there," she said, pointing at one of the assistant managers. "You talk to him after we dance—if you still want me to go with you. I'll be right back. I have to take a piss."

"Okay."

Sonya walked rapidly in the direction of the women's room. On her way she stopped beside one of the bouncers, one for whom she'd done a favor or two in the past. "Dimitri, know anything about the little guy I've been sitting with? Say's his name's Gregor and he's a new member."

The bouncer stared into the darkened room a minute. "His name's Orlov, Gregor Orlov, and he is a new member. We were told to keep an eye on him. He's got a reputation for making trouble when he's really smashed."

"Know anything else about him?"

"Why?"

"He's talking about buying me out and I'd like to know as much as I can about him."

"All I know is his name and that he sometimes makes trouble when he's drunk."

Sonya wanted to ask more—where was he from, what did he do—but she didn't dare. Anyway, Dimitri probably didn't know anything more.

"Thanks, Dimitri," she said, kissing him on the cheek.

She then hurried to the staff dressing room, grabbed her cell phone and retreated to the far end of a rarely used corridor. By the time she opened the phone and began dialing, she was sweating and her heart was pounding. Whatever Gregor's words had meant, she was now convinced they were both important and dangerous. If her own intuition hadn't settled it, the look the grub had given her when she left the table had. And walking around with that sort of information hidden inside you was just as dangerous as walking around with a pocket full of diamonds. Somebody might decide to cut it out of you.

"Yes?" said the phone after ringing a few seconds.

"Jacob, this is Sonya." Jacob was the only name by which the girl knew her Agency contact.

"Yes?"

"A drunk named Gregor Orlov, a new member of the club, has just bragged to me that he's completed a deal with 'the richest people in the world' and that the Jews will soon be getting a very unpleasant surprise. I don't know what it means, but it seemed important."

"What business is he in and where's he from?"

"I don't know."

"Did he tell you any more about the deal?"

"Nothing."

"What does he look like?"

She described him as best she could.

"Go back and feed him more drinks."

"I think he suspects he's told me too much. He's also talking about buying me out tonight."

"That's not good. Can you avoid going with him?"

"Maybe, but it will be held against me by the club."

"I don't want you going out with him. If you can get more from him in the club, okay. But don't go out with him."

"Is the information that important?"

"I don't know, but I don't like the sound of it."

"At first I thought he was talking about the Americans."

"I'm not sure they're the richest people in the world anymore. Don't go with him!"

The phone went dead, and Sonya returned to the table where she'd left Gregor. He was gone. She went up to the assistant manager. "Did that little guy talk to you about me?"

"No. What about you?"

"Nothing."

* * *

The ancient dhow's second day on station dawned clear, with the wind continuing to blow out of the northeast. Ali watched the horizon turn from black to gray to pink and began to feel that life might well be worth living, after all. He then checked his Kalashnikov and ate a bowl of spiced beans mixed this time with rice.

"A ship!" shouted one of the lookouts shortly before noon. As he shouted, he pointed to the south.

Suleiman grabbed his binoculars and studied the tiny black pimple on the southern horizon. "He's headed north. In two hours we'll have them."

The dhow continued to plod ahead slowly, rising, falling and twisting in the still-choppy seas.

"Get the boat ready," ordered Suleiman an hour after the ship had been spotted. "Light the smoke pot," he then ordered. "He must see our smoke before he sees us. And all of you get below, get down in the hold. All but you four," he added, pointing at the most experienced crew members. "I'll call the rest of you when it's time to launch the boat."

Within a few minutes of climbing down into the hold,

Ali felt as if he was going to be sick again. The smell and the rolling were overpowering. He stuck his head up onto the deck and saw the oil drum filled with oily rags emitting a tall plume of smoke. Acrid, choking, gut-wrenching smoke. The men who had remained on deck were already waving and shouting as if the dhow were truly on fire.

"You, get back down there," shouted Suleiman when he noticed Ali's head above deck. "If I see your head again, I'll kick your teeth in."

Ali had started to back down the ladder when there was another shout from behind him, in the hold.

"We're sinking! Allah protect us."

Ali turned and looked down in time to see a small wave of greasy water roll past the base of the ladder. It hadn't been there five minutes before. "Captain," he shouted, "we're sinking. The hold is filling with water."

The son of Ibrihim stormed over with a scowl on his face and looked down. Another wave, a deeper one, rolled across the hold as the dhow rolled. "Quickly!" he shouted, "find where the leak is." As he spoke, he climbed down and started to search himself.

"Here, Suleiman, here," cried Ali, now down on his hands and knees. "I can feel the water coming in here."

The captain joined him and pulled up a section of the sole—the floor of the hold. He then shoved his hand down into the bilge. "Yes, that's it. I can feel it. One of the hull planks has come loose."

"Suleiman," shouted the mate from the deck, "the ship has spotted us and is turning away."

"Allah curse him!" snarled the captain under his breath. The bastard was running away from them now that they really did need him. He reached down again to the loose plank. It felt even looser every time the dhow pitched. He knew he couldn't just jam something into the hole, because that would make the hole bigger.

"Bail, all of you," he shouted to the men in the hold, most of whom had horrified looks on their faces. "Find something to pick up the water with and pass it up to the men on deck." He then bounded up the ladder. "Nur!" he shouted at one of the more experienced crew, "come over here."

Nur, who was the strongest swimmer aboard, knew what was coming. "Yes, Captain?"

"I want you to go over the side and see if we can push that plank back into place. You are our only hope. I will place two men with rifles to guard you against sharks."

Nur looked down in the hold then around at the limitless white-crested blue of the Indian Ocean and then at the steamer that was racing as fast as she could toward the east. There was always the attack boat, he thought, they could use that for a lifeboat. But he knew they couldn't all fit into it. Not in seas like these. "Yes, Captain."

A badly worn and stained length of half-inch nylon line—taken over a year before from a captured yacht—was tied around the swimmer's waist and over the side he went.

After hitting the water, Nur paused. From where he was the tiny dhow could have been a supertanker. It was a frightening sight, pitching and plunging, bucking like a terrified horse, throwing its sharp, sweeping bow in the air only to crash down again.

Nur continued to tread water as the waves occasionally broke over his head. The sight of the dhow bludgeoning the face of the ocean caused him to loose all fear of sharks. They were the least of his problems.

"Go down, Nur. Find the hole," shouted Suleiman impatiently.

For a moment Nur considered refusing, but he realized he couldn't. Even if he managed to survive the sinking, Suleiman would have him killed for defying him. If not at sea then some dark night ashore.

His heart pounding, he took a deep and desperate breath and dove under the hull, roughly where he thought the loose plank was located. Without a mask he was able to see little, so he had to try to find the plank by feel. He tried to get close to the barnacle- and weed-encrusted bottom, only to have it leap up and away from him. And then slam back down.

Desperate, his hope running out as fast as his air, he forced his shoulder and side up against the bottom and felt around frantically. Just as the pain in his chest was becoming unbearable, he came to it, farther forward than he'd thought. He quickly reached up—before it could fly away—grabbed its edge and pulled down gently. He then turned and breaststroked down and out from beneath the hull and back toward the surface, his lungs by now feeling as if they were being carved by a thousand knives. With every stroke, he was painfully conscious of the dhow's mad gyrations just inches above him.

Once he made it back to the surface, using the nylon line to hold his head above the waves, he forced more air into his lungs. And went down again.

This time he knew where to go. As he worked his way under its hull, the dhow never stopped moving. It pitched forward and slid down the back of a wave, driving its stern high into the sky and briefly exposing the slowly turning propeller to the sun. Seconds later the bow plowed into the face of the next wave and rose, causing the stern to slam down with a smacking sound and a small explosion of spray, crushing the unfortunate pirate. A moment later, what was left of Nur popped up to the surface and started to drift away.

"Allah!" cried Suleiman, his anger and frustration infinitely greater than his shock. "Pull in on that line."

Ali, who was standing near the captain, leaned over the rail and looked at the swimmer. He couldn't be alive, he thought with a shudder. There was blood coming out his eyes, nose and mouth.

"Haul him aboard," ordered Suleiman. "He may still be alive." Within a minute or two it was clear to all hands that he wasn't.

For a moment Ibrihim's son appeared shaken. Maybe he was sad about the death of one of his crew. Perhaps he was concerned that the crew might be angered to the point of mutiny by their shipmate's death. Whatever his temporary preoccupation, he had little time to indulge it. The dhow was sinking!

Suleiman returned to the hold. If he wished to live, he not only had to somehow keep the boat afloat but also had to maintain the initiative. And maintain control. When he reached the bottom of the ladder, the water was up to his knees and the wormy old hull was beginning to rise and fall more sluggishly. Holding his breath, he got down on his hands and knees and felt the hole again.

It might just be possible, he thought. "Get me some of that wire from the engine space," he shouted on deck. "And the line from Nur."

He took the wire and twisted it into an eight-inch circle, then attached the line to it. Back again on his hands and knees and working by feel, he managed to fit the wire circle around the loose end of the plank. "Pull!" he shouted, gasping for breath as his head appeared above water.

Four men pulled. Suleiman took another breath and went

down again. Praise be to Allah! The loose plank had been pulled back almost into place—the wire was thin enough to fit through the seams on each side of it. He felt carefully— water was still coming in but much more slowly.

"Keep that line tight and secure it," he instructed. "Then everybody bail. We're heading home."

Inshallah, he thought, that the rest of the plank didn't come loose. Or the one next to it. Or the one next to that. Then he cursed himself for not thinking of the solution sooner—before he'd sent Nur over the side.

* * *

Thanks to the heavy overcast and the continuing snow, dawn had arrived late in Moscow, making it all the more surprising that the two patrolling militiamen were able to spot the blond girl's body so quickly. When they did stumble on it, it was already covered by a thick shroud of snow and lying in an alley ten yards from the Metro station. It was the blood, of course, that gave it away. The blood that colored the otherwise pure white snow.

* * *

The small twin-engine jet banked and started its approach to the old Garowe airport just outside the "capital" of the semiautonomous region of Puntland. While construction on a new airport had started, it had not advanced as far as it might have because a significant portion of its funding was either missing or had never existed at all.

The instant the plane's wheels touched the packed sand-clay runway, a trail of red dust exploded behind it. As soon as it had rolled to a stop, the copilot appeared, opened the door and folded down the stairs.

Mandy, followed respectfully by Abdul, walked forward along the narrow aisle and stuck her head into the flight deck. "We should only be here an hour or two. Do not leave the plane."

"Certainly not, madam," replied the French charter pilot. There was nothing in Garowe of any interest to him, and he feared that if he left the plane, he might not find it where he'd left it. For that matter, it was possible that he might not find it at all. Of course, if he and his crew did stay aboard, he'd have to run the air-conditioning, which would use fuel. That might be a problem since he had no intention of trusting his life to the fuel he might end up with here. However, he felt confident that he did have enough to make it back to Djibouti with some to spare.

Mandy turned, ducked and stepped out onto the stairs. There was a far-from-new black SUV parked next to the airstrip. It looked as if it might be armored. Standing next to it were two Somalis in slacks and sport shirts. She expanded her gaze and spotted a half dozen heavily armed men spread out around the plane. Nowhere did she see a uniform. No customs. No immigration. No official record of her visit—except the invoice for the charter plane.

"Miss Cochran," said one of the men as he stepped forward without offering his hand. "Please come this way."

Mandy and Abdul followed and soon found themselves seated in the rear of the SUV. The two men settled into the front seats.

The instant the last door slammed shut, the SUV rocketed down the dusty road toward the city. On either side were barren, almost naked fields, fields that seemed barely capable of supporting even the few anorexic little goats that were rummaging through them. Within a few minutes the road narrowed as a succession of single-story, concrete buildings rose along its sides. Here and there an ancient car or small truck was parked. As the SUV was forced to slow, the man riding shotgun checked his automatic rifle carefully, looking out at the dozen or so citizens—most dressed in what might, by many, be defined as near rags—as they attended to whatever business they could.

The driver suddenly leaned on the horn and the SUV shuddered to a halt. The guard jammed his finger into his rifle's trigger guard. Through the windshield Mandy could see four men struggling to load a tattered bed and an equally decrepit couch into the back of a tiny, rusty white Toyota pickup that blocked most of the street.

Mandy tensed, reaching for her sidearm. Was it an ambush? She studied the surrounding buildings—their often doorless doors and windowless windows. And the alleys alongside them.

The laborers paid no attention to the SUV—and neither did the half dozen spectators—but two small boys did, pressing their noses against the tinted glass and trying to look inside. The guard opened his window, shouted something and waved at them to stand back. Wide-eyed, they complied. The driver then blew his horn again and worked his way past the front of the truck.

As they approached the center of the city, they passed a few larger, three- and four-story structures. One, Mandy knew, was the legislature, another the presidential palace. One was clearly a mosque, its tall, white minaret towering above everything around it. A few of the buildings had arches and other minor architectural details, but most were decorated—if at all—with faded, peeling advertisements for Coke or some medicinal or household product that probably hadn't been available since the last civil war had trashed the city.

A large two-story building came into sight. Abdul had advised her in advance that it was an important government office building, so she expected to stop, but they rolled past. Mandy looked at Abdul, who just shrugged his shoulders. She was about to demand to know where she was being taken when the car coasted to a stop in front of a newly built two-story structure that looked very much like a moderately upscale condominium.

The gunman riding shotgun got out and opened the door for them. "Please follow me. Sheikh al-Abbas is in here, waiting for you."

Mandy and Abdul followed their guide into a small lobby and then through a door into what looked like a combination living and dining room. Seated at a table in the center of the room was a tall, handsome Somali dressed in a white robe and small, fezlike cap. "Ms. Cochran," said the man, standing as he spoke, "welcome to Puntland. I am Hussein al-Abbas."

Mandy took the sheikh's extended hand.

"And Mr. Jones," continued the sheikh, shaking hands with Abdul. "Will you have some tea with me?"

I can't believe this, thought Abdul. *He always refuses to speak English with me.*

Even before Mandy could answer, the sheikh signaled to a small man who had replaced the guard in the door. The man disappeared.

"I trust your flight was uneventful," said the sheikh.

"Yes," said Mandy, looking around the room. "You have a somewhat unique office," she continued, hoping the comment might be taken as the sort of preliminary pleasantry she knew was appropriate but with which she tended to have difficulty.

The sheikh chuckled. "I have several. In my current position, as you might well imagine, there are times when I find privacy useful."

The little man returned with tea, which the sheikh

served. After several more minutes of chatter—about the world economic crisis and the new American president—the sheikh appeared to decide that the preliminaries had been sufficient. "I understand you wish to talk with me about the piracy problem along our coast."

"Yes."

"Let me assure you it is of great concern to us. If we are to grow and prosper, we must increase our trade with the rest of the world, and obviously, this brigandage will not help us do so. It also, I might add, is an embarrassment to us. Unfortunately, as we all well know, my nation is badly divided. We have a national government that fears to occupy its own capital. We have Somaliland to the west, which claims to be independent, while we in Puntland recognize the authority of the national government in principle but find that we have to fend for ourselves. Then we have a half dozen other factions—everybody from the Islamic radicals to Communists—each with its own army and more than willing to attack any established, democratic authority that might stand in its way. Within each of these entities the politics—clan and religion—is incredibly complicated, much more so than the politics you are accustomed to in your own country."

"But you do wish to end the piracy, don't you?" demanded Mandy, cutting off the sheikh.

"Clearly. Of course," replied the Somali, a slight haze of irritation drifting across his face. "I have already told you that. We have, on occasion, apprehended and punished some of these people, but as I have explained, the practical power of the Puntland government is limited."

"Have you managed to infiltrate any of these groups? Found a way to learn in advance where and when they plan to act?"

"As Mr. Jones has undoubtedly explained to you, these groups tend to be very regional, very local. They have all known one another for their entire lives. Their families are interconnected. Even if you are a Somali, if you're not a member of their clan then you are a foreigner. And nobody here trusts foreigners."

At that point Mandy—who had never been known for her diplomacy—lost her cool. "I also understand that many of these groups are under the protection of, indeed led by, some of your local leaders," she blurted out.

If the sheikh was offended by her blunt accusation he showed no sign of it. "Such is said to be the case. Some of those I suspect of such behavior are too powerful to act against. Your own agency, as I am informed, finds itself in a similar position at times. With respect to others, I don't have enough evidence to act. And please allow me to remind you that armed robbery is only one of the many security problems with which I have to deal. I have five or six private armies—especially the Islamic radicals—to keep at bay before they topple our young government."

"Would you consider sharing what information you have and then allowing us to act upon it?"

"I assumed this was where our conversation was going to lead. I am more than pleased to share with you what I can. I have been doing so with Mr. Jones. But I cannot permit you to take any actions not authorized by the government of Somalia or that of Puntland. Surely you understand this."

The sheikh's message was clear, although the relaxed smile had returned to his face. "I will do absolutely everything I can."

It's now or never, thought Mandy. "It has occurred to me that it might be desirable for us to establish a special arrangement, with you personally, to facilitate the flow of intelligence concerning any terrorist activities going on in this region."

The sheikh looked closely at her. Clearly he understood what she was proposing.

"Ms. Cochran. My total loyalty is to Puntland. And Somalia. Just as yours is to your homeland."

Mandy tried to smile as she finished her tea. "This has been a most fruitful meeting," she finally said. "We now understand each other."

"Yes," said the sheikh, rising, "understanding is the starting point for great things."

As he spoke, the Somali mentally thanked Allah that this irritating person, this woman, was about to leave. He and his peers, Puntland's mishmash of rulers, might disagree every now and then, but they far preferred an occasional intramural brawl to the prospect of having all the foreigners who kept buzzing around like flies tell them what to do in their own land.

The drive back to the airport was even faster than the earlier trip to town had been.

"We didn't learn shit," said Mandy as soon as they were back in the plane and the pilot was taxiing the twenty feet to the runway, "and he's not going to give us shit."

"That's not totally accurate," replied Abdul, who had been largely silent for most of the day. "He'll do what he's always done. Every now and then he'll tell us something, something that it's to his advantage for us to know."

"Which gets us back to how you're going to develop some resources for us."

"Very carefully. The sheikh will be considerably less polite if he catches me trying to recruit in his town. He and I get along, but that could quickly change."

"Find somebody who's greedy or has a grudge."

"I'll do what I can."

"You'll do what has to be done."

What the hell am I doing here, thought Mandy, playing right field in the minor leagues? "I'm not interested in reasons you can't do it, Abdul. I want action," she continued before lowering her seat back and closing her eyes.

7

It was snowing lightly in Langley, Virginia, as Paul Tracy, the CIA's manager of Russian covert operations, leaned back in his chair. "Connie," he said to one of his group leaders, "you're really not giving us much to work with."

"I know that, Paul," admitted Connie Barton. "On its own it could very well just be the boasts of some two-bit, trashed Russian thug, but the references to the richest people in the world and the Jews stuck in my mind. Then when the stringer was found murdered, I realized I'd better go over it with Tim Bryant at the organized crime group. He wasn't sure what to make of it but agreed that I should bring it to you."

"Who found her?"

"The militia, from what we can learn. They say she was knifed."

"Any suspects?"

"Since they're very sensitive about their crime problem, they'll undoubtedly round up all the usual ones, but Jacob doubts they have any idea who really did it."

"But we do."

"Yes. Jacob thinks this Gregor Orlov did it—or had it done—and I agree. B-girls are killed all the time, but this is one of those situations where the coincidence is just too strong. It looks to me like he decided he'd said more than he wished and did something about it."

"I agree that 'the Jews' probably refers to Israel, but I'm not totally convinced of your assumption that the 'richest people' are the Saudis. They consider each other enemies, but you rarely see the Saudis on the front line. They prefer to play the role of coat holders and behind-the-scenes financiers, not brawlers."

"I can't argue with you, but maybe they're financing whatever it is for somebody else."

"And you think we're talking about a WMD?"

"That or some sort of intelligence. What else could be important enough to kill the girl over?"

"Love? Money? People get killed over money all the time. Especially in Russia."

"I think we have to assume it's a weapon."

"What kind? Atomic, biological, chemical, what?"

"So far we have no idea, I'm afraid. But we all know that Russia's awash with them, and some of the guys with the keys can't be trusted. They have needs that the current system simply isn't filling."

"You think whatever it is has already been delivered?"

"We don't even know what we're looking for at the moment."

"What are you doing to learn more?"

"Jacob's working on learning more about Orlov. That might help us determine what we're dealing with and identify its source."

"What else do you suggest?"

"See if Jaleel can come up with anything from his people in Riyadh."

"That assumes it really is the Saudis."

"This assumes that it's anybody. Even I admit we have damn little to go on."

"But you consider it actionable?"

"I told you, without the girl's death, I'd suspect it was just the ravings of a Russian drunk."

Tracy stared at the ceiling a moment. "Until your Jacob can come up with more, the best we can do is put out the word—on a very limited basis, in-house only—that some sort of WMD may have been sold by somebody in Russia to we're not sure whom. It's possible that somebody may come up with something else that fits in."

"And pray it doesn't get out to the media before we know what we're talking about," said Connie.

"Amen," agreed Tracy.

* * *

"I'm certain they must be Americans," said Ibrihim Hassan into the cell phone. "They are violating our sovereignty and endangering our fishermen."

"Were any of your men killed?" responded Sheikh al-Abbas, not that he really cared about the men, but a death or two would have great potential political value.

"No, but I can see it is part of a plot by them to interfere with our activities."

The sheikh considered a moment. Hassan was not an exceptionally powerful clan leader, but he did have enough influence to be worthy of attention. And, like so many, al-Abbas didn't trust the Americans' intentions. Once they arrived, they could be depended upon to stay. To see the thing through.

"I had a meeting with their new 'piracy czar' not four hours ago."

"He came to Garowe?"

"It's a she and yes."

"A woman? They send women to order us around?"

"Yes."

"Did she mention this?"

"No. She seemed most interested in having me provide the intelligence she has so much difficulty acquiring herself. What do you expect me to do for you?"

"I need a half dozen good, shoulder-fired missiles. Quickly."

"From what you told me of their catamarans, you will still be at a disadvantage, even with those."

"Not if the missiles are onshore, on Ras Xaafuun, and my boats lead them right past."

"You have the money to pay for them?"

"Yes."

"I'll give you a name. He'll be able to get them to you within one day."

"Good. I'm convinced these Americans are going to cause us a great deal of trouble if we fail to act. They already are."

"We'll talk again."

* * *

As carefully scheduled by Captain Papadis, *Eastern Trader* arrived off the breakwater at Colombo, Sri Lanka, in midmorning. As he slowed, a Sri Lankan gunboat approached. "It would probably be best if only five or six of your men are visible, Colonel," he remarked. The Saudi officer, who was standing beside him studying the gunboat through a pair of binoculars, nodded, then spoke into his shoulder microphone.

"That naval ship isn't trying to board us, is it?"

"No. They would have signaled us by now if they planned to do so."

"I understand your logic, Captain, but we both know there is a civil war going on here. I will have all my men posted, but they will not be obvious."

"As you wish, Colonel."

Papadis doesn't take security as seriously as he should, thought the colonel. And neither does his crew of third world loafers. But then none of them had the slightest idea of what it was all about. Which was as it should be. He and his men could handle anything that might come up.

Fifteen minutes later the pilot boat came alongside and the pilot—a short, dark, cheerful man—made the long climb up the Jacob's ladder to the ship's deck. Before continuing into the superstructure to take the elevator to the bridge, he looked around him and noted what seemed a large number of heavily armed security guards. All were dressed in slacks and polo shirts, all had close-cut hair, and all appeared to be Arabs.

There was nothing extraordinary about their presence, he told himself, especially with the piracy problem exploding everywhere. But maybe there *was* something a little odd. He felt certain they weren't the mercenaries most merchant ships carried. They were military, not former military. And they weren't Greek—even though the ship was—or Americans. They appeared much more on edge than were the guards aboard most ships that visited Colombo.

When the pilot reached the bridge, Captain Papadis greeted him. The colonel had retired to the main salon, not wanting to risk drawing attention to himself.

"How are things to the south?" asked Papadis, referring to the civil war that had sputtered painfully and fatally for decades in Sri Lanka.

The pilot shrugged his shoulders. "It does seem endless, Captain."

"It is a very sad thing. You have such a beautiful country."

"Yes," agreed the pilot in between giving rudder commands to the helmsman. "I understand you had an incident in the Strait of Malacca."

"Yes," said Papadis, wondering how much the world really knew about it, "several boats attacked us in a squall, but our security people managed to hold them off. We were very lucky."

"Your security people look most competent, Captain. I'm sure it was more than just luck. What is important is that you are safe."

"Yes."

Forty minutes later the ship was moored to a dock located on the inside of the long breakwater, the pilot had left, and thousands of gallons of fuel were being pumped into her tanks. As Papadis had predicted, all the proper officers—customs, immigration and health—had arrived and none had stayed very long. Why waste time when the ship would have no significant contact with shore?

"Why is that gunboat anchored there?" demanded the colonel, who had just returned to the bridge. He pointed at the small ship, which was anchored two hundred yards away.

"As you pointed out, Colonel, there is a civil war going on here. I very much doubt they have any special interest in us, but it's understandable that they feel they can't be too careful."

"Yes. You're undoubtedly correct."

"I should remind you, sir, that the authorities in Mumbai will be considerably more nosey. There we will be alongside the pier, unloading some containers and taking others. They will be very interested in everything we do."

"I'm already reconciled to that, Captain."

By late afternoon *Eastern Trader* was under way again, making sixteen knots across the open Indian Ocean, and Papadis was certain he detected an air of relief surrounding Colonel bin-Sharif.

* * *

Jacob—known to her coworkers as S. I. Andreyev—sat at her desk in the Gazprom building in Moscow and looked out the window at the falling snow. She'd liked Sonya and felt very badly that she'd died as she had, hacked to pieces on a sidewalk a few yards from a subway station on a bitterly cold night. The girl had been a little confused about her goals, but then most young people today seemed just as confused as she'd been. Once, many years before, when she'd been certain of her beliefs and less tolerant of those that seemed to conflict with them, Jacob might have thought of Sonya as a little blond tramp. In the world of today, Jacob saw that she was no different from most of her countrymen—doing what she had to survive. Nothing had changed in fifty thousand years.

As a young woman Jacob had possessed high hopes when the Berlin Wall fell—and with it much of the communist system—but over time she'd become disillusioned. Her countrymen, and especially their leaders, simply did not seem interested in the free, open and honest world of which she had dreamed. Although she still considered herself a loyal Russian, she had no compunction about telling the Americans things when she thought she should.

She'd never told them everything they might have wanted to know, only what she thought they should know.

Not only was Jacob inclined to forward intelligence on a selective basis, but she was very well positioned—as a supervising auditor for Gazprom, Russia's petro giant—to collect intelligence. A large part of her duties involved looking over the shoulders of local Gazprom auditors at thousands of projects and facilities from one corner of the country to the other. Looking for incompetence and carelessness. Looking for evidence of corruption that was not officially sanctioned. She was expected to ask all sorts of questions and demand all sorts of information. Nobody would be in the slightest surprised if she demanded to know more about a known wheeler-dealer named Gregor Orlov. Where did he operate? What did he buy and sell? Was he, perhaps, connected in some way to the fifty extremely valuable drill tools missing from the warehouse in Novosibirsk—the diamond-tipped bits used for drilling?

The implications of Sonya's message worried her, and the girl's violent death offended her.

She turned her attention away from her window and back to her computer monitor to see if the name Gregor Orlov could be found in the Gazprom security files. Or any of the many official files to which she had access.

An hour later Jacob leaned back in her chair, took off her wire-rimmed glasses and rubbed her eyes. In a perfect world Gregor Orlov should have popped up almost instantly. The files she'd been exploring were built specifically to catalog people like him and their unsavory activities. But so far she'd come across nothing. She was going to have to do it the hard way. E-mails. Phone calls. Jacob had contacts all across Russia, both within Gazprom and the government. Jacob was expected to ask

questions about people like Gregor Orlov. It was her job.
Even Putin would agree.

* * *

It was dark and damp, and a strong wind was blowing off
the Gulf of Aden. Abdul Jones stood in the shadow of a
pile of beat-up wooden crates, all marked "Product of
France," in the old part of Djibouti Port—the section
where the small coasters and fishing boats tied up. He
stood where the girl had told him to stand and he waited
as she'd directed. As always, he felt totally out of place.

Abdul had been born and raised in coastal North Carolina. And there he'd been raised a proper Christian—even
though the name by which his parents had baptized him
might suggest otherwise—and gone to college. In a fit of
patriotism he'd joined the Agency to fight Islamic terrorists, and almost immediately he'd been noticed. Not for
what he'd done but for how he looked. One of his superiors had decided that he looked just like an everyday Somali, so he'd been sent off to learn the language and
customs of the nation from which he did not come. He
knew he had some North African blood and was proud of
it, but none, absolutely none, of the ancestors he'd been
able to trace had originated in East Africa. Except, of
course, in the very beginning, maybe a hundred thousand
years ago.

When he'd first arrived in Djibouti he'd slipped over
the border into Somalia several times to recruit resources.
Few of the Somalis had shown the slightest interest in
helping him. Not really helping him. Those who were
less-than-devout Moslems—not to mention those who
still thought fondly of the older, African gods—were willing to drink the beer he bought for them, and then they

disappeared. Those who were more faithful to the Prophet rarely even spoke with him.

Then one truly scary night it all came to a head. He was walking down the street when a crowd of Somalis gathered around him, all shouting angrily that he was an Ethiopian. He never knew who or what had triggered the rumor, but he knew that it was enough to get him killed. He knew the Ethiopians and the Somalis had been at war, on and off, for centuries. Who knows, maybe millennia. There was a religious problem. There was a cultural problem. There was a territorial problem—for either centuries or millennia, Ethiopia had coveted Somalia's coast. Her access to the Indian Ocean.

Abdul had started to explain that he wasn't Ethiopian but then realized that they no longer cared what he was. They expected little of life and gave it little value. They were just in the mood for a little killing. Fortunately, most of his attackers were smaller than he was. It's also possible that many were really more interested in shouting and terrifying him than they were in actually beating him to death. He was able to burst through the crowd and run like hell. When he reached his car, he dove in and almost destroyed the vehicle by trying to fly it over the indescribably bad roads. Within hours of making it back to Djibouti, he told Preston Olbrig he needed two weeks of leave. Or else. Olbrig sympathized and got him on the next flight out.

After this brief return to sanity—which he defined as North Carolina—Abdul returned, determined to get on with it. Back into Somalia he went, with the greatest of care. The local power structure always knew who he was but didn't seem to care. And he got lucky. He came across an old man—a clerk in an insignificant bureau of the barely breathing Transitional Federal Government—who seemed willing to throw him scraps every now and then. He also found a young prostitute in Basalilays who seemed to have a strong desire for money.

He was convinced he couldn't trust either, but what choice did he have? Thus, here he was at ten thirty in the evening, breathing deeply of the harbor air—a mixture of wet, salt and diesel fumes, all overlaid by the faint memory of organic decay—and waiting to talk to a Somali sailor who the girl said had something important to tell him.

And there, he suddenly realized, the fellow was. Another figure standing in another shadow about twenty feet away. "Are you Mohamed?" asked the other figure.

"No, I'm Haji. And you are Habeb?"

"No. I am Jama."

"Very well, the girl said you had something to tell me."

"Do you have the money?"

"Yes," said Abdul, checking to make sure the pistol in his sport coat pocket was cocked.

"One thousand U.S. dollars. Show it to me."

Abdul showed him the cash with one hand while he kept the other on the pistol.

"What do you have to tell me?"

"Two nights from now three fast boats from Basalilays will join up with the trawler *Ina Boqor* near Ras Xaafuun. They will then all go east, past Socotra Island."

"That's interesting but not worth one thousand dollars."

"There's more. Many of the pirates are afraid of those boats you send to attack them along the shore. In order to show them there is nothing to fear one of the clan leaders will be in one of the boats with them."

"Then he will get aboard the trawler?"

"No, he will go ashore at Ras Xaafuun. Once they are with the trawler, they do not fear those boats."

"How do you know all this?" asked Abdul, thinking it might be of some value to catch a clan leader with a boatful of weapons.

"I have a distant cousin who is one of the pirates."

"And he told you?"

"No, his wife overheard it and told me."

"Why did she tell you?"

"Because he has dishonored her many times and she wants revenge."

"And why do you tell me?"

"Because he refuses to share his money with his relatives. He is a disgrace to the family and I have to get money from somewhere."

This is insane, thought Abdul. But then, this is Somalia. Well, Djibouti, but they were talking about Somalia. Did he believe the story? Maybe, maybe not. He'd not yet met a Somali who'd stay bought—unless the buyer was another Somali, and even then it wasn't a sure thing. Did he think it was worth a thousand dollars? Possibly. Did it make sense? Yes, in a Somali sort of way. But what he thought didn't matter. A thousand dollars were the same as one dollar. Not one of them came from his pocket, and Mandy had approved the expenditure. Mandy had insisted that he go through with it. He'd tell her exactly what this fellow had told him. He'd also tell her he had his doubts. Serious doubts. That way his butt would be covered. He handed the Somali the wad of cash, and the informant disappeared into the shadows.

Mandy was desperate for intel, and Abdul was heartily sick of being the whipping boy when she couldn't come up with any. Clutching his pistol, he walked back to his car, peering deeply into every shadow he passed. Even in Djibouti, life was cheap. Especially if people thought you were an Ethiopian.

* * *

Mike was standing on *Wake Island*'s flight deck watching a company of embarked marines doing a very strenuous set of exercises under the hot sun when it hit him—Jill's birthday was in two days and he'd failed to arrange anything for her. Should he run down and do a little Internet shopping? He really wasn't sure what to get her. After all these years he was still rarely sure what she really wanted. He should have thought of this weeks ago. They'd been married for twenty years, so she wasn't going to fall apart if he didn't send anything. Then again, after putting up with him for twenty years she deserved more than he could ever give her. Something was required. A gift certificate, he decided, to that dress store she so liked. And a phone call.

Determined to do what he could to save the situation, Mike turned and headed for the superstructure just as Alex walked up waving a cell phone. "It's Mandy, Boss. She wants to talk to you."

"Calling to remind us not to start World War Three?"

"No. She has some intel that actually may be useful to us."

Mike took the phone. "Hello, Ms. Cochran."

"Hi, Captain." Her voice sounded almost young and enthusiastic, thought Mike. "We think we may have come up with something that you are best prepared to deal with."

"Okay, we're always ready to try just about anything. Although we do have our limits, I suppose."

Mandy made laughing noises. "Here's the story. We've developed a new resource who says three small fast boats will be rendezvousing with a trawler named *Ina Boqor* near Ras Xaafuun tomorrow night. They're all then going on toward Socotra. That big island to the east of Ras Xaafuun. It's some sort of big nature preserve the Yemenis are

trying to develop into a tourist attraction, if you can believe that. The interesting part is that one of the clan chiefs
will be aboard one of the small boats. It seems all your
bad behavior has actually frightened some of the pirates,
so the big guy is going along to show them there's nothing
to be afraid of."

"Oh? How good is this source?"

"To be honest we don't know yet. This is our first
transaction with him."

"Do we know which clan chief?"

"No."

"Why not have CTF 151 send a ship in to follow them
and nab them in the act?"

"Because the chief isn't going with the trawler. He's
going ashore at Ras Xaafuun. Aren't you the one who's
said it would be nice to get one of the bosses?"

Yes I did, sighed Mike to himself.

"Having seen you operate, I'm sure you can keep control of the situation," she continued. "If it's nothing, it's
nothing. If it is something, you might bag a midlevel terrorist. He might know a lot and we'll both look very
good."

All very logical, thought the naval captain. And if we
make fools of ourselves it would be much easier for everybody else—including Mandy—to say they knew nothing; that Mike and his team were just a pack of loose
cannons.

"Captain, are you going to act on this or *should* I go to
CTF 151?" Her almost girlish tone had disappeared.

"We'll handle it, Ms. Cochran, and I'll let you know
what comes of it just as soon as I have anything to report."

"Excellent!" The phone went dead. Mandy must have
learned phone procedure at the same school as Alan
Parker, thought Mike. Then he hustled off to get that gift

certificate for Jill, hoping it might give her at least a little pleasure even though he considered it totally inadequate. He started to blame the nature of the naval life but caught himself. The navy hadn't forgotten about Jill's birthday. Mike Chambers had.

* * *

The night was warm and clear, with a brilliant full moon rising slowly from the horizon, as the two Trident cats approached the great rock-and-sand pile that was Ras Xaafuun, the easternmost point on the African continent.

"Do you have them, Trident?" asked the radio.

"Affirmative, Mamacita," replied Mike. "Both of them."

"Roger."

Mike watched as what was obviously the trawler worked its way along the long, low sandbar that connected Ras Xaafuun to the mainland, while the three blips of what must be the boats raced out from the south, between Mike's cat and the shore. "You think those are the same three boats we've tangled with before, Captain?" asked Ted.

"I assume so, which means they've got radar and can probably see us. At least the Agency's intel seems to have been right on."

"We're going to stop them this time, right?"

"First we'll try swamping them again. See if they'll shoot. If they don't, we'll stop and search them. See if they have a load of weapons. If they do, we grab the chief. Later, if somebody says just having the weapons doesn't prove they're pirates, we'll still have had a chance to chat with one of their leaders. He may find it very embarrassing."

"You're still convinced they're in it for the money rather than the greater glory of Allah?"

"I am."

"Then it's always possible this guy might be interested in some sort of deal once we get our hands on him."

"That's how I see it, although the exact details are a little hazy at the moment."

"What about Mandy Cochran? She's going to want to get her hands on this guy. Get him to say he's Al Qaeda."

"Don't know yet. If we have him long enough, we may have to turn him over to Mandy or someone else, but unless they actually shoot at us, I'm sure he'll be out on bail in no time."

"This whole thing doesn't feel right, Boss," said Ray, who'd been standing quietly off to one side looking out along the silvery moonbeam. "They must know we're here, yet they act as if they don't."

"I'm nervous too, but we've got to play a few more cards until we see what develops."

"You work your way a little closer to Ras Xaafuun," said Mike into his headset, "and prepare to pass ahead of them when I tell you to execute harassment."

"Roger," replied Alex, who was in the second cat with Jerry, between the pirate boats and the shore.

Eyeballing the radar, Mike concluded that the cats' courses would intersect with the boats' in about ten minutes. "The fifty all prepped?" he asked Ted.

"Aye, Captain."

While he waited for the situation to develop, Mike allowed his attention to drift to the same moonbeam that had so fascinated Ray. They really are hypnotic, he thought. Almost reluctantly he turned back to the radar. Damn, the boats had speeded up.

"Ray, does it look to you like they've speeded up?"

The marine officer studied the display a moment. "They sure as hell have, sir."

"Ted. Get to the fifty and get ready, but don't fire unless I tell you."

"Aye, sir."

"Trident One, this is Trident. The boats from the south appear to have speeded up."

"Roger, Trident. And the trawler looks as if it's slowed down."

"Man your fifty and stand by."

"Roger."

The minutes ticked by; the night remained surrealistically beautiful.

"Captain," snapped Ray, "those boats are splitting up."

"Roger. This is going to screw up our maneuver."

"They've turned toward shore. Toward the other cat. Two to the east of her and one to the west."

"Shit!" Were they headed for shore or headed for Alex and Jerry? If they were headed for the other cat, they'd have her boxed in between them and the shore. He didn't know the answer, and he began to get the feeling that he was losing control of the situation. He then realized with disgust that they probably could see him illuminated by the moonlight. He'd been suckered. He considered calling in a helo gunship but then thought better of it. He couldn't tell them to open fire until the pirates had done something. He also considered aborting the operation but knew he couldn't do that either. His mission was to get close, and that's what he was doing. There'd been risks all along.

"Hang on!" he ordered, jamming the throttles forward and bracing himself. "We're going to circle wagons with Alex and Jerry."

Engines screaming and spray flying, the cat surged forward through the night then healed sharply as Mike turned toward Ras Xaafuun and the other cat. It became clear almost immediately that the three pirate boats had turned again and were now converging on Alex and Jerry.

We've still got time, he thought. They won't be within effective rifle range for another few minutes—assuming they really did intend to open fire rather than just playing tit for tat. Then the boats were visible—hopping around in the choppy seas—as was the great mass of Ras Xaafuun, highlighted here and there by the silvery moonlight.

It also soon became clear that Mike's assumptions were all wrong. Ibrihim Hassan had changed the rules again.

Mike realized his error the instant six flashes of light flared partway up the side of Ras Xaafuun and then continued to burn as they arced out toward the other cat. For a split second he watched in horror, then opened his mouth to order evasive action.

"This is Trident One. Incoming!" reported Alex before Mike could say a thing.

"Roger, Trident One." There was a brief pause while the entire team concluded from the way the missile tracks seemed to be curving toward Alex's cat that they were heat-seekers. An eventuality for which they were totally unprepared.

"This is Trident One. We're ditching. Out."

That was easy, thought Jacob as she read the e-mail from
Pavel, one of Gazprom's auditors in Vladivostok. According to him, Orlov had been making deals in the dark corners of Siberia for years. Once or twice he'd even run
afoul of Gazprom, although nothing had ever come of it,
for all the usual reasons—primarily because one of the
other parties involved was influential enough to prevent
any problems. Orlov didn't appear to be a really big-time
operator, but he did seem to have contacts. Of course, he
would have to! Otherwise he would never have survived
even as a small-timer.

Unfortunately, Pavel had no idea what Orlov had been
peddling recently. The fact that he conducted much of his
business in Vladivostok did, however, provide a frightening array of hints. Although the city was now more or less
open, it had been closed for many years. Not only because
it was right on the North Korean border, but also because

it had been the home of the Soviet Pacific Fleet and a number of other sensitive military facilities.

She'd have to dig harder, she told herself. But she did have enough to forward to Langley.

* * *

"Shit!" growled Ted. "How many did you see?"

"Six," said Ray. For a moment he found it difficult to take his eyes off the flaming arcs created by the weapons' burning tails.

Mike, his muscles now tense, his eyes and ears attempting to reach out into the surrounding dark, just grunted in anger as he continued to steer for the other cat, which the pirate boats had already passed, now headed for shore.

Then there were three searing flashes directly ahead. Three booms—running into one another in their haste to announce themselves—followed.

"Anybody see the other three?" asked Ray. "I could swear I saw six fired."

"No," reported Ted. "I saw six too, but I don't see any more now. Must have crashed."

Damn it, thought Mike, it's combat now. "Stand by," he shouted. "We're going after them."

"You see what happened to the other missiles?" repeated Ray. "I thought I saw more than three launched."

"No idea," said Mike. "And it doesn't matter now. If they were going to hit us, they would have already."

"One of those boats is turning back toward us," shouted Ted.

"I hope to hell they're not carrying more missiles," said Ray as he stepped around the center console and stopped next to the fifty.

Gritting his teeth, Mike jammed the throttles forward and turned east to attack, the cat healing violently, throwing spray in all directions. Soon they were screaming down the pirates' now-visible wake. He turned slightly to port, then back so that the boat was now clearly—if distantly—observable in the very same moonbeam that had made the cats so visible a few minutes before. "Open fire, Ted."

A thundering, pulsing crash erupted from the cat's bow almost before the words were out of Mike's mouth, causing the whole boat to shake and pound as it thrust forward, cutting the tops off the dark waves. As the cat screamed through the night, Ray stood beside Ted, feeding him ammunition, while the tracers arched toward the faintly visible target and the well filled with spent brass casings.

* * *

"Alex!"

"I see them, Jerry."

"They're following us. Must be heat seekers."

"Shit. We'd better bail."

"At this speed we may kill ourselves hitting the water wrong."

"Roger."

Alex yanked the throttles back and the boat fell backward off the plane as she called Mike.

"It's now or never," said Jerry, his glance moving from the flames of the approaching missiles to the water alongside.

"Go. I'm right behind you."

Jerry bounded up onto the gunnel and continued on over the side into the dark water. Alex followed. Her foot slipped on the gunnel and one leg fell back into the boat, momentarily wedging itself between a bracket and the hull as her body continued forward, over the side.

She felt a brief bolt of sharp pain course up her leg and screamed quietly. Then the leg came free and she fell into the water as the cat continued past her.

Alex was still in shock, facing toward the shore, when the missiles detonated and the massive shock wave thrust out in all directions, through the air and through the water. She felt the blast of heat slam into the back of her head and, almost simultaneously, shuddered as the water pounded her back. For a moment she wondered if she really was going to die. Then it was over, all but the painful throbbing of her leg. And the salty water splashing into her mouth.

Dizzy and disoriented, at first she floated, looking up at the dark sky. Then she remembered Jerry. She looked around and could see nothing. A wave rolled under her and lifted her, and there, off to the south, she spotted a strobe light. Still dizzy and feeling weak but determined, Alex forced herself to breaststroke in the direction of the strobe, dragging her leg behind her and continuing to swallow water.

When she finally reached the strobe, she found Jerry, floating upright thanks to his life vest, not moving. "Jerry," she tried to shout. No response. She felt for a pulse.

* * *

Ali was terrified when the vicious, knife-like flashes of light appeared where only the dark shadow of the pursuing cat had been seconds before.

"Shoot them, shoot them!" screamed Mohamed Hassan as he turned the rolling, pounding boat around toward the cat and tried to force the outboard's throttle even farther past its stops. "My father has sunk one of them and now we will sink the other."

Ali, like the other four pirates aboard, raised his Kalashnikov. Before he could pull the trigger, before he could even aim, he heard a distant, rapid, thudding bark, then the boat slewed wildly to one side and jumped into the air. The crew members all grabbed at the thwarts, or the gunnels, desperate to not be thrown overboard. One even dropped his rifle over the side. Although the boy managed to hang on to the Kalashnikov, he continued to find it impossible to aim and shoot. And then it didn't matter because the heavy, horrible fifty-caliber slugs began to zip through the dark air and slam into the boat and the men around him, pounding holes in the fiberglass and hacking his shipmates to pieces.

Allah, protect me, he thought. It was too dark to see the blood, but he could see the shadowy, twisted bodies lying twitching in the bilges. And hear the heavy pounding of the gun. Then he could feel the searing pain as one of the huge slugs tore through the paltry coating of meat that surrounded his arm. This was worse than anything he'd ever imagined. Infinitely worse than the dhow. Without even realizing it, he was shaking with terror. Then he was in the water, hanging on to what was left of the boat's shattered hull.

* * *

A minute or so after commencing fire, Mike thought he spotted a flash near the shadowy, bouncing mass that was the pirate boat. Then a second. Although the range was still great, the gun's output was torrential, and Ted was known for having a knack with fifties—and just about everything else. Which was one of the less objectively verifiable reasons he belonged to the Trident Force.

There was another, larger flash. Mike looked at the radar. The boat seemed to be slowing. He shifted his attention to the other two. They were still on the screen, but they were now close in to shore. Working their way through the fringing shoals. It was a path he didn't dare follow. Because of the shoals and because of the additional armed pirates who were undoubtedly still occupying the cape's brooding cliffs.

And the trawler? She'd turned around and was approaching Hafun, the small fishing port at the mainland end of the sandbar. Even if he could go ashore to examine her, he suspected he'd find nothing but a fishing boat filled with innocent fishermen who'd swear they'd fled the minute they saw shooting.

Mike looked again at Ras Xaafuun. From where he was, the headland was nothing more than a darker mass in the dark night. Even with night vision gear he could see nothing. Yet he knew they were still there. Watching. Waiting. Preparing to fire another salvo of rockets?

How many could they possibly have?

Then they were there, almost on the pirate boat, or what was left of it. Ted had the barrel of the fifty depressed so far that it was spitting powder deposits on the fiberglass deck as he continued to pound the pirate hull, which was now nothing more than a whale-like shape wallowing in the rolling waters. Mike throttled back and the cat's stern fell off the step, the bow rising into the night a moment before settling down again.

"Shift target," he bellowed into his intercom. "Fire on the cliffs ashore."

At first there was no response, then he could see Ray pounding on Ted's shoulder. The rapid, thumping boom of the gun ceased, and despite the continuing growl of the engines, the night seemed almost silent.

"What should we aim at, Captain?" asked the marine.

"Just spray the area where you think the missiles came from. Maybe we can keep their heads down."

"Roger."

The fifty commenced pounding again while Mike turned on the searchlight and played it across the floating wreckage. The boat, or what was left of it, was awash and nothing but the waves seemed to be moving in its vicinity.

"Cease fire! We're going back to look for Alex and Jerry," Mike said as he turned away from the pirate wreck. "Then we'll see about these guys."

By now the other cat had disappeared from the radar screen, although small pieces of it decorated the surface of the Indian Ocean.

"I've got them, Captain," said Ray in something only slightly less than a shout. "I can see their strobes."

Mike followed Ray's pointing arm and saw the pulsing blue white strobes himself. He turned toward them and slowed.

"Hi," said Alex in a strange, small voice as she held on to Jerry's life jacket. "I think you'd better get Jerry first. I think he was facing the boat when the missiles detonated."

Ted grabbed Alex's vest while Ray reached over and grabbed Jerry's motionless form. Mike then leaned over the side and helped the marine lift Jerry aboard. Thanks to its great beam and stability, the cat barely heeled at all.

The chief boatswain's mate was breathing, but he didn't look good.

"Alex now," said Mike as he returned to the side while Ray tore off Jerry's gear.

"Ummh!" Alex groaned through gritted teeth as they pulled her over the gunnel. "My leg!"

Goddamn it, thought Mike as they deposited her on the deck and Ted started to remove her gear and examine her. I've really fucked up. But he had no time to dwell on his own stupidity. He had two team members who needed medical attention and he still had a mission.

"How's the chief?" he demanded.

"He's awake now, Captain," reported Ray. "More or less. I don't think he has any broken bones, but he says his chest and gut hurt."

"Any blood coming out of his mouth or nose?"

"Not now, sir."

They all knew that Jerry might well be—probably was—suffering from internal injuries caused by the concussion from the blast. He was in desperate need of real medical aid.

"Alex?"

"I'm okay, Captain."

"Bullshit," cut in Ted. "Something's definitely wrong with your leg. I bet it's broken, though nothing seems to be sticking out."

"Is that supposed to be a compliment? That I don't have anything sticking out?"

Ted just shook his head.

Again Mike paused. Both needed help. But he had his duty. "Make them as comfortable as possible. Then you two break out the riot guns. We're going to see if any of the pirates in that boat survived."

There was a pause, then "Aye, aye, sir" and "Aye, Captain."

The two broke out the weapons as Mike turned the cat back toward where he thought the pirate boat had sunk. He was soon able to pick out a fuel can and various scraps of lumber floating on the silvery water. There was also a head and a pair of arms splashing feebly among the wreckage. Mike pulled alongside and stopped so Ted could haul the survivor aboard. It was a boy. A young man. And he appeared to be suffering from shock.

After pulling the boy aboard, Mike searched for another twenty minutes then gave up and headed back to

Wake Island with the throttles jammed forward to the stops.

* * *

Much of the snow that had been plaguing Langley had melted, although the sky remained gray and the wind raw.

"Siberia?" repeated Paul Tracy.

"Siberia, Paul," said Connie Barton. "Jacob reports that while this Orlov is probably still in Moscow, he's lived and operated for most of his career in Siberia, around Vladivostok. She's also been able to confirm that he's been in on some pretty rancid deals."

"Like what?"

"She thinks he was involved in the theft and sale of several hundred tons of very high-quality oil drill pipe. And, possibly, the disappearance of over a hundred thousand barrels of crude oil. And drugs, of course."

"How does a hundred thousand barrels of crude oil disappear?"

"She thinks it only disappeared on paper in Russia and then popped up again in Poland or Hungary or someplace like that."

"You mean she thinks he works through the auditors she's supposed to be supervising."

"Probably. Through them or around them."

"But if all he deals in is oil and drill equipment, how does the girl's message make any sense?"

"Jacob's sure he does more than just petroleum-related thievery. Her sources tell her he's also into cars and art and whatever else will make a ruble."

"None of which sounds like WMDs. What makes you so sure he's dealing in them now?"

"The message."

"That logic's almost circular."

"I know. There are a number of military installations in Siberia and also several research facilities about which we know little."

"So we still don't know what it is or whether it's already been shipped."

"It must have been shipped by now."

"Then it must have been delivered by now."

"But it hasn't been used yet. As far as we know."

"Keep on it. Find out what it is and where it went."

"Okay."

* * *

"You say your name is Ali?" asked Ray in what he hoped was the local dialect of Somali.

"Yes. Ali."

As the boy answered, Ray studied him closely. He was banged up but not seriously injured, and he seemed to be recovering from the shock. Some food had helped. The marine felt a temptation to beat the shit out of him. He was a pirate. He'd helped break Alex's leg and mangle Jerry's guts. But Ray knew self-control was in order. This skinny, disoriented kid was the enemy, but he was also a valuable asset and you don't trash valuable assets. Handled properly, he might be a useful source of information. "How old are you?"

Ali seemed to have to think a moment before answering. "Fifteen. Almost sixteen."

"How long have you been a pirate?"

"One, maybe two months. Before that I was just a fisherman."

For the only survivor of a boat that had just been shot to pieces by a fifty, thought Ray, Ali really did look pretty good, after all. He had a bullet hole in his arm, a gash on his head and a broken finger, and he seemed tired, almost washed out, but other than that he looked healthy. At first they'd suspected he might have a concussion from the way his eyes seemed to wander, unable to focus. Then they decided he was just scared shitless.

"Why did you become a pirate?"

"Because I was starving."

"Do you have a family?"

"They are dead. I have only my friends."

"Did you know what you were going to do tonight?"

"Yes. Ibrihim Hassan wanted to attack you. To teach you respect."

"Who is Ibrihim Hassan?" asked Ray, reasonably certain he knew the answer.

"He is one of our leaders. A powerful leader."

"Is he the leader of your gang?"

"We do what he says."

"Where are you from?"

"Basalilays."

"Is that were the three boats came from?"

"Yes. They are usually kept there."

Probably the same ones we saw there a few nights ago, thought Ray.

"Have you always been part of that boat crew?"

"No. I sailed on a dhow for a while."

"Why did you change?"

"Because Suleiman told me to. The dhow has a very big leak."

"Who is Suleiman?"

"The son of Ibrihim."

"Was he in charge tonight?"

"He was on the trawler. His younger brother, Mohamed, was in charge of the small boats."

"Where is he now, do you think? Back in Basalilays?"

"I think he is probably dead. He was in the same boat I was."

"Who fired the rockets?"

"Ibrihim. He was on the shore with some of his men."

"Where did he get the rockets?"

"I don't know. They just arrived."

"You are afraid of the other pirates?"

"Some of them."

Ray looked at him a moment, his mind working furiously. "Do you know what will happen to you next?"

"You kill me because I tried to kill you?"

"No, we will probably have to give you to the Kenyans, and they will put you in jail."

Ali looked around him, at the bare, steel bulkheads, felt the sting and throb of the wounds he'd suffered and remembered the terror he'd felt when the bullets began to tear both the boat and his companions to pieces. Piracy, he thought, was for fools. It wasn't the road to guaranteed wealth. It was the road to misery and death. He'd made a terrible mistake joining Ibrihim's gang.

"The Kenyans," spat Ali, "they are no better than the Ethiopians. Why don't you take me to America? I want to go to America. Everybody eats there. Even when they're in jail."

"How do you know that?"

"Everybody knows that."

Amazing, thought Ray, how things sometimes happen. "You will wait right where you are. Do not move from that chair. I will be back very soon." That was a stupid thing to say, he thought as he stood. Even if he wanted to, the kid couldn't get very far with his ankle chained to the table leg. Ray then walked into the adjoining compartment and called Mike. "Captain, what's the word on Alex and Jerry?"

"They've set her leg—it was just a simple fracture, fortunately—and she's napping now. Jerry has some internal bruising, but they don't think its life-threatening."

"They going to medevac him out?"

"No, they're going to keep a close watch on him for now."

Fuentes stood, phone in hand, staring straight ahead into the blank bulkhead and thinking about Alex and Jerry.

"Mr. Fuentes," said Mike, a calculated edge to his voice, "do you have something to report to me?"

"Yes, Captain. Sorry. I think this kid can be turned. I don't know how long he'll stay turned, and I'm not sure what he'll be able to do for us, but he's better than the nothing we have. At the moment he's tripping over himself trying to be helpful."

"What does he want?"

"So far just to go to America."

"Have you already asked him?"

"No. So far he's just asked that we take him to America rather than giving him to the Kenyans."

"Okay. Keep on. See what you can come up with."

"Aye, aye, sir."

Ray returned to find Ali exactly where he'd left him. "You want to go to America?"

"Yes."

"Will you do some work for us?"

"You already have many sailors and I do not speak very much English."

"Can you read and write?"

"Yes, of course. So I can study the Koran."

"If we put you back ashore tonight so you can say you swam from the sunken boat, will you tell us things about the pirates' plans?"

Ali's expression changed as the implications of the suggestion sank in. For a moment a battle seemed to rage within him. Desire versus fear. "I do not swim well," he finally responded.

He's hooked, thought the marine.

"Not at all?"

"A little."

Ray thought a moment, tapping a pencil as he did. "You will tell them you floated ashore by holding on to an empty gas can."

As Ali considered the proposition, life seemed to return to his eyes. "How long before you take me to America?"

"A month."

"If they figure out what I am doing, they will kill me."

"We will help you keep them from knowing."

Ali sat in silence for several minutes. "I will work for you for one month, no more. Then you will take me to America and give me two hundred thousand American dollars."

Ray gave him the hardest look he could. "I will talk to my leader about that." He then wondered how the boy had settled on precisely two hundred thousand.

* * *

"We must call the boats back and have them look for Mohamed and the others," said Nasser, one of the clan chief's principal deputies, to Ibrihim Hassan, who was sitting on a small stool among the great, flat rocks of Ras Xaafuun.

The clan chief continued to stare out at the now-dark waters. Deep in thought. Deep in mourning.

From his vantage point he'd watched the battle develop. His three boats coming up from the south. The two American boats coming from the west and then splitting up, as they always had in the past—one positioning itself on each side of his boats. One to seaward, one on the land side. The situation had developed exactly as he'd hoped it would.

Ibrihim had given the order to fire the six missiles, and a slight smile had crossed his normally expressionless face as flames erupted from their tails and they took flight. A slightly stronger smile appeared when several of them struck the American boat and exploded. It had been just as he'd hoped it would be, and the awareness that some of the missiles had missed, burying themselves in the sea, was of little significance. Malfunctions were common with all the weapons he'd ever used in his life.

The one catamaran destroyed, Ibrihim had settled back to watch the second cat look quickly for survivors and then run like hell away. But it hadn't happened that way. Instead of running, the Americans had attacked one of his boats. The one with Mohamed in it. And in a matter of seconds they'd destroyed it. And the rest had been anticlimactic. They'd looked around the wreckage of their boat and of his, finding he had no idea what. Then they'd gone home.

"Mohamed is dead, Nasser. They all are dead, and I do not wish to risk any more boats tonight."

"But we must make sure."

"If any were alive, the Americans would have picked them up."

"But . . ."

"You and three others will stay and search the beach tomorrow. I must return to Basalilays."

"As you wish. We have won a victory tonight. We have taught the Americans a stern lesson."

A very costly victory, thought Ibrihim as he stood and started walking toward his jeep. All victories cost something, but this one had been more expensive than most.

* * *

"What's up, Mike?"

"Exciting things, Alan."

"So tell me."

"We were enticed into an ambush a few hours ago and lost one of the cats."

"Did we get more of them?"

"One of them."

"Casualties?"

"Alex has a broken leg and Jerry has some internal bruising, but the doctors think both will recover."

"What happened?"

"They hit us with heat-seeking missiles off Ras Xaa-fuun. The cat with Alex and Jerry aboard was blown to pieces, but they ditched just in time."

"Sounds to me like they waited too long to ditch."

"That's possible."

"And you got one of their boats?"

"Yes."

"One for one. That's not good enough. The media will make it seem we were defeated."

Mike started to tell Parker that he shouldn't say a word to the media, but then he realized there was no way the skirmish could be hushed up. The Somalis would raise hell about it and the two thousand e-mail–empowered officers, sailors and marines aboard *Wake Island* would all be wondering what had happened to the missing cat.

"Did you catch them in the act?" demanded Alan.

"Of what? Shooting missiles at us?"

"Damn it, Mike, this is still going to be an incident— you know, like on your car insurance. It doesn't matter whether or not you were at fault if they decide you're 'incident prone.' How'd you get into this mess?"

"Amanda Cochran in Djibouti, she's Agency . . ."

"Yes, I know."

". . . informed me that a trawler and three fast boats were rendezvousing off Ras Xaafuun and that an important clan chief would be aboard one of the boats. We moved in, and Alex and Jerry got plastered."

"How, exactly, did it happen?"

"I fucked up. You may quote me and leave it at that."

"You think the *Agency* set you up?"

"Of course not! Cochran warned me they had less than total confidence in the intel."

"Ummm."

"Tell SECDEF that we captured one of the crew of the boat we sank and Ray thinks he's turned him."

"You're trying to set up your own intelligence network ashore? What the fuck's the Agency going to say? And what about the Somalis and the Europeans? No major operations ashore! We learned that last time."

"We're not going to be ashore. We're doing this at sea."

"What makes you think you've turned him? Is he a secret admirer of Abraham Lincoln?"

"Ray thinks the boy's tired of living in hovels and gnawing on stripped goat bones. That's why he joined the pirates."

"Isn't that why they all became pirates. That and the chance to send a little cash to Al Qaeda or the Taliban."

"That's what Mandy seems to think. She's convinced the pirates are all Al Qaeda or Taliban."

"Aren't they?"

"The point is that this guy's very young. Ray, who's been interrogating him, thinks he's scared to death and wants an out."

"So what does he want?"

"He works for us for a month then we get him to the

United States and pay him two hundred thousand dollars cash."

"Mike, you're delusional. That's a lot of money for some two-bit Somali kid."

"Your buddies in the District are spending more than that every second to maintain the lifestyle of bankers who may or may not be honest but seem less than competent. Unless, of course, it's all a scam."

From his snort, Alan clearly didn't like that remark. "So what do we do with this orphan when he arrives?"

"Give him whatever papers he needs to keep from going to Gitmo, then give him the two hundred grand, then send him to school, then get him a job."

"That's asking a lot."

"The United States government does a lot more than that when it suits its whim. Like for Mafioso hit men."

"I've got to talk to SECDEF about this."

"No, you don't. We don't have time. We've got to get him back on the beach, or near to it, before dawn."

"Mike!"

"Alan! If it blows up in our faces, I have total confidence that you'll manage to cover your ass. That's why you're still there, three presidents later."

"I won't stop you, Mike, but I can't approve."

"If you don't promise me you'll cover for this kid— assuming he produces—then I'm not going to lie to him. Remember, both Jerry and I have enough time in to retire, and there are many days when retirement looks good to both of us."

"You think he's straight?"

"I don't know, but I want to try. If he's as bent as the Agency's latest source seems to have been, then he doesn't get the money and he doesn't go to the U.S. We're more alert than ever."

"Mike, you're going to hang yourself damn soon. You and all those other sketchy characters you cruise around with. But I will make this promise: If you tell me this guy performed, then we'll provide him with what you're offering him. If it blows up in our faces, then he'll get nothing and you and some of your pals will each get your own yardarm to dangle from."

"Thanks, Alan. I knew we were on the same side."

* * *

At two hours before dawn the brilliant full moon had moved on to beguile the other side of the planet. A twenty-foot hard-bottomed inflatable boat with two muffled outboards and a two-person kayak slipped out of *Wake Island*'s stern gate and headed toward the darkened shore some twelve miles away. The huge ship, totally dark, then turned and headed slowly back out to sea.

With their time incredibly tight, Mike ran the engines at full power for the first five or six miles, making the boat skip and bounce over the water and through the darkness. While Mike drove, Ray crouched with Ali, reviewing what sort of information they wanted and how the Somali could get it to them. The plan was a dangerous example of jury-rigging, but as long as Ali was willing to play, so were they.

When they were about four miles offshore, Mike slowed. While the portion of the cape where they planned to drop Ali was supposedly uninhabited, he wanted to make as little noise as possible. He also wanted to be well offshore again before the sun decided to make an appearance.

They continued on almost silently toward a location a few miles to the east of a very small fishing hamlet—no more than two or three huts—that somehow survived along the edge of the Ras Xaafuun sandbar.

Were the damn pirates still there? Mike kept asking himself, his back neck muscles growing tenser and tenser. Looking for their missing men? Sitting among the rocks, waiting for the Tridents? Sitting on the dark beach, chewing khat and waiting for them? The night vision gear revealed no reception party. But under conditions like these a negative indication meant nothing.

There was no way they could be sure. They just had to go.

"Roughly a mile now," said Mike to the marine captain as he put the engines into neutral.

"Okay," said Ray. "Now," he explained to Ali in Somali, "we get into this and I paddle us right up to the shore. Ready?"

"Yes."

Mike and Ray got the two-man kayak over the side, and Ray then lowered himself into it. Once he was settled, he signaled to Ali. Even though the boy had never seen a kayak, he had spent time in fishing boats and had little trouble taking his place. They cast off, and Ray immediately started paddling like hell through the chop that, if anything, had increased since they'd returned to *Wake Island* following the attack. The marine was just as nervous about a reception party as had been Chambers. He had less of a chance to worry about it, however, because he had to devote his full attention to getting his passenger in close to shore.

Twenty minutes and a great deal of sweat later Ray estimated they were about fifty yards off the beach. It was a location several miles south of where Ibrihim's men were waiting for dawn to look for survivors. Ray could see the white line of the two-foot-high surf and the faintly visible bulk of the sand behind. He could also see no sign of life. So far, so good.

"Are you ready?" he asked the Somali.

"Yes."

"Are you sure you can swim this far?"

"Yes. I will be able to do it."

Ray looked the boy over again. All the dressings that Ted had put on him had been removed, and the salt was probably going to sting like hell when he jumped in the water, but it couldn't be avoided. If he was going to play the part of a castaway, then it was best that he really be one. "Get in the water now," said Ray, preparing to shift his weight as necessary, "and good luck."

Ali slithered out of the kayak and over the side with as much grace as Ray had ever seen anybody do it. "Don't forget this," said the marine as he handed Ali a specially programmed EPIRB—an emergency position indicator beacon. "When you want us to come for you, just turn on that switch."

"Okay."

The marine waited a moment and watched as Ali headed for the beach. He was tempted to say a prayer for the boy, insane as that seemed, even to him. Ali had been the enemy twenty-four hours ago. He'd tried to kill them. But now he was on their side. He was a good guy. Until further notice.

Shrugging mentally, Fuentes turned the kayak and headed back for the HBI. Dawn wasn't far.

By the time the eastern horizon began to show its pearly glow, only the top of the rock pile at the tip of the cape was visible to Ray and Mike and they were totally invisible from the shore.

"You think he made it ashore, sir?" asked Ray.

"I hope so. We'll know in a day or two."

"You think he'll be able to get what we want for us?"

"We'll know in a day or two."

"I may have been wrong about him. He might switch sides again and tell them everything he now knows about us."

"As I said, we'll know in a day or two."

"How'd it go last night?" asked Mandy Cochran after Mike had identified himself over the secure satellite phone.

"We were set up. One of our boats got blown to hell."

"Any casualties?" Mandy sounded suitably—but not convincingly—concerned.

"Two of my people got pretty badly beaten up, but they'll survive."

"The other guys?"

"We sank one boat."

"Survivors?"

"No," lied Mike. He didn't want Mandy knowing anything about the agent he was now running ashore.

"How'd they get you?"

"Heat-seeking missiles. We cruised right into it."

"I warned you that intel was questionable."

"I thought you meant that it might be nothing, not that

it was planted. And when did they start using heat-seeking missiles?"

"It's the first I've heard about it, but it sure as hell sounds like an Al Qaeda connection, don't you think? I mean, where else could they get them?" Mike thought she sounded elated at the conclusion.

"That's possible."

"It's more than possible. It's certain now. This confirms it."

"You have anything new for us?"

Mandy paused for a moment. "Captain, I *am* sorry this happened, even though I warned you. It doesn't look good for me. I'm going to have one of the internal security teams flown in today for a chat with Jones, the guy who came up with the intel. It's not that I don't trust him, but you can never be too careful, and now that I'm convinced we're dealing with an Al Qaeda operation, I want to focus even more closely on it."

Mike grunted something noncommittal then added, "Let's keep in touch."

"Let's do that."

* * *

Ali felt himself going mad with thirst as he dragged his battered body along the narrow, rocky beach that bordered Ras Xaafuun. His every thought was focused on water and the bone-dry desert that was his mouth. He could think only of water. Nothing else registered. Not the pain in his arm and finger. Not the Americans. Not Ibrihim and Suleiman. Not where he had been or where he might be going or why. Water.

The sun beat down, and the fine, salt-tinged sand blew into his eyes and nose and between his swollen lips. Every now and then he raised his eyes and looked ahead. All he saw was blue ocean on one side, gray rocks on the other and endless, waterless sand before him. He stopped and stared at the blue water. He knew he shouldn't, but the temptation was overpowering. He knelt down on all fours and drank of the Indian Ocean.

At first it felt wonderful so he had some more. Then he vomited, and very soon his guts were knotted and his mouth was drier than ever. But he was young and frightened, so he continued on down the beach.

Because Ali was a Somali, it would seem that he would be accustomed to walking long distances under the hot sun. But he'd lived most of his life in towns and, therefore, had little experience making long-distance treks across the hard desert that constituted much of his country.

By the time he reached the little cluster of wood and block fishermen's hovels—some little more than half-open lean-tos—he looked beyond death and felt the same. And at first he couldn't find a soul. Only after wandering around the decrepit structures for several minutes did he find anything that even resembled life.

"What do you want?" asked the mummy-like old woman who was sitting in the scant shade of one of the huts, carefully husking a small ear of corn while a beat-up aluminum pot of dried beans sat soaking beside her. Her bony, totally desiccated face showed a mix of suspicion and fear.

"Water," he croaked. "My boat sank last night and I had to swim ashore."

"Last night? There was shooting out there last night. Explosions." The woman's face and voice were emotionless—and displayed not the slightest hint of curiosity—as she reported the event. It was as if the ruckus had occurred on some other planet and was of no interest.

"We were attacked."

"We have nothing here. You can see that. Go away." This time her voice betrayed a hint of uncertainty, perhaps even fear. Ali knew as well as she did that nothing good ever came of strangers arriving and asking for things. Especially strangers who had been shooting the night before.

"Water. Please, water." As he said it, Ali had to resist the temptation to make her fears come true, to attack her, pound her into the sand, drive out whatever little life remained in her meatless body.

"I'll give you water, then you must leave. It is only a few miles more along the beach to Hafun. You can't miss it."

Ali drank the stale, ever-so-slightly brackish water she gave him in a cracked coffee mug—painfully jamming his broken finger in the process—and asked for more. The woman looked at him coldly, then poured another serving and returned the jar to inside the hut. The boy could have consumed the whole jar in one gulp but knew he could survive on what he'd had and didn't want to push the woman too far. It would have been easy enough to kill her, but then what if her family came back in time to catch him? Or tracked him down in Hafun? Somali revenge killings tended to be especially hard, as killings go, for the recipient.

"I'm tired," he told her, "very tired. And I ache all over. Let me lie down for a little while then I will go on to Hafun. I work for Ibrihim Hassan."

The old woman tensed even more than she already was. "You may lie down for a little while, but you must be gone when the others come back. They are all out fishing. And do not say that name. We are not of his clan."

Ali had no idea to which clan the old woman did belong, but it was clearly one that had suffered at Ibrihim's hand sometime in the past. He nodded then lay down on the hard ground in the shade of the hut while the woman went back to preparing the precious ear of corn. Before he fell into a deep, sweaty sleep, an overpowering feeling of depression settled over him. He hurt everywhere, and somehow he'd managed to get himself in an impossible situation. He might admit right away to Ibrihim that he'd made a deal with the Americans—it was the only way to escape them, he might explain—and swear to help the chief trap them again. But it was more than likely that Hassan would still kill him. Ibrihim had just lost his son Mohamed and would be thinking primarily of retribution. As for the Americans, Ali didn't really trust them. He knew he had no choice except to play their game. Until they betrayed him, which now, in the light of day, seemed inevitable, given their reputation for dealing with Moslems.

In retrospect, working for Osman hadn't been the worst of all possible lives. At least it was a life.

* * *

"Good morning, Commodore," said Mike into the sat phone.

"Good morning, Captain Chambers." His accent's more noticeable on the phone than it is in person, thought Mike.

"We had a little problem last night and I promised to let you know about such things. We were following three boats near Ras Xaafuun when one of my boats was blown out of the water by what must have been heat-seeking missiles."

"My sources have informed me there was shooting in that area. Did you have any personnel casualties?"

"Two. One broken leg and one man with internal injuries."

"Serious?"

"Less serious than I'd originally feared. The woman with the broken leg is already hobbling around. The chief petty officer with the internal injuries is expected to fully recover, although they want to keep him under observation for a few days."

"Please keep me posted. Now, about this incident. Are you sure they were missiles? Were they fired from one of the boats?"

"I'm quite sure they were missiles, but they were fired from shore."

"They were waiting for you?"

"I'm afraid so. We were acting on information that I suspect was intended to suck us in."

"These things happen, especially when you are playing the sort of game you've chosen to play. I must inform you that the Puntland government has already complained to me and the UN and just about everybody else they can think of. Their version of the story is a little different. I believe yours. I have assured everybody that I will look into the matter, but I am an old man and it takes time for me to look into things these days. There may eventually be repercussions, but I think you still have some time. I assume you will continue your experiments until somebody tells you to stop. Or manages to kill you. Can you tell me what you plan to try next?"

"I think the harassing tactics we've been using have been effective in a limited way, but we'll never have enough resources to track and heckle every potential pirate vessel. I've been hoping now to catch one of the pirate kingpins in the act at sea. In fact, that was the bait that made me careless last night. Nobody wants to waste time on the minor players, but I think a chief would be of more interest to everybody, including the courts."

"A kingpin? You mean a leader?"

"Yes, sir."

"How did the pirates know that was your objective?"

"I doubt they knew, but they're not stupid, and that's the sort of bait that's worked over the centuries." As he explained, Mike felt a wave of embarrassment build within him. He'd fallen for a trick that had been used ten thousand times.

"Very well. Despite the risks, it does sound worth a try. Please keep me posted."

* * *

"Ms. Cochran, this is Sheikh al-Abbas," said the voice on Mandy's telephone.

"Good morning, Your Excellency." As she said it, she tensed, knowing perfectly well what the call was about.

"There was a very serious incident in the waters off Ras Xaafuun last night. Somebody attacked three of our fishing boats and sank one, killing the entire crew."

"I'm very sorry to hear that, sir. Do you have any idea who did it? Could it have been some sort of local dispute between two clans?"

"We all know perfectly well who did it. That gang of criminals you have racing around in speedboats terrorizing our innocent fishermen. The Somali people and the government of Somalia are very pleased for you to apprehend any real pirates that you catch robbing and killing at sea, but we do not want our fishermen attacked for no reason, especially close in to our shores."

"You have me at a disadvantage, sir. Nobody working

for me is driving around in speedboats harassing innocent fishermen. Such behavior is not in compliance with our policies. But I will certainly look into it."

"Yes. Do so. In the meantime I have reported this to both the Joint Task Force and also to the United Nations observer. The sovereignty of Somalia is just as sacred as the sovereignty of any other nation. Even the United States. You do agree, don't you?"

"I totally agree, Your Excellency."

Shit, she thought as she hung up. She'd known from the very start that Chambers and his crew were going to cause trouble for her, one way or another, if she didn't manage to get control over them. Now he'd really stepped in it, and she had to find a way of saving herself because he'd undoubtedly gotten some of it on her.

* * *

Late in the afternoon Ali raised his eyes almost hopelessly and was rewarded with the sight of little sharp-edged humps barely visible in the distance. Was it a mirage, he wondered as he trudged through the sand, or was it Hafun? His weary head dropped forward and he shuffled another hundred paces, then looked up again. The humps were still there, and some now even showed touches of color. His heart beginning to beat faster, he continued to shuffle. Perhaps an hour later he crept into the dusty town of a few thousand inhabitants housed in maybe seven hundred single-story boxlike concrete block structures.

Ali had never been in Hafun before, so he had no idea where the local boss would be found. And there was not a soul in sight on the sand-paved streets. He pounded on the door of a house with an old truck parked beside it. The door opened and a fierce, middle-aged man appeared.

"What do you want?"

"My boat sank last night, out there," Ali said, pointing toward the Indian Ocean. "How do I find the police?"

The man looked at him, his eyes settling on the wounds in his arm and head and his swollen finger. "Follow this street for ten blocks, then turn left and go another ten. You'll see the police station there." He then slammed the door.

Ali continued on until he found the police facility—it was two stories and had the Puntland flag flying in front of it. He dragged himself in and told his story to the scowling thug seated at a small desk in the reception hall.

At first the representative of law and order seemed on the verge of throwing him into jail, but Ali persisted, repeating that he worked for Ibrihim Hassan and that Hassan would want to talk to him. Looking intensely irritated, the thug made a phone call. Twenty minutes later, after being given water and a bowl of beans, Ali was in a tired old jeep on his way back to Basalilays.

The drive to Basalilays was a nightmare for the injured boy. Nothing had been done for his wounds, and the driver drove fast over the dusty, rutted track that passed for a road. Once again, Ali began to wonder about the wisdom of the path he'd chosen.

It was nearly midnight when he finally arrived at Hassan's compound. Both Ibrihim and Suleiman were waiting for him. "What happened to Mohamed?" demanded the chief before Ali had even managed to get out of the jeep.

"I'm sorry, Excellency, I don't know."

"Did you try to save him?"

"I did not even see him, Excellency, when I found myself in the water."

"Come in," said Ibrihim, leading him through the gate and into the garden.

"You are the only one to live?" continued the chief.

"As far as I know, Excellency."

"Why you?" demanded Suleiman.

"It was the sort of miracle that only Allah could have arranged," said Ali, tired and bruised and scared to death that he would somehow be held responsible for Mohamed's death. "I have thanked him a hundred times since I reached Hafun and shall continue to do so for the rest of my life."

"Sit," said Ibrihim, pointing at a low chair in the garden. "We have questions for you."

"May I please have water, Excellency?"

"Yes. And some beans I suppose. You are wounded?"

"My arm, Excellency. And my head and finger." As he explained, Ali attempted to draw their attention to each wound.

"Do you think any of the others survived?" demanded Ibrihim, still standing.

"No," said Ali, "I doubt it."

"How did you manage to get ashore?" asked Suleiman, hostility and suspicion evident in his voice.

"I held on to an empty gas can and kicked my feet."

"Why didn't the men I left to watch for survivors see you?" The suspicion in Ibrihim's words was just as strong as that in his son's.

"I don't know, Excellency. When I reached the shore, I set out to the south. I stopped in a small fishermen's camp and then went on to Hafun, where I insisted they call you."

"What did the Americans do?"

He had to be careful about this. He doubted either father or son was satisfied, but at least they hadn't drawn their swords. Not yet. "After they thought they'd chased the other boats away, they went and picked up their two people from the boat we destroyed."

"So they survived?"

"I think so, but I was in the water. It looked as if they picked them up. They may have been dead, of course."

"Then did they leave?"

"No. Then they came and looked around the wreckage of our boat."

"Did they see you?"

"No. I don't think they saw any of the bodies. Part of the boat was still floating. They looked at that then left."

"So they made no effort to see if any of you were alive?"

"Not that I saw."

"Pigs! They leave men to drown."

"You have done well, Ali," said Ibrihim, standing. Whatever his words, his eyes said he was not totally satisfied. But then, thought the boy hopefully, that was understandable. He has just lost a son. "Do you still wish to sail with us? To get back at the infidels and get rich at the same time?"

"Yes, Excellency."

"Suleiman?"

"Yes. But he will be of little use until his wounds have healed and his finger is better."

"Okay," said Ali.

Ibrihim nodded and the interrogation was over. A few minutes later the local medical practitioner appeared and examined Ali. He cleaned the wounds with alcohol and bandaged them, then splinted the finger and gave the boy some aspirin. Then Ali's water and beans arrived.

* * *

"Any word on your boatswain's mate?" asked Alan.

"He's going to be okay."

"You managed to create a major incident last night. You do realize that, don't you? The Puntland government claims you started it, that you were pushing too hard on innocent fishermen."

"Innocent fishermen don't shoot heat-seeking missiles."

"We know that, and I gather Commodore van Rijn believes your report, but a lot of people at the UN don't."

"Alan, this conversation is getting tiresome. In fact, this whole operation is getting tiresome. We're just screwing around. There's no endgame until the State Department manages to put it together. Van Rijn feels the same way although he's too diplomatic to say so."

Alan was silent for a moment. His contempt for the European tendency to try diplomacy before muzzle blast was well known, but he was also aware that he had just attacked the Tridents for being too aggressive and he hated to put himself in the position where he could be accused of flip-flopping.

"You're not going to get out of it that easily, pal. You just keep doing what you're doing and show a little more finesse."

Predictably, the screen went dead before Mike could think of a suitable reply to Alan's typically schizoid outburst.

* * *

"How'd you get back here?" demanded Ted when he walked into the team's quarters after taking a long walk around the flight deck, thinking about the ambush and trying to get his emotions under control. Emotions weren't permitted in the Trident Force, and Ted agreed in principal. It was putting the principal into practice that was difficult at times.

"I told them to bring me here," said Alex, who was lying in one of the bunks. "What do you think of my high-tech cast?" she continued, pointing to the blue thing wrapped around her lower leg. "It's all plastic and aluminum and it's lightweight and they say it dries out in no time."

She was talking coherently, but she still sounded a little strange to Ted. Must be some sort of medication, he thought. "Aren't you supposed to stay in bed with that?"

"Only tonight. They said it's a simple fracture and I can hobble about as much as I want tomorrow."

"Alex, if you'd ever been in the real navy, you'd know that whenever you manage to get yourself into sick bay, you stay there as long as you possibly can. They change the sheets once or twice a day for you and give you breakfast in bed. What's wrong with you?"

"He asked me to marry him," she said, out of the blue, as her eyes stared into space.

"Who? The doctor? The corpsman?"

"No. Bill, of course."

"The man of mystery to the rest of us?"

"Yes."

"What did you tell him?"

"That I have to think about it."

"You don't like him?"

"I love him, if I understand the meaning of the word."

"Then why are you thinking?"

"Because when I marry him I want to start a normal life."

"You tired of the rest of us?"

"Not yet but the day will come. Why haven't you asked Hannah?"

Ted paused. "Same as you, I guess. She doesn't like it when I have to run the hell off to who-knows-where whenever Alan Parker picks up his telephone."

"Shove off, sailor," said Alex, trying to turn on her side, "and turn off the lights. I want to take a nap."

* * *

"I hear you're the guy who controls Mike Chambers and his gang of loose cannons," said Mandy into the secure telephone after introducing herself.

"What can I do for the Agency, Ms. Cochran?" asked Alan Parker. Despite his pleasure in nailing Mike whenever he could, when it came to interagency warfare, Alan always knew which team he was playing on. Until he found it convenient to change sides.

"I want him out of here! Send him out to sea with the rest of his navy friends. Send him to Afghanistan, or Fresno for all I care. He's making a shambles of my operations. To be frank, I have doubts about the man's loyalty. He doesn't seem to take the Al Qaeda threat as seriously as the rest of us do."

"I'll forward your concerns to SECDEF, Ms. Cochran."

"I don't want forwarding. I want action."

"You should communicate your desires through your own director and then the director, National Intelligence."

"I'm communicating them through you."

"And I will forward them to SECDEF."

Alan then proved both his mettle and the speed of his reactions by hanging up before Mandy could.

* * *

"I can see him," said Ray, his eyes glued to a pair of very powerful binoculars, as the *Sea Dragon* clattered along the Somali coast, passing the impossibly small harbor at Basalilays.

"Where?" asked Ted.

"He's standing on the deck of that trawler."

Ted studied the fishing boat a moment. "She's a big one for these parts. Looks like she's steel too."

"The rust?"

"You think it's the *Ina Boqor*? The one they used to set us up the other night?"

"Probably."

"How the hell did they even get her in there?"

"God knows, although Jerry could undoubtedly provide a long explanation. Twist by turn."

"How do you know it's him?"

"Because he's wearing that same ratty shirt he was wearing when we pulled him out of the water. Damn, he's giving us the finger."

"That means he has something he wants to tell us, right?"

"Right. Either that or he's changed sides again."

"Sounds like we're going to have an exciting night."

"Just think of it as going ashore on liberty. A gift from Captain Chambers."

"Thanks. All the officers in this unit are so damn generous."

"It's just one manifestation of true leadership. Why don't you apply for one of the officer programs? You're totally qualified and I'm sure Hannah would be thrilled."

"I'm thinking about it. When you joined the Corps, was your wife thrilled?"

"We weren't married yet then. And she wanted me to be a college professor."

"I'm sure there's still time."

"Yeah. I can retire in less than fifteen years. Sandy's counting the days."

* * *

The city of Mumbai, India, is located on a peninsula that extends into the Indian Ocean, forming a large open roadstead to the east. It is an ancient city—once immensely wealthy and now beginning to come into its own again. The old port of Mumbai is located on the west side of this harbor, along with the city proper. On the southeast side of the roads is the immense new container port of Nhava Sheva—acres of piers and cranes and thousands of containers of all colors organized into ranks with military precision, waiting either to head out to sea or to head inland.

Eastern Trader slowed at the mouth of Mumbai harbor shortly after noon to pick up the pilot for the strait run in to the Nhava Sheva facility. As the ship moved purposefully up the channel, Colonel bin-Sharif remained on the bridge, carefully studying the Indian naval vessels coming and going from the naval station on the west side of the harbor.

"As you can see, Colonel," said Captain Papadis quietly when the pilot was out on the wing, "the Indian navy has no interest in us at the moment."

"I hope so, Captain."

Ever since Colombo, thought Papadis, the colonel has become more and more on edge. Maybe he's just suffering from channel fever—he wants to get home.

Within a few minutes the ship was slipping past Elephanta Island and two tugs had come alongside to ease her into her slot on the long, long pier. The instant she was moored, three uniformed Indian officials—customs, immigration and public health—scurried aboard, even as the first of the forty containers of farm machinery started to rise off the pier. Time is money, and *Eastern Trader* was scheduled for a three-hour turnaround.

Papadis had his papers all in order, and the officials soon left, leaving a policeman at the foot of the gangway just to make sure the crew didn't all jump ship. It was all going very well, the captain thought as he watched his chief mate supervise the securing of the containers.

"Papadis!" hissed Colonel bin-Sharif in his ear, "what's that man doing? That Filipino deckhand with the green shirt. He's talking with that Indian official."

Papadis looked where the colonel was pointing and saw a seaman named Gomez talking to one of the deputy harbormasters. His first reaction was to wonder how the deputy harbormaster had come aboard without his noticing. His second was to wonder what the harbormaster wanted. Only then did he wonder what Gomez might be saying to him. "I'll find out, Colonel."

Captain Papadis passed the word for Gomez to come up to the bridge.

"What were you saying to that official?" demanded bin-Sharif the instant the Filipino deckhand appeared on the bridge.

"He asked me where the boatswain was. He said he had some papers for him to sign. Then I asked him if the Taj Mahal is anyplace nearby because I've always wanted to see it. He said no then started to tell me that I should find a way of seeing it sometime. Then I was called up here."

It all sounded reasonable to Papadis, but the colonel was clearly not satisfied. He called one of his sergeants and told him to arrange for Gomez to be detained below incommunicado until the ship reached Jeddah. The captain considered arguing but didn't. He was eager to return to the Mediterranean. He was even more eager for this particular voyage to come to an end with as little disturbance as possible. Once the colonel's containers were ashore in Jeddah, along with the colonel and his men, Papadis could then forget about them and return to worrying about all the things normal sea captains worried about. Storms, reefs, engine breakdowns, pirates, bankruptcies.

Less than an hour later all the containers had been

loaded and secured. Two tugs were again alongside and a different pilot was on the bridge. Forty minutes later the pilot was back on the pilot boat and *Eastern Trader* was under way again, bound now for Jeddah.

* * *

The sky was mercifully overcast and the sea choppy as the two Trident kayaks approached the low, reeflike breakwater, paddling hard to avoid being tossed up on it. Neither Ray nor Ted said a word as they scanned the shore for any unwelcome sign of life. "Trawler," whispered Ted in a tone that could almost pass for the sound of a wave tumbling over the breakwater.

Ray directed his total attention to the dark mass that had to be the fishing boat and focused the night vision device on it. Even with the technical enhancements, the image was still almost useless. He could detect motion of some sort but had no idea if it was a person or just something flapping in the breeze. "Roger," he whispered back to the SEAL, who was now drifting a few feet in front of him. He then turned his attention to the shoreline. Almost immediately he spotted shadowy motion near one of the buildings.

"Pssst."

The marine lowered his night vision device and turned to Ted.

"That's definitely a person on the trawler's deck," said the SEAL.

Ray tapped on the deck of his kayak to indicate that he understood. He then returned his attention to the shore. Obviously, the pirates had not only upped the ante but also upped their security. They must have guilty consciences, he thought.

Twenty minutes later, convinced that they'd spotted as much life as there was to spot, the marine signaled to his partner to continue north and then creep in to the beach on the far side of a large rock that protruded into the water. Both paddled strongly but silently, with the chop occasionally breaking over their little vessels. Both knew perfectly well that an army might be waiting for them in the shadows, especially if the Somali kid had flipped sides again or somehow been discovered. But they had no choice.

With a three-foot surf breaking all around and over them, they guided the kayaks in to the beach, behind the rock, and immediately jumped out into the mildly foaming water. They waited a moment, hoping that if there was a reception party it would show itself right away, then nodded at each other and pulled the boats ashore.

The beach—which was strewn with a coating of dried seaweed—continued to be deserted, the only sounds the breaking of the surf and the rustle of the wind over the sand and brittle weed. Ray tapped Ted on the shoulder and pointed in the direction of the town. Ted nodded and they both crouched down in the sand.

"Now we wait," whispered the marine.

"Hi."

Both Tridents jerked even more alert than they already were and scanned the surrounding darkness.

"Up here," said a quiet voice in Somali. "On the rock, above you."

Ray looked up and realized that part of the rock was moving slightly. The little bastard had been there all along, watching them. If he'd been a bad guy, they'd have been dead by now. Or wishing that they were. "Hi, Ali."

"Hi. You stay where you are so you can't be seen. I will stay here so I can see if anybody is coming. And so that anybody who is looking can see that I am alone."

"Good plan." Then, to Ted, he added, "Keep a good

lookout because I can barely understand the kid at times and have to concentrate on what he's saying."

"Roger."

"How are your arm and finger?"

"They still hurt but not as much as before."

"Did they believe your story?"

"They didn't kill me, but Ibrihim and Suleiman are both very upset that you killed Mohamed. They plan to capture you and carve you into small pieces."

"Do they know what we look like?"

"All they know is that you're Americans and have that fast boat that you keep on that big ship that never comes near shore."

"What do you have to tell us?"

"You said you wanted to catch Ibrihim at sea."

We sure as hell do, thought Ray. That's the boss's highest priority at the moment. Catch the son of a bitch who zapped us.

"That is very difficult," continued Ali, unaware of Ray's thoughts, "since I think he has only gone once, but Suleiman, his son, is going out in two days on that trawler in the harbor with two boats. They are heading over past Socotra Island toward Aden. Maybe you can catch him. I think he will be useful to you."

Something about Ali's story sounded uncomfortably familiar to Ray. A clan chief going to sea?

"Will you be with him on the trawler?"

"No. I am to stay here and let my injuries heal."

"Ali," called another voice before Ray could answer. "Where are you?"

"Stay hidden," ordered Ali. "I'm here, Gouled, on this rock."

The Tridents remained hidden in the shadow of the

rock, not quite sure what they were going to do if Gouled—whoever the hell he was—managed to stumble on them. If they attacked him, it would foul the operation up just as much as letting him report them.

"Why are you sitting on the rock in the middle of the night?"

They could hear Gouled's breathing now. He was right on the other side of the rock.

"I am thinking. It's very frightening to have your boat sunk under you and the other crew members all shot to death. I'm also thinking about Mohamed."

"I can imagine. Have you decided on anything?"

"No, I'm still thinking. Do you want to come up here and think with me?"

"No. I'm tired. I just got up to piss and saw you weren't there."

"I'll be back soon."

"Okay."

The Tridents waited for Ali to tell them Gouled was out of sight.

"Three more weeks," said the young Somali quietly a few minutes later. "In three weeks you take me to America and give me the money."

"Yes. If all goes well," said Ray.

"What do you mean 'if all goes well'?"

"We could all be dead in three weeks."

"Allah will not allow that."

The optimism of youth, thought Ray. Something I'm beginning to lose, I'm afraid. Or maybe it was the optimism of desperation.

As they paddled out, Ray told Ted what Ali had said.

"Could be another damn trap," replied Anderson.

"I know. That's what worries me."

* * *

All was orderly and quiet on the bridge of USS *Wake Island*. The sun had disappeared behind the Somali coast—long since lost to sight—and the ship's haze gray hull was slowly merging into the pale gray sea and sky.

Mike was standing at the navigational plot with Commander Hartman, the ship's executive officer standing beside him. Roughly a hundred miles to the north—beyond the range of even *Wake Island*'s radar—the pirate trawler continued on its path to crime.

"So far, so good, Captain," said Hartman. "The satellite's only lost it once for a few minutes."

"Yes," agreed Chambers. "When we get farther north and the traffic gets heavier, we may have to edge in so your long-range search radar can pick it up, but for now this is working better than I'd hoped."

"Any idea how long he can operate without having to return to port?"

"I'd guess a few days. Maybe a week at most, round-trip."

"It doesn't really matter. We're here for the duration. The surgeons tell me they think your chief will come out of this intact and totally fit for duty again. I'm glad."

"I feel much better about it."

The XO nodded as a half dozen sailors and petty officers appeared on the bridge and started relieving those standing the soon-to-end second dog watch. "If you'll excuse me, sir, I have to take eight o'clock reports."

"I hope nobody has any unpleasant surprises for you."

"There's always something!"

With that the commander walked over to the ship's department heads who had assembled to give him the nightly report covering nonfunctioning machinery and other disasters, major and minor.

* * *

"Paul, I think we've come up with something major about Gregor Orlov." As she spoke, Connie tried to keep the excitement out of her voice but failed. The data both intrigued and frightened her at the same time.

"Jacob's came up with something?" asked Tracy, who'd been sound asleep beside his wife.

"Indirectly. One of her resources picked it up from an unhappy army officer."

"What is it? From the tone of your voice it sounds big."

"It is. Three weeks ago a complete Topol nuclear missile battery was disassembled and packed into shipping containers at a base near Habarovsk, about four hundred miles inland from Vladivostok. That's two mobile launchers and six missiles, with warheads."

"So? They're redeploying the battery. Maybe they're trying to hide it from us."

"The source thought there was something funny about it. The paperwork was all there, but it didn't really look kosher to him."

"Did he alert his superiors?"

"He suspects the superiors are the ones doing it. And he recognized Jacob's description of Orlov. Thought he'd seen him around but has never spoken to him."

"Damn it, Connie, this *is* serious. Where did it go? Where is it now?"

"The source wasn't sure, but he said they were put on truck trailers and driven off in the direction of Vladivostok."

"Who packed it?"

"He thinks it was some corrupt officers, but I think he thinks Putin knew about it."

"All right! Where are you now?"

"At the office."

"I want to see you in my office in an hour. I'm on my way, and I'll call the director before I leave home."

* * *

"Captain Chambers, this is Reynolds in the CIC."

"Yes, Reynolds." Thanks to years of training, Mike was instantly awake, even though it was still hours until dawn.

"Our target is in among three or four other ships and we're having trouble keeping them identified on the satellite system. I'll be more comfortable once it gets light, but at the moment we're not totally sure which is which."

"If we edge in closer, can you tell them apart on the search radar?"

"Yes, sir."

"Very well. I'll call Captain Browning and ask him to edge in to about seventy miles."

"Thank you, sir."

An hour later Reynolds called again. "Something's happening, sir. We've got the target both on radar and satellite, and she appears to have slowed or even stopped. She also seems to be within striking distance of two separate ships. I think this is it!"

"Please call Captain Browning. I'm on my way to flight ops, then the bridge."

10

The director of the Central Intelligence Agency was in California—trying to make peace with a congressman who'd been after his head for years—but every one of the three Agency officers sitting in the Langley conference room could feel his eyes on them from the teleconferencer at the head of the table.

"Then it's definitely a nuclear missile battery," said the director.

Paul Tracy nodded at Connie.

"We have to assume that, sir."

"And we're assuming that it's in the hands of the Saudis?"

Connie was tempted to offer that it might also be the Swiss—much of the world considered them excessively wealthy and they'd also managed to collect a number of enemies over the centuries—but didn't. The director was not known for his sense of humor.

"Or headed for them, sir," explained Tracy. "So far, our people in the Kingdom have been unable to come up with anything."

"Do we know how it was shipped?"

Again, Tracy indicated that Connie should answer. As she did, she was unsure whether he was giving her a chance to shine in front of the director or a chance to hang herself if her interpretations of the data were wrong.

"Considering its size and weight, there are four obvious choices—truck, rail, plane or ship. Both truck and rail seem very unlikely, both because they would be subject to inspection at far too many borders. Also, why would they truck them to Vladivostok first? That's out of the way."

"If they used a plane," interjected the director, "it would have to be a damn big one—a Globe Master or a Russian An-225 or some other monster like that."

"Yes, sir, and it seems very unlikely that the Russians would use their own plane after going to the trouble of working through this Orlov character."

"Which leaves a ship."

"Which is why I asked Paul to have Hal sit in."

Even though he was still three thousand miles away, the director's eyes seemed to bore in on Hal Nelson, the manager of the Asian maritime desk.

"Once Connie gave me the parameters, sir," said Hal, looking less than totally comfortable with the director's full attention focused on him, "it turned out to be surprisingly easy. Roughly one hundred ships sailed from Vladivostok during the month before the death of that girl in Moscow. Most were headed east or south—or to other Russian ports, and of those headed toward Suez only one stands out. A Greek registry containership named *Eastern Trader*."

"Why?"

"Several reasons. The company that owns her is controlled by the Saudis."

"Is there more?" demanded the director when Hal paused to catch his breath.

"Yes, sir. The ship was apparently attacked by pirates while transiting the Strait of Malacca and, according to a nearby ship, beat them off with unusual vigor—which suggests to me that they have an unusually strong security group aboard. Finally, one of the harbor pilots in Colombo who occasionally works with us confirmed that this same ship's security group looked exceptional to him. He also felt that it's composed of Arab commandos. Our guess in Saudis."

"Where's this ship now?"

"She's unloading some containers in Mumbai right now and is scheduled to be under way in a few hours. She should be off the Horn of Africa in four days."

"Then there's no time to get anybody aboard there?"

"I don't see how."

"She didn't go directly from Vladivostok to Jeddah?"

"No, sir. She has followed a previously scheduled run from Vladivostok to Colombo to Mumbai and only then to Jeddah."

"Would they be willing to steam all over the world with that sort of cargo aboard? Wouldn't they want to go direct?"

"You'd think so, but maybe they want to avoid any suspicion. They may also be relying on this security force they have to keep them out of trouble."

"This whole business is awfully damn iffy." The director stared at them all a moment. "Okay. Iffy though it may be, you've got enough to convince me. Unfortunately it's not enough for us to send a destroyer and board this ship.

Keep tracking her while I discuss this with the DNI, and he undoubtedly decides to go over it with the President."

"Thank you, sir," said the deputy director.

"Thank you," said the director. "Especially Connie and Hal."

* * *

"Ray," snapped Mike as he slipped into his blue coveralls, "the trawler seems to be making its move. I want you and Ted to get that squad of marines in the cat, light off and be ready to roll as soon as I get aboard. I want to go over the tactical situation one more time with Reynolds in CIC."

"Roger, Boss," said Ray, jumping out of his rack in the red-lit compartment.

"Good luck," said Alex, swinging her cast out of her rack. "You still want me in CIC?"

"If you feel up to it. I want you where you can avoid some of the communications problems that always seem to screw up operations like this. You understand us and the way we operate. *Wake Island*'s people may not."

By the time Chambers reached CIC, three helos—two gunships and a Sea Dragon, which was carrying the mission commander—were lifting off the flight deck, lights flashing in the first gray hints of dawn. Twenty minutes later, *Wake Island* slowed almost to a stop. Her stern gate opened, and the cat—carrying the three Tridents along with twelve marines and a Somali interpreter—slid out into the ship's glassy wake then turned northeast as Ted jammed the throttles forward to the stops. Almost immediately, the huge amphibious assault ship also turned to the northeast and cranked up to twenty-two knots, her very best speed.

"Trident, this is Mamacita One," whispered Mike's earphone a half hour later. It was the helo flight commander. "We're approaching the trawler. She's launched her two boats and they now appear headed toward the coastal freighter you guessed might be their target."

"Roger, Mamacita One. Can you see any weapons aboard the boats?"

"Afirmative, Trident. One of the gunships buzzed them and they waved rifles at it."

"That's it!" said Mike, almost jubilantly. "The attack formation by itself is enough justification for us, but the weapons seal it. Remember, you're to prevent the boats from getting close to their target. Also remember that the objective of this operation is to capture the pirates, not kill them. Avoid firing directly at the boats, and if it is necessary to fire on the trawler, aim for the waterline. My ETA one zero zero minutes. Hold them for us until we arrive."

"Roger, Trident."

* * *

Suleiman Hassan watched the three helos approach, recognized them as American and cursed to himself. They were hundreds of miles out at sea—how had they found him and his little squadron? Was it just a matter of luck or had they followed him?

"They're shooting, Suleiman," shouted one of the crew even as Hassan noticed the white puffs under one of the gunships and then the row of small geysers that erupted between them and the freighter. "They are so slow. We can shoot them down."

Suleiman was tempted to scream "Fire! Fire! Kill the pigs," but he controlled his rage. These were the whoresons who'd killed his brother. They were, to his mind, nothing more than another clan, a hostile clan who had killed one of his own and upon whom revenge must be taken. But Suleiman also understood that victory was the true goal and that the opposing clan—the Americans—would take time to defeat. Far longer than was usually necessary to drive away a marauding band of neighboring tribesmen. There could be no revenge if you did not win. And victory in a situation like this would result from calculation and self-control. If he shot back, that would give the Americans all the excuse they needed to sink both the two boats and the trawler.

"No!" he shouted to be heard above the outboard motor. "Lower all your guns over the side and we will return to the trawler and see what they really want."

"Even the RPGs?" demanded two of Suleiman's most trusted crew.

"Even the RPGs. We can get more."

When Ibrihim heard about this, thought the pirate captain, he was going to be furious. Furious with the Americans and furious with Suleiman. The chief's temper was even hotter than his son's, especially since they'd killed Mohamed. Indeed, shortly after learning of his second son's death, Ibrihim had detected a lack of respect in the demeanor of that girl Jasmine and beaten her severely. But then, she only existed to serve him in any manner he chose.

"Get rid of your weapons," he then instructed the other boat on the handheld radio, "and return to the trawler. Do not shoot at the Americans."

"What will they do now, Suleiman?" asked one of the crew as he lowered his Kalashnikov into the Indian Ocean. "Are they going to shoot at us?"

Suleiman looked up at the three helos as he turned the boat away from the target and back toward the trawler. What *did* they plan to do? Sink them? Drop soldiers on them from the big helicopter? It wasn't big enough to carry many. There must be a ship in the area. They're waiting for it to arrive, he concluded.

"No, they won't shoot at us. They are undoubtedly waiting for a ship to arrive. Then they may arrest us."

It's even possible we may be able to confuse them a little, he thought, as the boat surged up alongside the stopped trawler. They might have the money and the technology, but their brains didn't always seem to work very well.

* * *

"Trident, this is Mamacita One."

"Roger, Mamacita One."

"Be advised that both boats have returned to the trawler and are being hoisted aboard. Also be advised that they appear to be setting a trawl."

"This is Trident. Do I understand that the trawler is streaming fishing gear?"

"Roger."

Mike looked first at Ted, then at Ray—both of whom were now on the same communications circuit.

"These guys are unbelievable," remarked Ted.

"This whole mission is unbelievable," added Ray.

"All the more reason to grab this Suleiman and see if we can change the rules a little more. If we don't do something, we'll be here for the rest of our lives." As he said it, Mike thought about the family trip to Colorado that he'd scheduled for April. It was still only late February, but based on more than twenty years' experience, he knew it was possible that he might still be here in April. Duty or not, neither Jill nor Kenny would ever talk to him again.

"Mamacita One, this is Trident. Continue to prevent them from approaching their target. Our ETA now two zero minutes."

"Roger."

A few minutes later Mike noticed first one, then a second flash in the sky as two of the helos mirrored the rays of the now-risen sun.

"We have you in sight now, Trident."

"Roger."

Then Mike spotted two more gunships approaching from astern. While the Sea Dragon could stay over the trawler for several hours, the small, heavily armed gunships were very short-legged, limited to only an hour or so over the target without refueling.

"Ray, go over the drill one more time with the marines. Remind them again that we're here to grab one guy and that no matter how stupid it may sound, we don't want anybody killed."

"Aye, aye, Captain."

* * *

"Good to hear you, Peter," said the secretary of defense when he heard the director of National Intelligence's voice on the phone.

"I'm glad I caught you," said the DNI. "Our people have come up with a great deal more on that WMD alert, and frankly, it's a little frightening."

"Shoot."

"The Saudis seem to be in the process of acquiring a complete battery of the latest Topaz nuclear missiles."

"They don't trust us anymore?"

"The world's changing faster than we sometimes appreciate."

"Do they already have it?"

"As far as we can tell, it's aboard a ship named the *Eastern Trader*, which is right now on her way from Mumbai to Jeddah. And the ship appears to have a heavily armed and highly competent security force of Saudi commandos."

"Are your people certain enough so that we can send a

destroyer to board this ship without shooting ourselves in the foot?"

"I'm convinced, but I don't like the idea of running the risk of infuriating the Saudis if we're wrong. And neither does the President."

"What do you intend to do?"

"We're trying to work up some plans. Hal Nelson, the manager of the Agency's Asian maritime desk, reminded us that you have your own little group of sailors who have done some imaginative work on projects you've given them in the past. He also mentioned that they're in the area chasing pirates. He suggested they be brought into the loop. The fact is we have very little time. The ship will be off the Horn of Africa in three or four days and then will reach Jeddah in another three days. Perhaps your people can come up with something sufficiently off-the-wall to work."

"They're right there. Maybe they *can* come up with something. What about liaison with the Agency? We don't want them stepping on each other's toes."

"A woman named Amanda Cochran's in Djibouti. She's in charge of the Agency's antipiracy efforts and she's been liaising with your people already."

"Good. I'll get the word to Mike Chambers and see if he can come up with a way we can get a look inside that ship without embarrassing ourselves."

"Keep me posted, if you will."

"Don't hold your breath. Mike doesn't always tell me as much as I'd like until after the fact. But I'm not ready to fire him. Yet."

* * *

As the Tridents' cat approached the trawler, the low-lying sun made its rust-streaked sides seem almost like a work of intentional art. Mike's guts tightened, as did everybody else's. Were the pirates going to try to finesse the situation? Talk their way around and out of it? Play dumb? Or were they going to disregard the overpowering force of the helos and try to blow the cat and its entire crew to hell?

Then the smell hit him. Long-dead fish and diesel fumes. He would have liked to turn and approach from upwind, but there was no time. If this thing was to work at all, they had to move fast. Before the pirates had time to think up even more tricks and before some higher power decided to intervene.

"Samuel," he said to the Somali interpreter as he tuned the radio to the international hailing frequency, "tell them to recover their trawl and prepare to be boarded."

The interpreter nodded, not looking at all well. It may have been the stench or a touch of seasickness, or maybe he was just plain uneasy. It was one thing to work for the Americans at a desk in Djibouti. It was another to help attack your own countrymen. To be right there with them when the shooting started. It was easy to imagine what the pirates might do to a man who was caught serving with the enemy in a combat situation. Despite whatever misgivings Samuel may have felt, he called the trawler, but it failed to answer. He tried again and still no reply. Either they weren't listening—which was not likely since the traffic on that frequency would provide them with very useful information—or they were trying to be difficult.

Mike continued to head for the slow-moving trawler, the cat screaming across the waves as his gut tightened still more.

Over the years he'd known a number of men and women who seemed totally immune to the tension of an approach and attack. Some claimed that since they'd already done everything they could to prepare—and worked out a half dozen contingency plans—they had no need to worry. Others possessed an almost irritating sense of confidence. Confidence in their own abilities and in some sort of almost divine protection. Still others were total fatalists. And then there were the fools and fakers who didn't know any better.

Mike always made every preparation he could and worked out numerous alternate plans, but he also worried. And so, he knew, did Ted and Ray. They all thought too damn much. And so, based on their expressions, did most of the marines. Too much thinking, he reminded himself, could be fatal.

When they were about two hundred yards away and slightly forward of the target, he told Ted to fire a burst across the trawler's bow. There didn't seem to be any reaction. Now what the hell to do? By uttering a few words, he could direct the helos to destroy the trawler, but that would achieve nothing. "Get those troops ready, Ray. We're going alongside and board while still under way."

"They're ready, Captain. You going to let me go first?"

"I'll set the example. You right behind me."

"Aye."

"Draw cutlasses and get some fenders over the side. If we trash this boat, we'll be out of luck for the next adventure."

Ray limited his reply to a tense smile.

With Ted now at the helm and one of the marines on the fifty, the cat surged alongside the trawler and slowed. Mike was already up on the rail, hanging on to the windscreen on the steering console. He looked down at the water foaming between the two hulls then over at the trawler. A half dozen thin, ragged men were standing along the rail, watching and doing nothing, while one more stood on the bridge, looking down. Out of the blue a preposterous thought hit him—that it would be both embarrassing and very probably fatal if the Somalis took him prisoner instead of the other way around.

Sometimes, he reminded himself, you just have to step forward and seize what looks like an opportunity—and hope you're not really reaching out for the Devil's hand.

He was thinking too damn much again! "Time to go," he muttered as he launched himself across the two feet of open space, landing on the trawler's low rail. He jumped down to the deck and drew his sidearm, confident that the pirate mob would fall upon him and beat him to death if they didn't just shoot him. Then he realized he was looking right into the barrel of an old AK-47, with the snarling face of a young man behind it. He couldn't remember having noticed either before he landed.

Before Mike could pull the trigger on his Glock, a shattering boom erupted beside his right ear. One of the marines still in the cat had discharged a riot gun.

"Cease fire," bellowed Ray in his very best parade ground voice, even though everybody, including each of the marines, was wearing headsets. "I don't see any other weapons, but keep yours raised and ready."

His heart pounding and his ears ringing from the riot gun blast, Mike looked around. There were no more weapons in sight.

"Captain," asked the marine corporal who had fired, "did I overreact?"

"Absolutely not, Corporal," Ray reassured him. "We're here to take prisoners, but that guy obviously had his heart set on becoming a corpse."

Mike looked at his attacker, whose chest was soaked in blood. He must be dead, he thought, or very close to it. He heard a thump and turned to see Ray land beside him. Six more marines quickly followed, then the interpreter, who was helped across the void.

"What do you want?" asked the man on the bridge in English.

"You are to turn all your weapons over to us," said Mike.

"We are fishermen. We have no weapons."

"This fellow did."

"He was a fool. Don't give him another thought."

"I'm going to arrest you and your crew for attempted piracy."

As he spoke, the remainder of the marines clambered aboard the trawler and started rounding up crew members.

"But we have no weapons."

"We have photographs of your men with weapons, then throwing them overboard."

"What are you going to do with us?"

"Take you aboard our ship." As Mike spoke, he nodded to Ray, who nodded to the marine gunny to start handcuffing the crew. "And I want you to recover that trawl right now. Otherwise I will cut it."

"If you cut it, then many Somalis will starve."

In the briefest moment of weakness Mike wondered how many Somalis would starve when they succeeded in ending the piracy. "I will permit you four men and twenty minutes to recover your gear. Otherwise I will cut it."

The figure on the bridge called out four names. The men were released and headed aft while their companions remained sitting on the forecastle, manacled. As the winch started to grind, dragging the trawl wires in, Ray and two marines appeared on the bridge, surrounding the figure. "I will come down," said the trawler captain, who Mike had by then identified as Suleiman Hassan.

"Wait until I get there," ordered Mike as he and Ted headed up.

Prior to sending Suleiman down to join the crew on the forecastle, Mike and Ted studied the bridge controls—which were labeled in Russian, with Somali written over it in some cases—and decided they were pretty straightforward.

Mike looked around at the dirty, tired pilothouse and the rusty, dirt-caked deck and gear below them and then at Ted—who was at the helm of the slowly moving vessel—and laughed. "This is one hell of a command we seem to have ended up with."

"Definitely not up to my standards, Captain."

Mike then called *Wake Island* and reported that the trawler had been captured and secured.

"Roger, Trident. Our ETA one zero five minutes."

"I'll take the helm, Ted. You go aft and see how they're doing recovering the gear."

"Aye, sir."

Mike's earphones hissed a few minutes later. "What about the fish, Captain?"

"The fish?"

"Yes, sir. They've got the gear aboard now, and they're a half dozen good-sized fish in the net."

Fish, he thought. How many thousands of hours had he spent over the years trying to catch a few good-sized fish? But today he had no use for fish, and neither did the Somalis.

"Toss 'em back, Ted."

"I think they're tunas, Captain."

"It's a shame but toss them back."

"Aye, aye."

Mike then started to steam slowly in a large circle, waiting for *Wake Island* to appear over the horizon.

* * *

Ali sat in the shade and hugged himself in misery. Part of the misery was the pain he continued to feel. Despite the efforts of the medical practitioner, he neither saw nor felt any evidence of his wounds' improving. Much of his misery was loneliness. Gouled and the one or two other pirates he might be tempted to think of as friends were at sea with Suleiman, having left him with Osman and a few other old men and women. And even if they had been here, he still would have felt left out. At first, everybody had congratulated him for his bravery, but that had lasted at most a day. Then everybody, young and old, had returned to the all-consuming struggle to stay alive.

But the greatest part of his misery was the incessant fear that wrapped around him, clawed at his throat and squeezed his guts until they turned to water. If the Americans did get Suleiman, would Ibrihim assume it was just a matter of bad luck or would he realize they'd been betrayed? Would he realize Ali was the traitor? He knew Suleiman didn't like him. Did Ibrihim's last living son also suspect him and had he told his father of his suspicions?

Perhaps he should kill himself now. However he did it was bound to be less painful than what Ibrihim would do. Or maybe he should run out to Ras Xaafuun and activate the emergency beacon the Americans had given him. Then they would come get him.

But would they? They'd said he must work a month for them, and it had been only two weeks. Maybe they never planned to save him at all. Maybe after he'd worked for them, they'd just leave him with Ibrihim to be hacked to death while he was still alive.

Ali didn't know what to do, and that was the greatest source of his misery.

* * *

Mike watched the fifty-foot LCM-8 landing craft as it growled and rumbled toward the trawler from *Wake Island*, its big bow ramp looking like a cockeyed gray wall. As it neared the trawler, the LCM's coxswain made no effort to slow. He just turned alongside then backed down furiously, generating great clouds of blue white smoke.

The first person Chambers spotted standing in the landing craft was Chief Clarke, the chief engineman who had maintained the cats' outboards. He was standing with another chief, six sailors and a lieutenant.

"So we meet again, Captain," bellowed the engineman. "I've been sent to be the chief engineer of this yacht."

"How'd you get the job?"

"The engineering officer always gives me the jobs she doesn't know what to do with."

The LCM, which was almost as large as the trawler, was soon more or less secured, although each of them was dancing to its own tune. The lieutenant managed to make the leap with a reasonable degree of grace and was followed by the two chiefs and the sailors.

"Lieutenant Robert Rhodes, sir," he said as he saluted Mike.

"Michael Chambers, Lieutenant. Welcome to your new command. I assume it's your first?"

Rhodes, who Mike remembered seeing around *Wake Island* but had never met, looked around, a slight smile on his face. "The next few days are going to be a real adventure, sir, but I've got two good chiefs to keep me out of trouble." Then his slight smile developed into a full grin of delight—delight, Mike assumed, at the prospect of a good adventure. Rhodes, he decided, was going to do fine.

While Mike talked with Rhodes, the chief engineman and the other chief, a boatswain's mate, supervised the unloading of two weeks' worth of prepackaged meals and fresh water from the landing craft. Ray, Ted and the marine gunny then supervised the transfer of the prisoners to the LCM.

"Aside from the fact that the bottom may fall out of her at any time," remarked Mike, "your only real problem is that the equipment labels are all in Russian. With an occasional Somali annotation here and there."

"We understood that from your message and came equipped, sir," explained Rhodes. "One of the petty officers speaks and reads Russian fluently. His parents were both born there."

"Excellent," said Mike.

"We're ready, Captain," shouted Ray from inside the LCM.

"Very well," responded Mike. "Mr. Rhodes, is there anything I can do for you before I leave?"

"I won't know, sir, until after you've left."

"We won't be far. *Wake Island* is going to escort you to Djibouti. It would be a little embarrassing if another gang of pirates nabbed you on the way."

"Yes, sir. That'll give us a chance to practice station-keeping in formation."

The two then exchanged salutes again, and Mike hopped aboard the LCM, almost breaking his overaged neck in the process.

* * *

"The infidels have just captured my only remaining son," screamed Ibrihim into the telephone. "He sent me a radio message as they were boarding our trawler."

"So I have also heard," replied Sheikh al-Abbas calmly.

"It is irritating, but remember, no Americans or Europeans were injured or killed, so in the end it will lead to nothing."

"I'm not sure about that, my friend. I have suspected they are targeting me and my family."

"I don't doubt that. They have been changing their tactics, and eventually something may happen to cause them to lose their patience, but remember that Somalia still scares them. The last time they tried to occupy us, they were horribly embarrassed."

"We must act."

"We must wait awhile. What do you suggest? We have no nuclear weapons with which to threaten them."

"I will take this up with the other elders."

"That is your privilege. I'm confident, however, that Suleiman will come out of this matter whole and free."

"Inshallah."

After hanging up, al-Abbas stared up at the ceiling of his office. There would always be thievery in the world, but he and everybody else with a brain knew the current situation in the Indian Ocean would eventually come to an end. It had to. The Westerners would, as he suggested to Ibrihim, lose their patience. He and the other rational men who controlled Puntland would, in time, grow strong enough to govern all of Somalia. And once the land had a strong government, it would be in a position to wheel and deal. Somalia had more resources than even his friends were willing to admit. Start with a thousand miles of magnificent beaches and move on from there. Piracy was the here and now, but it was not the future. Allah had much bigger plans for the lands around the Horn of Africa.

Unfortunately, Ibrihim was not the sort of leader who could contribute much to the future. Perhaps Suleiman was, perhaps not. Time would tell.

Sheikh Hussein al-Abbas did not consider Allah to be a reactionary, backward-looking God. He considered Him the God of the future. And the future would be His.

* * *

"Congratulations, Captain. That strategy of yours seems to work."

Mike stared out a porthole aboard *Wake Island* as he listened to Mandy Cochran turn on the charm.

"Thanks, but we both know it's not going to solve the problem all by itself."

"No, but I'd like to have our people talk with that Suleiman Hassan you nabbed."

"We'll be off Djibouti later this afternoon, and they're all going to be heloed to Camp LeMonier then. They're supposed to be held in the brig until somebody can find a civilian court that's willing to try them."

"We both know they won't—not even the Kenyans will bother with an 'attempted' case. But I'm not interested in that. I want our people to get a crack at Hassan. I'm sure he can provide some solid connections with the people we're fighting in Iraq and Afghanistan."

There probably was some sort of vague connection, thought Mike. They all probably patronized the same vendors of used weapons. Many were undoubtedly resentful of the developed countries' wealth, and a few might even be highly religious—although nobody in this crew seemed to be. As far as he could tell, the trawler's crew was nothing more than a group of waterborne thieves—armed robbers—a profession that in many corners of the earth did not seem to be considered even vaguely disreputable.

Furthermore, Mike had his own plans for Suleiman, and Mandy was not getting her hands on him. Which was why he didn't bother to mention that Hassan would not be transported ashore with his crew.

According to Ray, the pirate captain was proving to be a fascinating specimen. Push the right button and he would fly into a rage. At one point he almost succeeded in getting his hands around the marine's throat—prevented only by the chain connecting his right leg to the leg of a table. Thirty seconds later he had returned to a combination of arrogance, confidence and a cunning cleverness. The son of a bitch seemed to have total confidence that nothing significant would happen to him. That he'd be back home in a day or two, none the worse for wear.

Suleiman was not, however, quite as worldly as he thought he was. As a result, he tended to blurt out information without seeming to appreciate its value—such as the precise routes by which money was being transferred out of the country, which tactics he had found most effective for trapping ships and the roles played by certain powerful Puntland clan chiefs.

And on the several occasions when Ray had had trouble with Somali words, Suleiman had helped him get them right, his aid reeking of scathing condescension. It was obvious to Ray that the prisoner had, indeed, been born into power and suffered from many of the shortcomings that men, and women, seemed to acquire along with such hereditary influence. The last time Mike had looked in, Ray and his prisoner were calmly drinking tea, the Somali trying to impress the marine with his feats of arms and the marine trying to keep track of all the little tidbits that he was being fed.

"I'm sure you'll get your chance to sort through them when they reach the brig," said Mike to Mandy, returning to their phone conversation.

"When will that be?"

"Late afternoon. I really can't predict it with any greater accuracy. *Wake Island*'s XO is handling the details now."

"Okay. See you at the Djibouti brig."

"I don't plan to be there."

Mandy, ever the high-powered mover and shaker, terminated the conversation without another word.

* * *

"Congratulations, Mike," said Alan Parker with less than sincere cheer over the secure teleconferencer, "your little program seems to have finally led to something, although none of us is quite sure what."

"So far Ray has learned quite a bit about the key figures in the piracy game around here."

"But he hasn't learned anything about Al Qaeda, has he?"

"There are connections, but they don't seem significant to me. It's like the Mafia once was; everybody ended up dealing with them—directly or indirectly—whether they wanted to or not. Everybody knows somebody who might be part of it. They probably use the same sources to get weapons. We were sent to do something about piracy."

"Al Qaeda's a much higher priority. You're to turn this guy over to Mandy Cochran immediately."

"Roger," replied Mike, thinking as he did how wonderfully noncommittal the word was. All it meant was "I hear you."

"And then you're to pack up your gear and return to Tampa. The entire nation's facing a financial crisis, and one of SECDEF's financial review committees has concluded that you're spending a lot of money without getting much results."

"Roger. Do we have time to take a day or two of liberty

and look around Djibouti? We've been operating pretty hard for the past few weeks."

"I suppose so. When should I tell Mandy you're going to give her this guy?"

"I'll touch bases with her. Don't worry about it."

"I'm counting on you."

* * *

"Ms. Cochran, you and your navy thugs have gone way too far this time."

Mandy stared out the window, her ear to the phone. "You have me at a disadvantage, Your Excellency."

"You are the American piracy czar. You know perfectly well that your people have seized an innocent Somali trawler and kidnapped the son of an important Puntland official."

The guy's Al Qaeda, thought Mandy. But at this point she wasn't going to bother to argue with al-Abbas about it, especially since she assumed he knew perfectly well. Instead, she started to say that she knew nothing about any such criminal activity, but stopped short. He knew perfectly well that she knew. It was a game. If she said she knew nothing, then she was suggesting that she wasn't in control of the situation, and that sort of suggestion would just make it harder to deal with this guy in the future. "I'll look into it, Your Excellency."

"It's a little late for looking into things. President Dr. Abdullah is very concerned. Of greater immediate importance, the father of the man you kidnapped is very angry and is, right now, arranging to get his revenge."

"Revenge! This is the twenty-first century."

"This is Somalia."

"What does he plan to do? Attack one of our warships?"

"He knows you are the pirate czar and holds you personally responsible."

"Me!"

"I urge you to leave Djibouti just as soon as you can. And certainly do not try to come to Somalia. When I have found a solution, I will contact you and you can consider returning."

"You can't be serious! What can he do to me in Djibouti?"

"Can you tell the difference between a Somali and a Djiboutian when you pass them on the street? You may, however, be safe as long as you stay in Camp LeMonier."

"This is ridiculous!"

"Yes, your actions have been ridiculous, but the threat to you is very serious. So serious that I have sent several of my people to try to ensure that nothing happens to you. Your death will not serve my purposes, nor those of the French."

The French, thought Mandy. Who cared about them? Ever since they'd managed to lose North America to the British, they'd been little more than pains in the ass.

"I'm not going to listen to any more of this."

"Either leave Djibouti or stay in Camp LeMonier and keep a careful eye on the servants. And do everything you can to have the chief's son released—before your superiors decide to send him someplace to be tortured."

Mandy couldn't think of a suitable reply so she just hung up.

11

Santiago Rizal, paintbrush in hand, leaned on the bulwark on *Eastern Trader*'s forecastle and looked to the north, in the direction of Pakistan, which lay far over the horizon some six hundred miles away. How are things going for Angel, he wondered, thinking of his brother who was in the American army in Afghanistan.

"You're supposed to be painting, man," remarked Macopa as he walked up with a new can of paint. "If we don't get this done today, the boatswain's going to be damn mad."

"I'm going to be damn glad when this trip's over," said Rizal to his Filipino countryman as he continued to stare to the north. "I should have jumped ship in Vladivostok just as soon as I saw those damn Arab guards. We all should have."

"The weather in Russia sucks."

"So does this trip. We're not allowed to send any messages home, and those guards keep creeping around looking at us like we're criminals. And then there's Gomez."

"You're his buddy. He tell you want they wanted? Why they roughed him up?"

"He won't talk about it. He's afraid they may hear that he talked about it. But I'm sure it's those containers we picked up there in Russia."

"Yes. What do you think's in them?"

"An atomic bomb, for all I know."

"We could go look some night."

"Are you nuts? They keep an eye on them. Now, open that paint can so we can finish up before the boatswain gets on our asses."

* * *

Ray walked into the compartment in which Suleiman had been confined. It was an unoccupied berthing space almost identical to the one the Tridents were in. Steel bulkheads, bunks, a table and chairs, all secured to the deck. It was the same compartment in which he'd interrogated and hopefully turned the boy Ali.

"Have you been ordered to send me home yet?" demanded the pirate before Ray could even sit down.

"Not yet, *amigo*," replied Ray, smiling.

"It will be soon."

"While we're waiting, would you please tell me a little more about your connections with Al Qaeda. I mean, they're everywhere in this part of the world."

"Al Qaeda!" shouted Suleiman, anger filling his face. "They are out to destroy my country. You saw what they did several months ago when they started blowing themselves up. They are radicals who have no interest in Somalia. Religious fanatics. They used to be connected with the

ICU—the Islamic Courts Union—but my father and his associates drove the ICU into Kenya."

"Then there's no connection between you and them? You're not sending them money?"

"We do what we do to eat. Our mullahs do not demand jihad. They want a decent respect for God and food for His people."

"You act as if Al Qaeda is a threat to you."

"Of course they are. They threaten our traditional way of living."

Ray decided not to push further for the moment the matter of what constituted the traditional Somali way of life. Instead, he allowed the conversation to morph into the sort of almost collegial exchange the pirate seemed to enjoy. Not for a second, however, did he forget that, given the chance, Suleiman would gleefully stuff a spit through him and roast him over the nearest fire. Whether or not he was a religious fanatic, he was the enemy. Grudges are just as strong as faith.

A sly smile suddenly appeared on the prisoner's face. "You have never told me how you knew where I was. It was almost like magic the way you suddenly appeared."

"Suleiman, we've been using radar to watch and track you for weeks, you know that."

"Yes, but I think there is more. I think you have an informer in my crew."

Shit! thought Ray, forcing himself to stare right into Suleiman's jet-black eyes. He just might know. Somehow.

"It's that boy, isn't it?"

"What boy?" asked Ray. "Tell me about him."

"He never really was one of us. My father insisted we use him because his father once served my father well, but I never have trusted him."

Even if he's only guessing, we're going to have to get that kid out of there *pronto*, concluded the marine. Certainly before this guy or any of his crew manages to get himself set free. Which they undoubtedly would in time. Mandy Cochran might think she was going to inherit Suleiman and his pirates from the Tridents, but he suspected she was in for a surprise. Somalia, at the moment, wasn't Iraq, Afghanistan or Pakistan.

* * *

"Mike, I'm going to miss you and your team," said Pat Browning, *Wake Island*'s CO, as he and Chambers sat down in Browning's small, private dining room for the noon meal. Because it was Sunday the ship was a little quieter than usual, as she steamed slowly through the blue waters. "Not only have you broken the monotony, but I think you actually have done some good."

"Thanks, Pat. We both know these things happen."

"You going to take those pirates you've parked in my brig with you?"

"That's not yet decided. The Agency wants to get their hands on them, but CTF 151 and some of the others want to send them to Kenya. It's a shame because I was hoping to use the leader, Suleiman, as an opening to get to his father, the local clan chief."

"So you're telling me that they're my problem? That you're going home and the hell with it?"

"Orders is orders, old buddy."

"I thought I'd been a better host than that. Did any of my people ask you any embarrassing questions?"

"You've broken your back for us, Pat. I'm sorry to leave this little mess for you to handle."

Browning's phone buzzed. He picked it up, listened,

said, "Very well," then hung up. "Your favorite deputy secretary of defense wants you in the comm center."

Mike looked at the very juicy steak that had just been placed in front of him and sighed. Then he took a bite and chewed it. "This is fabulous, Pat." Then he took another bite and savored it. "I'm sorry to do this to you, but maybe I'd better see what Alan wants now."

"My XO hasn't scheduled any general drills for today, so it'll be right here waiting for you. We'll keep it warm."

With a sigh of regret, Mike pushed back his chair, stood and marched out the door. Three ladders later he was seated in front of the teleconferencer, staring at Alan Parker.

"There's been a change of plan, Mike," started Parker with no preamble. "Forget about coming home. There's work to be done, and it's much bigger than tracking a pack of raggie pirates. You're going to find a way to board and inspect a Greek containership that's headed your way."

"Why don't you just send a destroyer?"

"There are complications."

"Well?"

"The ship is Greek-flagged but owned by the Saudis, and it appears to have a very strong security group that we believe is composed of Saudi commandos."

"Get to the point, Alan."

"We believe she's carrying a complete battery of the latest Topol nuclear missiles to Jeddah."

"Send a destroyer."

"Can't. The Agency has good reasons to believe the missiles are there, but they're not confident enough to board openly—which would be tantamount to accusing the Saudis of breaking the Nuclear Non-Proliferation Agreement—and be certain of finding them. Remember the last time we accused an Arab of having a pile of WMDs in the desert? That war's still going on, and we really can't handle any more than the three or four we already have. For some reason SECDEF thinks you might come up with a solution, although, frankly, I'm not sure there is one."

"Where is she?" asked Mike.

"Northeast of Socotra."

"She's pirate bait, then."

"What? She had no trouble beating the shit out of some Malay pirates two weeks ago."

"Yes. The security group will be a real problem, but we may be able to come up with something. What's her present position, course and speed?"

Alan provided them.

"It's a real long shot, but I want to talk with my people. I'll get back to you."

"If you do come up with something, you have two days—maybe less—to pull it off."

"I'll get back to you."

He then picked up a phone and called Pat Browning. "I'm not going to be able to make it back to finish dinner. The world has turned again and we're now playing a totally new game. Would you please turn northeast and plot a course to intercept a ship currently located at 140 degrees, 12 minutes North, 54 degrees, 46 minutes East, and making fifteen knots on course 260. And have Rhodes in the trawler come along." He paused. "I guess we have to use Rhodes's best speed as our best speed."

"Do I have a need to know?"

"You sure as hell do. The Agency believes—but they're not sure—the ship is carrying a battery of Topol nuclear missiles for delivery to the Saudis, and we have to board them somehow without pissing them off."

"If it turns out Langley's right, they'll be damned pissed off, no matter how gracefully you arrive."

"I've no real idea what happens if it turns out Langley is right. I'm not even sure what we're going to do to get aboard, but in an hour or so I think I may have a plan, and you'll be among the very first to hear about it."

"Thanks."

Mike then called Alex, who was in the medical department checking on Jerry, and told her to assemble the team—all but Andrews—in their quarters as fast as possible.

* * *

Mandy Cochran was trying to decide which was more promising—putting some real pressure on the Al Qaeda pirate captain that Chambers was eventually going to deliver to her or focusing on playing a central role in the *Eastern Trader* business. Al Qaeda was big, but so was the Nuclear Non-Proliferation Treaty. Which should she concentrate on? Which would do her the most good? Could she possibly multitask successfully? Do both at the same time?

Her phone rang. It was Gutermann, the head of the internal security group she'd called in.

"We've decided to take Mr. Jones with us for some enhanced debriefing. We're convinced there's more to it all than he's telling us."

"If that's what you think best. I'll tell Olbrig he's losing his assistant."

"Okay."

Maybe, she thought, the Djibouti station chief would be more helpful to her once he'd appreciated what was happening to Jones.

* * *

"I see it, Chief," shouted Rob Rhodes as he remained down on all fours, studying the leaking lube oil fitting under the pounding diesel engine and trying to keep his head from spinning out of control from the heat and noise. "Are there any spares aboard?"

"No, sir. I doubt they've had any for years," replied Clarke. "The engine—the whole damn boat—is mid-1960s Russian and this fitting that's leaking isn't the one that's supposed to be there. The Somalis jury-rigged it at some point."

"Can you improve on their jury-rigging? We'll never make it to Djibouti if we keep losing oil at this rate."

"I can, sir. But we'll have to stop for at least an hour."

Rhodes nodded, looking around the hole that passed for an engine room. Everything was shaking and rattling, and it was at least eight hundred degrees. And the stench— the bilges and the petroleum—was overpowering. But then the whole boat stank. And leaked. How the Somalis could survive wrecks like this was beyond him.

"Very well. I'll get permission to stop."

The prize master's head was just emerging from the engine room hatch when one of the sailors walked up to him. "*Wake Island* has just ordered us to turn northeast and follow them. They say they'll provide more details soon."

"Very well," he said, taking a deep breath. "I'm on my way to the bridge." As he mouthed the phrase, he felt a brief desire to laugh. Bridge? Who was he kidding?

There's not much to the northeast for hundreds of miles, he thought. If we can't make it to Djibouti, then we certainly can't make it to wherever they were now supposed to be going. He didn't want to be the one who fouled up whatever was going on, but they simply had to stop.

The whole problem might have been avoided if the trawler weren't a little too big to fit into the amphibian's well, but she was too big for anybody's comfort. Especially Captain Browning's.

* * *

There was a rumor going through the harbor area that Ibrihim was coming to visit. To build the morale of the pirates who hadn't gone on the captured trawler—although maybe "building morale" wasn't quite the right way to describe it. According to the rumor he was so furious that his oldest son had been captured that he had nearly beaten one of his serving girls to death. He'd lost one son ten years ago in the civil war, another in the incident a week ago, and did not intend to lose his last. And eldest. They said he was going to bring some of his soldiers along and ask some hard questions about how Suleiman could have been captured.

Ali's nerves, already badly frayed, snapped in terror. He knew he couldn't possibly face the chief without blurting out the truth. He found an empty one-and-a-half-liter soda bottle and filled it with water. He then ambled off to walk on the beach. Once out of sight of the port, he started to jog north, toward Ras Xaafuun and the little yellow beacon that he'd hidden there. If he was still in Basalilays when Ibrihim arrived he was certain he would soon be in even greater pain than he already was. And then, dead.

* * *

"I understand the basic plan, sir," said Ted. "But what happens if the ship doesn't stop? Are we going to fire rockets at their bridge or something like that? And what if they refuse to let you board?"

"Whatever happened to the good old days," asked

Mike, "when all anybody said to a captain was 'aye, aye, sir.'"

"Well, sir, there is a very simple answer to Petty Officer Anderson's question."

The whole team, which was sitting around the table in their quarters, turned and looked at the door. "You're supposed to be in bed, Chief," observed Ray.

"Alex said something big is up and then I noticed the ship had turned. I had a word with the chief corpsman who talked the surgeon into letting me take a short walk to stretch and rejuvenate my thoracic muscles. I really feel quite good."

"Your what?" demanded Ted.

"My muscles around here," replied Jerry, pointing at his chest and gut as he did.

"Before I send you back, what's your plan?" asked Mike.

"We're going to use that trawler for our pirate ship, right?"

"Yes."

"Are her trawls still intact?"

"More or less. They're not in very good shape."

"I'm sure they'll do. I learned this trick from a deck ape I knew twenty years ago. He was a minesweeping boatswain's mate—from back when they actually swept mines—and he told me a story that was very informative."

"Out with it, Chief!" Of all the team members, Jerry was the least likely to come up with off-the-wall schemes, but when he did they generally hit the spot.

"As you will see, sir, you're going to need me to pull it off."

"Nobody's indispensable, Chief."

Jerry explained his plan. Mike then called the surgeon to get his real opinion about Jerry's condition. According to the doctor, if Jerry were a civilian, he should be in bed. But since he was in the navy, he could get up, just as long as he avoided heavy lifting and violent motion.

* * *

Mike was standing with Pat Browning, Commander Hartman—*Wake Island*'s XO—the ship's navigator and the rest of the Tridents, next to the tactical display in CIC, when a messenger appeared and handed Browning a sheet of paper.

"This is it," said Browning. "ComFifthFleet has designated me the officer in tactical command of this drama and attached the destroyer *Charles L. Dodgson* to our pirate squadron. You sure you want it this way, Mike? You should really be the OTC, you're quite a few numbers senior to me."

"If this thing works, I'll be boarding *Eastern Trader* and in no position to exercise command. You'll be a great tactical commander. And if something goes wrong, they'll know just who to call about it."

"Thank you."

"To review," continued Mike, "Captain Fuentes, Anderson and I will be leading the boarding party while Chief Andrews will be with the pirates working his miracles. Ms. Mahan, much to her disgust, will be left behind in your CIC, where she'll attempt to keep our communications straight and fend off any interlopers—such as the Agency."

Alex gave him a thumbs-up. The truth was that her leg still hurt, and she was willing to miss out on some of the fun. This time.

"Chief, the LCM is loaded and waiting for you, so you'd best head off. You've got a lot of work ahead of you."

"I'm on my way, Captain. Good luck."

"Good luck to all of us."

* * *

Rob Rhodes stood on the trawler's tiny bridge and hung on as *Ina Boqor* pitched and rolled in the Monsoon chop. Although his rusty command was under way again after the engine had been repaired, she was almost stopped as she waited for the LCM to come alongside her. Rhodes watched the boat approach and felt even more out of the loop than ever. So far, nobody had explained where they were now going. Or why. And the boat was filled with a ragtag group of black guys in filthy shirts and trousers. For a moment he assumed they were the pirates Captain Chambers had carted off a few hours ago. Why the hell were they being sent back to him? He had no way of guarding them. Then he recognized some of them. They were petty officers from *Wake Island*. They were the petty officers you went to when you wanted something done right. Leaving a boatswain's mate on the helm, he climbed carefully down a wobbly ladder to the main deck.

"Mr. Rhodes, my name is Andrews, Chief Boatswain's Mate Gerald Andrews, and this is Chief Hopkins." As he spoke, Jerry pointed at one of his disreputable-looking companions. "Chief Hopkins is not only a boatswain's mate, but as a young man, he sailed in a shrimper for a while. I bring orders, explanations and apologies from Captains Chambers and Browning." As Jerry spoke, Rhodes couldn't help but notice that Chief Hopkins and another petty officer were helping him over from the landing craft to the trawler.

"That's quite an opening line, Chief. Are you sure you're all right? You don't look well. Aren't you the chief who was injured in that gunfight that none of us are supposed to know about off Ras Xaafuun?"

"I got careless, sir."

Rhodes looked at him, then laughed. "Welcome to my ship, Chief. And what the hell's going on? What's the story on the costumes?"

"You're going to love it, sir. And I've brought along costumes for you and Chief Clarke. Along with some face paint for the three of us."

While Jerry explained the plan to Rhodes and Clarke, Hopkins supervised the two crews—the original one and the pirates who had arrived with Jerry—as they unloaded sections of lightweight ceramic armor and a variety of weapons, including several shoulder-fired missiles. The LCM was cast off, and the crews then set to work positioning the armor to make small "bunkers" in the engine room, in a portion of the cabin and in the small cubicle under the fantail that housed the trawler's steering gear. Several hours later the trawler, which had once again taken station behind *Wake Island*, slowed to receive the returning LCM. The original crew jumped aboard and returned to *Wake Island*, leaving Rhodes and his new crew of ill-dressed pirate petty officers following and wallowing in the big amphibian's wake while they gritted their teeth at the trawler's smell and incessant leaks.

* * *

Colonel bin-Sharif stood amidships on *Eastern Trader*'s main deck and watched as one of his men—standing far forward on the bow—pitched an empty paint can over the side. "Ready," he said to the commando standing beside him. The man, his M-16 already raised, nodded. He then opened fire and with two shots sank the can.

"Well done."

In a few days this long trek would come to an end, thought bin-Sharif, and all was going very well. Since they'd left Mumbai, they had only seen two ships—neither any closer than the horizon. The waters that lay directly ahead, especially the Gulf, did have him a little on edge, but he was far from alarmed. Both the threat of pirates and the threat posed by the Joint Task Force—none of whose governments would look kindly on his mission—had been considered from the start, and neither had been considered an insurmountable problem. The Somalis, in his opinion and that of Prince Saeed, were little more than larcenous children, and the Western governments were still hopelessly addicted to the Kingdom's oil. They might say this or that, but he was certain they would not dare interfere with his operation.

Bin-Sharif turned and looked forward, nodding at the man on the forecastle. "Ready," he then said to the next commando.

* * *

As the sun set behind it, *Wake Island*'s strange little formation continued to steam northeast, its speed controlled by that of the trawler. Of the one thousand officers and enlisted sailors aboard the amphibian, and the eight hundred embarked marines, only maybe two dozen fully understood the ship's current mission. Almost all, however, were desperate to know why they were hanging out with the ugly, smelly little boat that was following them.

"I hope Jerry's still okay," remarked Ted as he and Ray played poker in the team's quarters.

"I'm sure he is. If not we would have heard."

"That boat's a pigpen. It'd make anybody sick."

"Amen to that."

"He'd damn well better remember that chiefs aren't supposed to do hard manual labor. They're paid to supervise and shout at people. I think he may have developed some bad habits by hanging around with us."

"The man's all-navy. He's not going to forget the important stuff."

"I'm really looking forward to seeing him in blackface. It'll be a totally new Jerry."

"I'm not sure how well he's going to be able to pull off the ethnic bit. He's such a plain-vanilla gringo. You do know where he's originally from, don't you?"

"Minnesota. But they're not going to get that close a look unless something goes really wrong."

"Right. Full house. Beat it."

"I can't."

Ray looked at his watch. "Be back in an hour or so."

"Where are you going?"

"Mass."

"Good man. May I use your cards while you're gone, to get in a little solitaire?"

"Fine, but don't you dare mark them."

"Captain!"

After watching Ray walk out the door, Ted spent the next twenty minutes carefully scrutinizing the cards to make sure Ray hadn't already marked them himself.

*　*　*

"Mr. Rhodes plans to pass them on our port side, right?" asked Chief Hopkins as he adjusted the four-legged chain bridle on one of the otter boards—the big, wood doorlike hydroplanes that, when properly rigged, "flew" like kites through the water, at an angle, holding the mouth of the trawl net open.

"Affirmative," replied Jerry, who was sitting on a hatch

with his back resting on the trawl winch. His guts felt a little shaky, but he wasn't about to mention that, not even to another chief boatswain's mate. It sounded too much like whining. "You think that gear's going to hold up?"

"It's a total mess, though I've seen worse, I suppose. The bridles on the boards are almost totally rusted through and the wires are badly pitted, but it should all hold together long enough for our purposes. You okay?"

"Tired. I have a few aches, but I'll make it another day."

With that, the two became aware of a gentle but noticeable grinding sensation. Then the engine's beat changed radically and the trawler almost sighed as she slowed.

"Goddamn it!" growled Chief Clarke as he burst out of the deckhouse door, next to the ladder to the engine room, his walkie-talkie in hand.

"What's the problem, Chief?" asked Jerry.

"I can't hear myself think down there and Mr. Rhodes can't understand a word that I say."

"What's that noise?"

"Damn bearing. I've got McGill down there pouring oil over it, but we can't keep it up forever." He then concentrated on the walkie-talkie.

"Aye, sir, I've already slowed way down. We're going to have to stop again. . . . We don't have time to request permission, Mr. Rhodes. . . . Thank you, sir."

"You going to be able to fix it?" asked Chief Hopkins.

"I can fix anything so it'll last at least a few hours. That's all we need, right? A few more hours?"

Jerry nodded. "Aren't you glad to be part of our team now?"

"You warned me that you guys find yourselves up to your asses in politics," replied Clarke. "You said nothing about this sort of shit, although I suppose I should have guessed."

"You want out?"

"Of course not! Don't pay any attention to my sour expression. I don't like abused engines. Otherwise, I haven't had this much fun in years."

The engineer then disappeared back down the hatch to prepare for surgery on the ailing bearing.

* * *

It didn't take Ibrihim long to discover that Ali had disappeared. Or that since his return from the waters off Ras Xaafuun, he had started acting a little strangely and keeping to himself.

It might be his injuries, thought the clan chief. Or the experience of almost getting killed. But he found neither explanation totally satisfying. Suleiman had been right to be suspicious of him. But where had he gone? As far as the clan chief knew, he had no family anywhere. They were all dead. And he'd lived most of his life in Basalilays. Ibrihim looked around the group of ragged, nervous fishermen assembled before him.

"You," he said, pointing as Salem. "They say he used to live with you. Where has he gone?"

"I don't know, Excellency," replied Salem, quailing. "I haven't spoken to him since Suleiman called for him. Once he joined the gang, I was of no interest to him."

Ibrihim scowled distrustfully at him a moment then turned to Osman. "He worked for you."

"Yes, Excellency, but I know little about him except that he was lazy and stupid and if I didn't watch him carefully he would try to steal from me."

"Are there any boats missing?" demanded Ibrihim.

"No, Excellency," replied Osman nervously. "None that I know of." The old fisherman then looked around at the others, who nodded no, hoping to avoid attracting attention to themselves.

So where has he gone? repeated Ibrihim mentally. The answer was clear. He'd gone to rejoin the Americans. After they'd sunk the boat and murdered Mohamed and the rest of the crew, they must have rescued the boy and bribed him to join them. Then they would have put him ashore again, probably on Ras Xaafuun.

Had he returned to Ras Xaafuun? It made sense. But the Americans might have arranged to pick him up anywhere along the coast. Or even inland, using a helicopter.

"Are any cars or trucks missing?" he asked of nobody in particular.

The fishermen all nodded no, carefully looking at one another rather than at Hassan.

He could have gone in any direction, thought Ibrihim, but the odds are that he went north. The clan chief turned to Nasser—who, much to his personal glee, had not sailed with Suleiman on this particular expedition—and told him to send out parties in all directions. And to send twice as many men to the north than to the west or south. The boy was on foot. How far could he get?

12

"That damn engine going to make it for another twelve hours, Chief?" asked Rob Rhodes as he, Chiefs Andrews and Clarke and a helmsman were all jammed into the trawler's tiny, darkened pilothouse.

"One way or another, sir." Clarke sighed. "We'll just keep patching and whatever."

"Good."

Rhodes sniffed the air and realized that he and his crew already smelled as bad as the trawler did.

"And you're all set with the trawl, Chief Andrews?"

"Aye, sir. Chief Hopkins has it all rigged to fly to port. He's a little concerned about how deep it'll fly, but he thinks it'll be okay."

"Good."

The sun hadn't yet made its appearance, but the wind had, building four-foot seas into which the trawler's ancient, leaking hull was pounding vigorously and occasionally groaning as tired old trawlers sometimes do. *Wake*

Island's white stern light was visible a hundred yards ahead. The ship herself was still largely invisible, although her immense mass could be sensed if not seen.

It was decision time now for Rhodes. He was far from certain that his "command" would survive even another hour in these seas, and the plan itself required a great deal of faith and some preposterously good luck, but the job had to be done, so it would be. Mike Chambers had just radioed to ask if it was go or no go, and Rhodes now gave him the answer. "Mamacita, this is Sea Queen. All systems go." As he said it, he had to smile at the temporary voice call. According to Chief Andrews, the woman member of their team had come up with it the first time she'd laid eyes on the trawler.

"Roger, Sea Queen. Good luck."

By the time the sun arrived, *Wake Island* was just disappearing over the horizon, and the trawler was on her own, pounding northeast on a course to intercept the ship that might—or might not—have a cargo of illicit nuclear weapons.

* * *

"Damn it, what are they up to?" demanded the pirate czar.

"I know no more than you do," replied Preston Olbrig. "As far as I know, they're still scheduled to bring in those prisoners late tomorrow."

"That's not what Langley says. They say the satellite shows they're headed north, toward Aden. And they've still got that pirate boat with them."

"Sounds like they're headed for that containership Langley alerted us about."

"Yes."

"What does Fifth Fleet say?"

"Nothing. Not to me, anyway."

* * *.

The Sea Dragon hovered over the destroyer *Dodgson*'s helo pad a moment then settled onto the platform, which was itself rising and falling in concert with the seas.

Ray, Ted and the four marines unbuckled their seat belts and headed for the door, following Mike. "Be careful," bellowed the Trident CO. "None of you will be of any use with a twisted ankle or a broken nose."

"Unload the gear," he then instructed Ray, while he climbed down a short ladder to the main deck, where Commander W. L Ingram, *Dodgson*'s captain, was waiting for him.

"Welcome, Captain Chambers," said Ingram as he saluted. "I see you had no trouble finding us."

"No. You're right where we hoped you'd be, Captain," said Mike, shouting to be heard above the helo's slowly whooshing blades.

They paused to watch as the helo lifted off. "Up to now your orders have been very clear, sir," said Ingram as they headed into the superstructure, "but I'm still totally in the dark concerning the objective."

"You won't be for long if you'll collect up your XO. It might be best if we meet in your quarters, since there are one or two things only you two need to know at the moment. Meanwhile, do you mind if my people join yours for lunch?"

"Our pleasure, sir. What about you?"

"I'd love something. After our chat."

Once the XO had appeared in Ingram's office, Mike got right down to it: "I'm going to give you the most sensitive part first because that's the reason for the whole drill—there's a Greek-flagged containership named *Eastern Trader* about two hundred miles to the northeast of us at the moment. We have good reason to believe she's carrying a battery of Topol nuclear missiles for delivery to the Saudis. We also have good reason to believe it's protected by a very efficient security group—probably Saudi commandos."

"Isn't it highly risky for the Russians to give nukes to the Saudis?" asked the XO.

"The Agency guesses that it's not the government, at least not directly. They think it's the new Russian capitalists working with the government."

"A public-private partnership, sir?"

"That's one way to put it."

Ingram glanced at his XO, then at Mike, wondering just how much of a sense of humor the mysterious captain really had.

"If we were sure the missiles are there, we'd just steam up, tell them to heave to, and board," continued Mike, "but we're not totally sure and we don't want to piss the Saudis off—for obvious reasons—so we're going to have to con our way aboard."

"Interesting," mumbled the XO.

"About a hundred miles to the west is an ancient Somali trawler. Up until two days ago it belonged to a gang of pirates. Now it belongs to the United States Navy and is manned by us, although you wouldn't believe it from looking at it. It still looks for all the world like the Somalis are running it."

Ingram started to smile. "You're going to have your gang of pirates attack the containership? But if these commandos are as good as you suggest, how do you plan to capture it?"

"We don't. The pirates will only disable the ship, then you'll come rushing to its rescue and drive the pirates off.

After that, I and my team will board to render assistance and, while we're there, snoop a little."

"They may tell you to go to hell, sir," offered the XO.

"There are several holes in the plan, and that's one, but if we do manage to disable them, it'll be very difficult for them to shoo us off, and they certainly won't start shooting, not if you're sitting there with a big smile on your face."

"When, sir?"

"The curtain will rise at dawn, tomorrow."

"I love it," said Ingram enthusiastically. "I really do get tired of chasing virtual submarines all the time."

"Food, Captain Ingram? Did you mention lunch? We can go over the fine points later."

"Absolutely, sir."

* * *

Ali lay in a small scrub thicket a hundred yards inland of the settlement where the old woman had given him water, and watched as a jeep, its lights swinging from side to side and bouncing over the rocky patch, ground its way past him and down toward the beach.

The old bastard's no fool, he thought as the car stopped at the edge of the beach and two men got out and immediately started walking back toward Basalilays. Then the jeep turned and retraced its path inland, where a narrow track headed north, to Ras Xaafuun. It would undoubtedly wait for him to arrive.

He stood and started to run, hoping to keep the jeep— which continued bouncing and rolling as it picked its way slowly over the ravaged land—in sight as long as possible, hoping to see if it stopped to let off more ambushers or if whoever remained in the car stayed there until they reached Ras Xaafuun. If they did all decide to wait for him to arrive, then he might have a chance. The rock pile was big and it had a lot of places to hide. If they dropped people off along the way, he'd have trouble avoiding them.

* * *

It was still dark when the watch officer aboard *Eastern Trader* called Captain Papadis to report that there was some sort of a small vessel about fifteen miles ahead and it appeared to be on the reciprocal to their course. Papadis, who was in his night cabin, made it out and onto the bridge in seconds. He studied the radar display for a minute or two and then called Colonel bin-Sharif.

"Unless they change course they will be close aboard in an hour, Colonel," remarked the captain while the soldier studied the display. "Do you want me to change course a little? If they then also change course, we will better know their intentions."

The colonel studied the radar, a sneer beginning to form on his thin face. "Unless we turn around completely and run away, they will still be able to close in on us."

"That's true."

His men had made short work of the Malay pirates, and those brigands had a much more fearsome reputation than the Somalis. Indeed, in his mind, the Africans were backward, inept, seagoing muggers whose successes were the result of luck and the timidity of their victims.

"Continue as you are, Captain. I have full confidence in my men. These pirates are timid little men accustomed to firing a few shots and having their victims stop. We will not stop even if they fire one or two rockets. This is a big ship and my men are both dedicated and well trained."

The truth, Papadis suspected, was that the colonel was

still more concerned about the warships that might be patrolling in the area—one of which seemed to be about forty miles to the north—than he was about the pirates. And although Papadis lacked bin-Sharif's seemingly total confidence, he still agreed with the colonel. The objective was to complete the voyage as quickly as possible before some new, totally unexpected complication appeared—as complications often seemed to do just when you thought you had everything under control.

* * *

Forty miles to the north of *Eastern Trader* Mike Chambers stood in *Dodgson*'s CIC and saw much the same reality that Papadis saw, although he knew what it meant. The containership was charging west at sixteen knots. The trawler was struggling east at eight or nine knots, and the destroyer was loitering, waiting to step in and play her role as the rescuer of the damsel in distress.

"The boat and the boarding party are on station, Captain." Mike looked up at Ray's red-tinged face. He looked tense. Everybody who understood what was happening looked tense. "Thank you, Ray."

"Let's hope Jerry can pull it off."

"Let's hope Mr. Rhodes's first command doesn't disappear in a hail of gunfire."

"Or doesn't just spring a leak and sink," offered the marine. "At the worst possible moment."

* * *

Everybody who knew her knew that Alex Mahan never got excited and never lost her cool. As the sun rose over the Somali coast, however, Alex was fidgeting with the zipper on her coveralls and wondering if she should take up smoking while she watched the drama develop on the satellite display in *Wake Island*'s CIC. Feeling the need for action, she stood and started to pace, dragging her high-tech cast slightly behind her. Thanks to her inattention, it snagged on a chair and sent her crashing to the deck. A flurry of action followed as the CIC watch officer and three others helped her up and to a chair. "Does it hurt?" asked the watch officer, assuming it did and knowing that his question probably sounded stupid. You just don't ask special operations people if their leg hurts, even if it's lying on the deck in two pieces.

"Yes," admitted Alex through clenched teeth.

"You two, get her down to sick bay," he said, nodding at two sailors.

"No. I can't leave now."

"But you probably tore up your leg again."

He's right, she thought, I probably did. But it only feels a little worse than it did before. "You're going to need me in a few minutes, once the action starts," she informed him in a slightly shaky voice.

He looked at her skeptically.

"Anyway, it's really only a throb. No sharp pains. I'll be okay."

"Okay," he agreed reluctantly. He'd never figured out if these special ops types really were made of steel or if they faked a lot. Or if they were just plain stupid.

* * *

While Mike, Ray and Ted had spent a comfortable—if uneasy—night aboard *Dodgson*, Jerry, Rob Rhodes, Chief Hopkins and their crew of navy-approved pirates had not spent the same aboard their boat. The trawler had rolled and pounded all night. They were severely shorthanded, so Rhodes had spent the entire time on the helm, while most of the others had devoted the dark hours to babying the engine and keeping the bilge pumps running. Jerry and Chief Hopkins, when not helping in the bilges, had spent their time measuring, remeasuring and checking the fittings on the ancient trawl.

Shortly after dawn, Rhodes, who'd been growing a little groggy, snapped alert when he spotted the container-ship's high green bow growing out of the dim horizon. Ahead and slightly to port. Oh my god! he thought. We're right in position.

"Chief Andrews, Chief Clarke," he practically shouted into his walkie-talkie, "the target's in sight. Make all your final preparations and get all hands into the bunkers."

"Roger."

"Roger."

"Doty," he said a half hour later to the first-class boat-swain's mate who was sitting on a stool in the corner of the pilothouse, "this is it. Take the helm while I get to the steering flat. When I tell you I'm on station, get yourself down to the bunker in the cabin and get ready."

"Aye, sir."

Rhodes sprinted down the ladder to the main deck then aft along the fantail, dancing around the trawl net, boards and wires, all of which were laid out on the open deck. Having managed to avoid tripping, he jumped down into the steerage flat, a small compartment with at most five feet of headroom located all the way aft, under the fantail. Within the compartment was the steering quadrant—the device that connected the rudder to the steering cables that led to the pilothouse—along with a second-class boat-swain's mate named Jenkins, who was sitting on the deck holding a steel tiller that was secured directly to the rudder post.

"Nice to see you, Mr. Rhodes," said Jenkins.

Rhodes squatted down to talk to him. The space was

small and stifling and the bulkheads were covered with damp rust. He could appreciate the petty officer's discomfort. "Always a pleasure, Jenkins. Ready?"

"Aye, sir."

Rhodes then stood up so that his head was about a foot above the fantail deck. Although he was unable to see directly ahead—thanks to the presence of the deckhouse—he could see reasonably well out to the two sides.

"Doty," called Rhodes, "we're on station. Now get the hell below."

"You have control?" he asked Jenkins a moment later.

"Yes, sir."

Now it was up to him. "A little to starboard," he directed. With a grunt, Jenkins pulled the tiller toward him, and after a moment the trawler's bow edged over to the right.

"Midships."

"Midships, aye."

After the trawler had steadied up and he was convinced that he and Jenkins had control, Rhodes turned back onto the course that would lead to a close port-to-port passing. Unless the containership changed course.

Good, goddamn it, he thought, trying not to hold his breath. The target was right where he wanted her to be— slightly off to port and coming fast.

"Chief, you and Chief Hopkins stream that secret weapon of yours," he shouted when *Eastern Trader* was about a mile away. "Then get into that bunker."

Calmly, methodically, Chief Hopkins tossed the drogue over the stern. It paid out a short distance then started dragging the net after it. As the mouth of the net approached the stern Hopkins carefully tripped the otter boards from their storage frames. "Pay out slowly, Chief," he shouted at Jerry, who was at the winch controls. "Keep your head down, Mr. Rhodes," continued Hopkins, "while the wires take a strain."

Rhodes glanced to each side at the wires as they started to dance then hop up into the air and suddenly become rigid, quivering slightly as they ran from the winch, two feet over his head and out through the stern blocks

Hopkins stood and studied both the trawler's wake and the behavior of the tow wires. Almost as soon as they disappeared below the choppy surface, the boards started to "fly" like horizontal kites, dragging the whole assemblage off to port.

"Looks good, Chief," said Hopkins, standing with his hands on his hips. "Even the depth looks right. These things can be unstable at times, but I think we've got it right."

"Damn it, Hopkins, get the hell over here, under cover," shouted Jerry, who'd already left the winch and crawled into the bunker.

"I'm coming, although it ain't much of a chief's club you've got there."

With the two vessels meeting at a combined closing speed of about twenty-four knots, it was all over in a few minutes.

One minute after Hopkins crawled into the bunker, Colonel bin-Sharif's men opened fire. With M-16s at first, raking the trawler's empty decks and punching holes in the superstructure. Then, with a *woosh* and an immense *boom*, they fired a missile into the pilothouse—which bulged and essentially burst at the seams—causing the whole boat to shudder.

Having abandoned all hope of living through the day, Rhodes watched as the containership's high, flaring bow raced past, and all he could see were her rust-spotted, wall-like sides. The colonel's men then added hand grenades to the concert.

While the commandos showered the trawler with gun-fire and hand grenades, Rhodes continued right along the containership's side, praying that he didn't get shot. "Left full rudder," he shouted as calmly as he could to Jenkins, who immediately shoved the tiller over. The trawler turned sharply to port right under *Eastern Trader*'s counter, drag-ging the trawl toward the containership's rudder and pro-peller.

As the trawler crossed the containership's stern, Doty and another petty officer who were sheltering in the super-structure bunker, stood and fired two antitank rockets into the counter, hoping to hit the containership's steering flat and disable her steering mechanism. Just in case the trawl failed to catch anything.

The extra precautions didn't prove necessary, for just as the rockets were fired, Jerry noticed the trawl wires jump as if they were fishing lines with a fish striking.

"Damn it, Chief, we've caught the son of a bitch," Hop-kins said exultantly. A second later the wires jerked up out of the water, now as rigid as bars of steel. The trawler staggered and the winch started shuddering.

Crack. Crack. Jerry had flicked a toggle switch on a small hell box, firing two explosive cutters, cutting the tow wires.

Her superstructure burning and still under heavy fire, the trawler continued past *Eastern Trader*'s stern and scrambled away, not stopping until she'd put a mile be-tween herself and her now-crippled quarry.

"Any casualties?" asked Rhodes—who was miracu-lously uninjured—over the walkie-talkie. As he spoke, he realized he was shaking. The adrenaline in his system must already be crashing, he thought.

"One man in the deckhouse," reported Chief Clarke. "He was hit in the leg, but we've got it under control."

"Chief Andrews?"

"We're good here, sir."

Rhodes then looked again at the containership. He could see she was slowing. Her course also seemed to be wobbling, as if her steering was damaged.

We did it, he thought. "You stay here," he said to Jenkins, "in case we have to get under way again."

"Can I get some fresh air, sir?"

"Of course. Stand where I've been standing. Just be ready to steer with your feet if necessary." Rhodes then jumped out of the hatch and started forward to see if the pilothouse was worth saving. He stopped to congratulate Jerry and Chief Hopkins. Then, as he turned to continue forward to report to Mamacita, there was a sickening crack and rumble that ran through the whole trawler.

* * *

When Andreas Papadis first realized the pirate trawler was going to pass close aboard his port side, he, like Colonel bin-Sharif, assumed the attackers would attempt to put grapnels over and pull themselves up them. When the trawler failed to slow—or to turn to parallel *Eastern Trader*'s course, he began to have his doubts. The vessels would pass too fast for the grapnels to be useable. Only when the trawler had reached his ship's bow did he realize that she was towing something. A split second later a vague suspicion formed in his mind. He started to open his mouth to order the shaft stopped, and to warn bin-Sharif, but it was already too late. He gritted his teeth, certain that disaster was within seconds of striking.

* * *

Ali continued to run long after the jeep's taillights had disappeared into the night. As long as he didn't see the lights, they hadn't stopped to let anybody off, he assured himself. So he ran, frequently tripping in the dark, painfully bruising his arms and face.

Several hours before dawn he realized that the great, dark bulk of Ras Xaafuun was filling the sky to the north. He stopped, panting and aching, and tried to reach out with his eyes into the night. As he looked, he listened, but all he could hear was the sound of the wind roughly caressing the rock and sand.

Were they out there, waiting for him?

They must be, but where?

He crept forward, desperate to get his wheezing, rasping breathing under control. He froze when he thought he saw motion over on the beach. How many were there? Where else were they?

With every one of his senses as alert as those of a hunted fox, Ali worked his way slowly north, thankful there was no moon. Several hours before dawn he finally scrambled over the edge of the ravine in which he thought he'd hidden the EPIRB. Panting, shaking, his mouth even drier than the surrounding wastelands, the boy collapsed into the ravine then started to crawl around, looking for the beacon.

He was certain he'd buried it next to a large rock on the south side of the ditch, fifty-three paces from the ocean. After a half hour of desperate scrambling the length of the ravine—stopping frequently to crawl up and look out over the edge—he still hadn't found it. Neither the EPIRB nor the rock. Only when the first gray light of dawn began to surround him did he guess that he was in the wrong ravine. Desperate now and cursing—but taking care not to blaspheme Allah—he stuck his head up again and spotted another ravine about two hundred yards to the north. He paused, looking for any sign of Ibrihim's men, and not seeing or hearing any, he crawled over the edge and staggered to the next ditch, his breath rasping down his bonedry throat into lungs that felt as if they were made of crumbling concrete. Once again he tumbled over the edge and slid to the bottom.

Allah be praised! There was the rock. He was sure of it. He crawled over to it and looked for where he'd buried the device but could find no evidence of digging. The wind must have smoothed the sand. He started to dig where he remembered digging—and found nothing. Could somebody have found it?

No. Impossible.

He dug next to where he'd just dug and, a foot below the surface, came upon the little yellow transmitter. He grabbed it and sat back, holding it to his breast and telling Allah just how much he really did love him. Then he flicked the toggle switch, took a deep breath of relief as the light came on and lay back to wait, hoping the ravine would provide cover for at least a while. He was convinced that if the Americans didn't arrive soon, he'd be dead. From thirst or at the hand of Ibrihim Hassan.

* * *

"Cease fire," snapped Colonel bin-Sharif into his communication unit. For the first time since the colonel had walked aboard, Captain Papadis saw what he thought was true emotion on his face. The colonel was angry.

"Something's wrong. What has happened?"

"They've damaged our steering system. I've ordered the engine stopped."

"Those explosions?"

"Yes. I think they've also wrapped something around the rudder. That trawler was towing something as she passed us."

"Have you sent somebody to check?"

"Yes. Two engineers are going to the steering flat right now."

"And what about the rudder?"

"I've already tried to turn it manually and it is partially jammed."

"Allah!"

Papadis now recognized another new emotion on bin-Sharif's face. Mixed in with the arrogance was a hint of fear. What, he wondered, would happen to the colonel if the ship was taken? Papadis might lose his job, but he was just a hired hand—they'd never even told him what was in the containers. But bin-Sharif bore the ultimate responsibility for protecting the ship—or the cargo. It was he who would truly pay the price for failure.

The phone buzzed and Papadis answered it. "Yes? . . . I see. . . . Very well. Do what you can. I will send help."

"What is it?"

"There's a fire in the steering flat. They can do nothing about the hydraulic system until the fire is out." The captain then picked up the phone again and ordered the fire party mustered and sent aft to the steering flat.

The colonel picked up a pair of binoculars and focused on the trawler. "They're on fire. Probably also afraid to continue the attack because we're too strong, so they sit like the carrion eaters they are and wait. They must be expecting their friends." It seemed to Papadis that the colonel was trying to reassure himself.

"Or they are too busy attempting to save their ship."

"Lieutenant," said the colonel into his communicator, "the ship's steering has been damaged. We must stop until we know more. Be prepared for an attack at any time. Keep the men alert. And remind them that the ship is not to be taken by anybody. And when I say that, I do not mean that I merely expect them to fight to the death if necessary. I mean that they are not to allow the ship to be taken."

* * *

Even though she was a hundred miles from the action, Alex knew what was happening. It was all right there on the satellite display. The circle that was the trawler had passed alongside that of the containership a few minutes before. For an instant they'd merged, then they'd separated again, and now the containership appeared to be stopped. Jerry's part of the game was over, and it was now up to Mike, Ray and Ted to somehow pull off the second half. Somehow.

"Ms. Mahan." It was Reynolds.

"Yes?"

"This message just came in for Captain Chambers."

He handed her the sheet of paper.

Oh God! she thought as she scanned it, then read it again. The EPIRB they'd given the Somali kid had been activated. He wanted to be picked up. Probably had to be picked up, she guessed. But everybody was off playing pirates and couldn't be interrupted.

Everybody but her. She glanced again at the message. As she expected, the beacon was transmitting from Ras Xaafuun, probably where the kid had left it the night Ray and Mike dropped him off. *Wake Island* was about four hundred and fifty miles east of that location. Within range of one of the amphibian's Sea Dragons, although they wouldn't have much fuel to spare.

"I have to see Captain Browning right away. Where'd he be? On the bridge?"

"If he's not here at a time like this, he'll be on the

bridge." Reynolds checked. "Yup, he's there. Should I tell him you're on your way?"

"Yes."

* * *

"It's as bad as I had feared," reported Papadis to the colonel after he received the report from the fire party. "Our steering system has been disabled. We are unable to steam on our own. We will have to request a tug."

"Get a Saudi tug."

"We need a powerful salvage tug, and as far as I know the Kingdom does not possess any. The only one I know of is Dutch. It's homeported in Djibouti."

"If we must."

"We must also request a warship. The tug will not come unless it is confident that it will be protected."

The colonel felt a sudden tightening across his chest. The situation was rapidly progressing from being just out of control to being totally out of control. He would not panic, however. There was nothing the Somali scum could do that couldn't be dealt with. Papadis was right, as far as his knowledge permitted him to be. But there were still actions that could be taken. The ship's cargo would not be revealed or captured. It was just that simple.

"Very well. Send out an SOS."

* * *

Alex found Pat Browning standing next to the satellite display on the bridge. "It looks to me like your boss managed to pull off the first phase of this operation. I just hope it didn't cost any of those fake pirates I provided. They're the best I have, which is probably why they seem to be so good at piracy. I wish Rhodes would report the status there."

"Yes, sir."

"How's your leg and what can I do for you?"

"As I think Mike mentioned, we left a specially pro-grammed EPIRB with a Somali kid—one of the pirates—who's been working for us. That beacon's been activated, which means he wants out. Or has to get out."

"Where's the beacon now?"

"Ras Xaafuun."

Browning studied the display a moment. "A Sea Dragon can make it. It might be a little tight. Like every-body, though, I'm a little allergic to sending my helos too close to shore, let alone landing and trying to pick up somebody. Is this kid really worth it?"

"I think we have to, sir. We've made promises and he's provided the goods."

"Is Mike going to want to be consulted?"

"He is, but I'm worried that we don't have time. He's undoubtedly concentrating on boarding the container ship."

"This could be a trap, you know. Or maybe some kid found it and started playing with it."

Alex sighed. "That's all possible, but Ali was told to hide it carefully."

"He may have given it to them."

"Yes, sir. I can't deny any of that."

Browning studied her a moment, then looked out over the Indian Ocean.

"Very well. Mike seems to have a lot of confidence in you. I can get a bird up in twenty minutes."

"Thank you, sir. Please ask them to wait for me."

"You've got a broken leg."

"I know the kid and nobody else aboard does. And I assure you I'm not going to do anything stupid. I tripped on a chair leg a few hours ago, and it hurt too much for me to repeat the performance."

"We're all big boys and girls, aren't we? Good luck. If promises were made, then they should be kept."

"I just hope I'm not engineering another disaster."

"If you are, you'll be right there to enjoy it firsthand."

13

"Trident, Mamacita, this is Sea Queen. Attack successful. Target now dead in the water. Prior to stopping, target's steering appeared erratic."

"Roger, Sea Queen," replied Captain Ingram, a big smile on his face.

"Be further advised," continued Rhodes, "that Sea Queen has one injured, not life-threatening. I say again, not life-threatening. Also be advised that Sea Queen is on fire and taking water. Currently stopped one mile from target. Request you arrest us as soon as possible. All hands consider manacles preferable to water wings."

"Roger," acknowledged Ingram. "Am heading for your position at slow speed. As soon as we receive an SOS, we will increase speed."

"And if they don't send an SOS?"

"We'll increase speed anyway."

"Rhodes has quite a sense of humor," he then said to Mike.

"He does. Pat Browning, CO of *Wake Island*, chose him, and I think he chose very well." Let's just hope he's not too good, thought Mike, too stiff upper lip. The thought of arriving and finding his personal crew of pirates swimming with the sharks was not attractive.

"Bridge, this is Comm," blared a speaker on the bulkhead. "We have just received an SOS from the containership *Eastern Trader*."

"Roger," replied Ingram. "Tell them we're on our way."

"If you would, Captain," said Mike, "please prepare your motor whaleboat to go arrest the pirates. I'll use the rubber boat to board the containership."

"Aye, aye, Captain."

"Ray?" said Chambers, turning to the marine.

"Ted and I have already rigged the inflatable and briefed the crew. A few asked what we're going to do if they tell us to fuck off. I told them we'll think of something. They're good men. That seemed to satisfy them."

* * *

No matter how hard Ali tried to hide from it, the rising sun still managed to find him. For a while the edge of the ravine protected him. For a few minutes the big rock protected him. Now there was no place left to hide. No trees. No caves. Nothing.

He lay at the edge of the ditch, scanning the flat sand-and-rock surface that stretched in all directions, alert for the slightest sign of Ibrihim and his men. The only motion, besides the glittering of the sun on the breaking waves, was a hawk, high in the sky, looking for breakfast. Ali tried to forget his thirst. He couldn't forget his growing fear that the Americans would never come. Where were they? Usually they were close by, watching and waiting.

Were they still close by, watching and waiting for him to get caught or to die of thirst?

He couldn't bear to believe it, yet he was beginning to suspect he had no choice. Should he stand up and shout for Ibrihim's men? Tell them to come and get him? How would that help? If he stayed where he was, he would soon die of thirst. If he gave himself up, there was a very good chance Ibrihim would hack him up a little and then leave him out in the sun to die slowly.

Allah!

* * *

"You mind if I stick this thing here?" asked Alex as she shoved her cast in beside the Sea Dragon's pilot's seat.

"No, that's fine," said the pilot. "I'm O'Brien. The co-pilot is Fiske. And the big guy back there," he added, pointing his thumb over his shoulder, "the cabin attendant, is Martin. And you're Ms. Mahan?"

"Right. Alex, if you wish. Thanks," said Alex as she tried to settle back into the third chair in the cockpit, the one installed for the use of a flight commander when one was aboard.

"All comfy?"

"If you have an imagination."

"Okay. Let's head out." With that, O'Brien goosed the throttle, and the engine's quiet roar became deafening as the gray and blue helo rose, the sun glinting off its sides. Within seconds *Wake Island*'s flight deck was falling far below and the six smaller helos lined up on it looked more and more like toys.

Once clear of the ship, O'Brien turned west toward Ras Xaafuun. "This is a long flight, even for a Dragon," he remarked. "Can you swim with that thing on?"

"They told me it's fully waterproof to three meters, but I'd rather not have to test it."

"Roger. You ever been where we're going?"

"Cruised by a couple nights by boat but never set foot ashore."

"Let's just hope you don't get your chance today."

"I plan to stay aboard and cheerlead."

* * *

With a bone in her teeth and her steaming ensign snapping smartly in the breeze, *Dodgson*—being the good beat cop she was—managed to reach the victim of the piratical mugging in less than ninety minutes. Commander Ingram slowed from the thirty knots they'd been making, then stopped a hundred yards from *Eastern Trader*, directly between the smoldering pirate wreck and the containership.

"Now away the assistance party," instructed the PA system. Mike and his lightly armed team climbed down into the inflatable and headed off, bouncing across the waters between the destroyer and *Eastern Trader*, which had already lowered a Jacob's ladder.

"Now away the boarding party," boomed the speakers as soon as Mike was clear. The ship's motor whaleboat—filled with a heavily armed party—was immediately launched and headed, pitching and rolling as it went, for the trawler.

"Captain Michael Chambers, United States Navy," said Mike after climbing the ladder and swinging his leg over the containership's bulwark.

"Andreas Papadis," said *Eastern Trader*'s captain, saluting as he did.

Despite an unfortunate shortness of breath from the long, swaying vertical climb, Mike breathed a silent sigh of relief. Nobody'd told them to fuck off. Or shot them. At least not yet.

"Those bastards seem to have done quite a job to you," remarked Mike, pointing at the trawler as he did.

"They've crippled my ship," said Papadis, clearly upset, "but none of my crew has been injured, thank God."

Mike looked around at the crew. Some were young, some were old. Filipinos, he guessed, and some blacks, along with a sprinkling of Greeks and who knows? None seemed particularly alarmed. Or threatening. They stood there occasionally chatting but mostly just waiting.

But not the security guys. They were totally alert and tense, their fingers in the triggers of their weapons. They were ready to act the instant they were told to.

"Captain, you seem to have enjoyed a very ill-fated voyage. I understand you were attacked by pirates in Malacca."

"Yes. Fortunately we have a very effective security group aboard." Papadis paused a moment, then continued. "Let me introduce you to Mr. Sharif, the head of that group."

The colonel stepped forward, his hand outstretched, his eyes boring into Mike's.

This guy's all the proof I need, thought Chambers. He's not a mercenary. He's active duty and probably something of a fanatic. He's the one the security team is waiting for. He'd never be here unless there was something really big aboard.

"I understand you've requested a tug from Djibouti."

"Yes, it should be here in two days."

"Very good. We'll deal with the pirates who attacked you and stand by, just in case some of their friends show up, until the tug arrives."

"Thank you."

"You! What are you doing?"

Mike, Papadis and the colonel all turned and looked forward where one of the security group, his M-16 raised, was running toward Ray and Ted, who were standing near some containers with black boxes in their hands.

"This is very routine, Captain," said Mike, his heart in his throat. He then realized that at least ten more armed men had appeared and were all pointing their weapons at his party. He glanced at Mr. Sharif and was startled by the look of fury on his face.

The son of a bitch knows he's been set up, thought Mike. He might not know precisely how, but he's obviously recognized the result. Was he angry or desperate enough to launch a bloodbath?

* * *

The overcast was nonexistent and the wind was light when the great mass of Ras Xaafuun came into sight.

"We don't know precisely where this guy is, do we?" asked O'Brien as he stared at the barren, rutted headland and the waves breaking along its shore.

"No," replied Alex. "Get as close as you can to the location on the display, and then we have to use our eyeballs. And before we go in, we'd better take a quick look around just to make sure they're no unfriendlies in the area."

"Roger," grunted the pilot as he pulled back on the controls and the helo rose. The possibility of a trap had occurred to all of them but been mentioned by none.

"God, what a sterile pile," remarked Fiske a few minutes later. "I can't see a living thing."

"Keep your eyes opened anyway," said O'Brien.

"I can," said Alex, binoculars to her eyes. "About a mile to the south there's a truck of some sort headed north.

It looks like it's having trouble getting through the rocks and sand."

"You don't want to go in for a closer look, do you?"

"No. We have to assume it's hostile. They must be looking for our passenger."

"Okay," said O'Brien, turning the Sea Dragon to the north.

"If we believe the display, we're here," reported Fiske a moment later.

All eyes scanned the ground.

"I don't see a damn thing," said Alex, her frustration building as her leg started to ache.

* * *

"I order you to leave this ship now," said the colonel, his eyes still blazing.

I knew it would come to this, thought Mike. Obviously they're hiding something.

"I'm afraid I can't," he said, staring back at the colonel. "Both the captain of that destroyer and I have our orders."

Mike waited, expecting the security guys to open fire any second.

The colonel turned and looked at the destroyer then turned back to Mike, a look of resignation on his face. Resignation but certainly not surrender. Still keeping his eyes on Mike, the colonel twisted his head and mumbled something into the microphone clipped to his shoulder.

Mike felt a sharp rumble, followed by another and another and another.

Goddamn it, he thought as the rumbles continued, maybe twenty in all. The bastard was at least one step ahead of him! He'd detonated a chain of scuttling charges. Undoubtedly more than enough to sink the ship. But how fast? Did he have time to sort through hundreds of containers, find the ones of interest and get photographs? From the expression on the security chief's face, and his failure to tell his men to shoot, he clearly didn't think Mike had enough time. And neither did Mike.

"Ray, you and Ted get below and see how much damage has been done."

"Aye, sir."

"I'll show the way," offered the ship's chief mate, who up to now had said nothing.

Even as the inspection party disappeared below, Mike thought he noticed that the ship was beginning to list. He tried to tell himself it was his imagination.

"Trident, this is Eclipse," reported *Dodgson*. "The boarding party reports that it has detained all the pirates and is now heading back to Eclipse. The boarding officer believes the trawler is beyond saving. It is still on fire and taking water badly from a broken back and sprung plates. He estimates it will sink within a few minutes."

"Roger," acknowledged Mike, almost absentmindedly. Damn it, the containership was already listing.

"They've done a damn good job, Captain," reported Ted as he emerged from the hatch a few moments later. "They placed them all along one side and the ship's flooding fast. I think she'll turtle in a half hour. Maybe a little less."

Mike wanted to explode but managed to calm himself. He'd almost gotten his hands on the evidence, but now it was about to disappear into six or seven thousand feet of water, and the whole damn thing would probably turn into a major incident.

But then again, who was in any position to complain? Certainly not the Saudis. When confronted, they would be most eager to finesse the whole matter. Ally to Ally.

The game, he concluded, was essentially over for him and this Mr. Sharif, whoever he really was. It was now a matter of state, and the President himself would probably end up having to do something about it.

But there were still one or two odds and ends left to wrap up and appearances to maintain. "It appears you have lost your ship, Captain," he said to Papadis. "I'd like to offer you and your people the hospitality of the United States Navy."

"Will we be prisoners?"

"I can't imagine why. Greece is a valued ally of the United States, and as far as I know nobody has committed any crime. You've been attacked by pirates and your ship was fatally damaged. I assume you will be treated as is customary with shipwrecked seamen. Either your owners will arrange for everybody's return to home or to some other port, or your consular representative in Djibouti will attend to it."

"Thank you, sir," said Papadis.

"I'll ask the destroyer's captain to come alongside. Tell your people there's no time for them to get any possessions. They must leave with what they have right now."

"Yes."

Something big broke loose below and *Eastern Trader* shuddered from bow to stern.

* * *

"I've got him," reported Fiske. "Down in that ravine. Skinny little guy. He's waving at us. Looks weak."

O'Brien leaned forward to get a better look. "Okay, I see him now. I'll try to land as close to the ditch as possible. Keep a good lookout."

"Roger," replied Fiske.

With that, the helo turned and dove. Then, when it was

only a few feet off the ground, the pilot cut power and settled down with barely a shudder.

"His name's Ali," shouted Alex as Martin threw the door open and jumped out. "And the guy he made the deal with is Ray."

"Does he speak English?"

"A few words. Not really."

"Okay."

Martin nodded then ran to the edge of the ravine and disappeared over the side. A minute later he reappeared, carrying Ali's limp and painfully insubstantial frame under his arm. The airman, dressed as he was in a flight suit and helmet, looked more than a little like an astronaut running across the moon's barren, burned landscape.

"Oh shit!" The copilot groaned, pointing to a low rock outcropping that overlooked their position. A group of a half dozen figures were standing there, pointing weapons at the helo. "How the hell did they get there? They were a couple miles to the south."

"Must be another group, Ace. This country's bad joss for Americans, I guess. No matter what the fuck we do."

Zing! Clang! Puffsh!

"They're hitting us, goddamn it!" shouted O'Brien.

Alex pulled herself erect and, after spinning in the narrow space, dragged her leg aft to the opened door. "Move it," she shouted at Martin. "We're under fire."

Martin, who was already running as fast as he could, didn't bother to respond other than to lean forward and try to run even faster. Suddenly he toppled forward with Ali still under his arm.

"He's down," shouted Fiske as he pulled himself out of his seat and headed for the door, only to run into Alex, who was also heading for the door. "What the hell do you think you can do for him?" demanded the copilot. Alex looked at him a moment then flushed in embarrassment. In her current condition all she could do was make the situation worse.

"He's up again," shouted O'Brien. "Fiske, you get back up here."

Sure enough, Martin, whose right foot had slipped on a flat stone, was up again and running.

"Get him in," shouted O'Brien.

Alex could have screamed with frustration. There was nothing she could do until they reached the door.

Psst. A hole appeared in the helo's side. Then a second. All she could think of was what everybody else had been thinking about all along—the Black Hawk helicopter and its crew that had gone down in Mogadishu ten or fifteen years ago. It had ended up a horror show. A nightmare. And how much worse would it have been if there'd been a woman involved?

Martin staggered to the door. Alex grabbed his shoulders and pulled as he dove through, dragging Ali with him.

"They're in," she shouted just as soon as she thought the three of them were far enough from the door not to disappear out it again.

Cursing to himself, O'Brien revved up and lifted off— generating a huge cloud of dust in the process.

"Ladies and gentlemen," he announced in a somewhat breathless voice several minutes later, as the barren rock pile shrank behind them, "this is a nonstop flight directly to USS *Wake Island.* If that isn't the destination shown on your ticket, you are free to get off at any time."

* * *

Captain Ingram aboard *Dodgson* had heard the multiple detonations and seen the containership shudder and could easily guess what it meant. Mike's call requesting him to come alongside and pick up all hands was, therefore, not a surprise.

"I don't like this one bit," remarked Ingram to his XO as he studied the listing ship and planned his approach. "If we go along her low side, some of those damn containers may fall on us. Or the whole damn ship may roll over us. And the high side's almost as bad—if she does roll, she'll probably bash our bottom in. We're going to edge on up to her stern."

"Aye, sir." That was always a safe response, thought the XO.

"Okay. Have the first lieutenant get those fenders and lines in position." He then picked up the radio microphone and notified Mike that, unless otherwise directed, he would come alongside the containership's stern. Mike concurred.

Creeping ahead, Ingram maneuvered alongside the containership and stopped several feet downwind from the ship's now-angled stern. "Get those lines over but keep them slack," he directed. "And get hold of those man lines they're trying to pass."

"One at a time on each line," Mike reminded the *Eastern Trader*'s crew as hands aboard the destroyer grabbed the man lines. "This will be done in an orderly fashion," he continued as the containership's crew started lining up at the three lines. It took less than ten minutes to transfer *Eastern Trader*'s thirty-six crew members along with the security group across the narrow strip of open water. Most were able to jump, holding on to the man line as they did. A few had to work their way across hand over hand.

"Mr. Sharif," said Mike to the colonel when they and Captain Papadis were the only ones left aboard, "you're next."

The colonel looked at him with a strange expression—

at the time Mike suspected that he was about to refuse to go—but then grabbed the line and lowered himself to the destroyer.

"Captain Papadis?"

"Allow me to be last, sir," said Papadis with a note of sadness in his voice. "I'm quite certain this is my last command."

With Papadis right behind him, Mike grabbed one of the lines and jumped over to the destroyer.

"Cast off!" bellowed Ingram from the bridge.

The destroyer's white nylon lines were retrieved and her fenders taken in and the warship stood off, now carrying the survivors of two vessels—a pirate trawler and a containership.

Mike and Ray watched from *Dodgson*'s bridge as the containership healed farther and farther. There was a sudden screeching, grinding roar, then a half dozen containers broke loose and tumbled into the water. A few minutes later a loud rumble filled the air, followed by a great whooshing sound as air and water erupted all around her. *Eastern Trader* rolled over on her side and more of her stacked containers broke loose and crashed into the foaming blue waters. Some sank immediately; some floated for a few minutes before disappearing tiredly into the Indian Ocean.

In one final effort to retain her dignity, the containership slowly rolled upright as her hull settled, finally disappearing almost on an even keel.

* * *

"More," said Ali in English, still clutching the now-empty container of electrolyte-enhanced fluid as he lay propped up against the helo's side.

"Wait," insisted Alex, who was half sitting, half kneeling in front of him. "I'll give you more in a few minutes. Now I'll work on your arm."

"More. Please."

Alex didn't know if he'd really understood her, so she tried again, in her mangled Arabic.

Ali frowned but still didn't seem to understand, so she tried yet again, changing the accents on some of the words she suspected she might have mispronounced.

Ali stared blankly at her—although he stopped thrusting the container at her—as she finished cutting off his shirtsleeve to examine the wound. Even without looking at the discolored swelling, she knew—by the smell—that there was a serious problem.

"You have any of those antibiotic shots in that kit?" she asked Martin as she tried to clean the wound's exterior without causing too much pain. "The kind you use when you don't really know what the hell you're doing but are certain you need it."

Martin looked in the bag and pulled out a syringe, which he handed her. She quickly stuck it into the boy's arm before he could realize it was headed toward him. She then tried to reposition herself. The way she'd been sitting was growing painful. Feeling slightly more comfortable, she sat back. The helo went on rattling and swaying as it continued to the northeast, toward *Wake Island*, which was now only about an hour away.

"Alex," said O'Brien's voice in her headset, "you remember that fuel leak I mentioned?"

"Affirmative."

"Well, it's just gotten worse. Whatever they hit has broken some more."

What next? thought Alex. "We going to make it back to the ship?"

"No."

"What are our choices? You have a plan?"

"We could ditch at sea and pray, but in my mind that's a nonstarter because practically everybody goes down with the ship when you do that. Or we could try for Socotra Island. It's about sixty miles north. You know anything about it?"

"It's Yemeni and it's some sort of big nature preserve—all sorts of unique plants and animals. Not much of a population, and I don't think they get as many tourists as they might like these days."

"They're going to get five more in a few minutes. If we can make it."

"You're the captain."

"So I am," said O'Brien. He then turned north and notified *Wake Island* of the situation.

"You know Socotra Island, Ali?" asked Alex, again struggling with Arabic.

"Belong to Yemen."

"Yes. We're going to have to land there. We are running out of fuel." She wasn't sure he understood, or even cared for that matter.

"More water."

Alex opened another bag of fluid and gave it to him. She then sat back to wait. Would this be her last helicopter ride? Her last ride of any kind?

* * *

Pat Browning was standing in CIC when the helo's message came in. He looked at the CIC watch officer. "Those passengers of ours seem to get themselves, and their friends, into more trouble than anybody else I know."

"We *are* on speaking terms with Yemen, aren't we, sir? Just in case they make it?"

"As far as I know. I get the feeling Socotra is a little out

of the real political action. I hope so, because we're sending the other Dragon to pick them up, whether the Yemenis like it or not. Hopefully they'll be able to get in and
out before anybody notices they're there. Then maybe
they'll let us go back someday to get what's left of the
helo."

"If they have to ditch over water?"

"I didn't hear you ask that."

Browning called flight ops and told them what he
wanted. He then notified both Fifth Fleet and CTF 151 of
the emergency and asked them to notify the Yemeni government that neither the first nor the second Sea Dragon
had the slightest hostile intent. Not, he figured, that they'd
have time to respond, even if they wanted to, because the
south shore of Socotra—as he understood it—was essentially uninhabited. Finally, he called Mike Chambers
aboard *Dodgson*. Mike, who felt he'd already had a less
than perfect day, cursed. There was nothing else he could
do at the moment.

* * *

"There it is, ladies and gentlemen, directly ahead, the island of Socotra, said to be the garden spot of the Gulf of
Aden." O'Brien and Fiske watched, holding their breath,
as the flat, dry island grew on the horizon. Both expected
the engine to die at any moment, and when it coughed
loudly, neither could resist the temptation to take another
look at the fuel gauge. It continued to show a few dregs,
although neither really believed it.

Alex and Martin, who were in no position to see forward, just held their breath, while Ali still seemed unaware of what was really happening.

And then the suspense came to an end. With a roar the
Sea Dragon shot over the rocky beach and the low beige

cliff behind it. Below lay a rocky plateau, gray brown with a sparse coating of green here and there.

"You see any hostiles?" asked O'Brien.

"Don't see anybody. Just sand and a few flat-headed trees in the distance. And even if I did see hostiles, what the hell would we do about it?"

Concentrating intensely, O'Brien cut power, and the helo, after coughing again, settled down, shrouded in a great cloud of dust. As O'Brien continued to cut power, he exchanged a very long glance with his copilot. "Alex," he said into the intercom, "we're here. The nature walk will be beginning shortly." He then reported their safe landing to *Wake Island*.

"Roger, Zero Nine Seven," replied the ship. "Zero Eight Three is already on its way. ETA your location seven seven minutes."

"Roger."

"Can I open the door? It's already getting hot back here," asked Alex.

"Good plan," replied O'Brien. "I might even get out and stretch my legs a little. This kind of drill always makes me a little tense."

Everybody got out and stretched his or her legs, wandering behind a rock for a little privacy.

"Flight boss is going to be a little pissed about the holes in his helo," offered Martin, who was lying on his back on the rocky sand.

"O'Brien's going to take a little shit about this," Fiske reassured him. "Flight Ops doesn't like excuses—or anything he considers such."

"Okay, Fiske," said O'Brien, "we've got work to do. Get out the inventory of classified stuff. We're going to pack what we can to take with us and burn or trash the rest."

"Roger."

"And, Martin, you can help."

For the next fifteen minutes the helo crew bagged, bashed or burned the limited number of classified documents and devices they'd carried.

"I thought this area was uninhabited," growled Fiske a few moments later after looking out the cockpit window. Alex, who was seated outside the helo, opening another bag of fluid for Ali, looked up.

"Supposed to be. Why?"

"Because somebody's coming. Some sort of SUV."

Everybody but Ali stood and watched the approaching cloud of dust. A Range Rover soon appeared from within it and pulled up next to the helo. A young woman, about Alex's age, climbed out. She was dressed in a khaki uniform and had a sidearm on her hip.

Alex greeted her as best she could in her fourth-grade Arabic. The woman nodded then walked over to the Sea Dragon. Spotting one of the bullet holes in the fuselage, she ran her index finger around it and then stuck the finger in gently. She turned back to Alex. "Welcome to Socotra," she said in American English. "I see the navy has sent you to enjoy the many wonders of our park. Are you the pilot?" Then she started laughing.

"I wish my Arabic were better," said Alex, "and Lieutenant O'Brien is the pilot." As she said it, she pointed at O'Brien, who smiled. "Are you in the army?"

"No," said the young woman after nodding at O'Brien, "although there are several small army installations on the island. I'm a game warden. This is a natural park. We've got all sorts of fascinating stuff here. Stuff that only evolved and survived because this island has been isolated from the mainland for thousands of years. We keep hoping tourists will come, but most people can only get here from the mainland, and Westerners are a little reluctant to travel there at the moment. Not everybody has their own helicopter. And before you ask, I went to school in the United States."

Then her eyes settled on Ali and her smile disappeared. "You *are* the navy, aren't you?"

"Yes."

"Is this boy your prisoner? Are you taking him someplace to interrogate him?"

Alex groaned inwardly. Technically O'Brien was in charge, but he knew very little about Ali or the operation. Furthermore, the game warden seemed to want to deal with Alex. "No, he's been helping us, and now we're trying to get him out of Somalia before some other people get their hands on him." As she said it, she looked at Ali. The kid sure as hell did look as if he'd been tortured.

The game warden started questioning Ali in rapid Arabic, much too fast for Alex to even hope to understand. Ali answered slowly, slurring his words, probably from fatigue. As the Yemeni woman listened, she studied the boy's face intently.

"Okay," she finally said. "He says he was helping you against the pirates and you promised to take him to the United States. He seems to want to go with you, so I'll let you take him and I'll figure out how to explain it later. Somebody *is* coming to get you, aren't they?"

"Yes. Another helicopter should be here in about a half hour. We're going to have to leave this one, though. No gas." Alex looked at the helo. "It's kind of junky, I'm afraid. An eyesore."

"Yes, it is. I'm sure our government will expect you to remove it just as soon as possible. In the meantime I'll keep an eye on it. Make sure nobody steals the hubcaps."

"Thanks."

"I think I see your ride," said the game warden, pointing at the horizon. "And I wasn't kidding about our wanting tourists. If you're into nature, Socotra is a must. You might consider using a different airline, though."

"But I'm a damn good pilot." O'Brien huffed. "I got us down in one piece."

The game warden chuckled. "Maybe I was being too hasty."

14

Pat Browning watched with a great sense of relief as the Sea Dragon, his only remaining airworthy Sea Dragon, settled onto *Wake Island*'s flight deck. Not feeling any particular need to stand on ceremony—he was, after all, the captain—he walked out to the helo while its rotors were still turning and waited for the door to open.

"Welcome home," he shouted as O'Brien appeared and jumped down onto the deck.

"Thank you, Captain. I just wish I'd managed to bring the helo back."

"Don't worry, they won't dock you more than five hundred a month. You'll get it paid for in no time."

Fiske and Martin appeared, helping Alex and Ali out. Browning studied Ali a moment. "This is the kid, eh? Well, the operation itself seems to have been a screaming success. From the look of him we'd better get him to sick bay right away."

"You *were* able to round up a translator, weren't you, sir?" asked Alex.

"Three. Two marines and a petty officer. None are Somalis, but they all speak some kind of Arabic. We'll just have to give each a try and see who can get through."

"Thank God," said Alex. "I've been having a hell of a time."

"And I want you in sick bay too. For a checkup."

"It'll be a pleasure, Captain. About the real pirates?"

"They're all safely locked up with a flock of marine nannies to keep an eye on them."

His hosting work done, Browning gave the helo's pilot a thumbs-up sign then marched up to his bridge to prepare for *Wake Island*'s arrival off Djibouti. The Sea Dragon was refueled and dispatched to pick up Mike and company— including the fake pirates—from *Dodgson*.

* * *

Shortly before midnight the secretary of defense's limo pulled up to the side entrance of the White House. It was a cold night in which the drizzle gave every hint of turning to sleet. After passing through a half dozen checkpoints— and being scrutinized by guards and agents he'd known for at least ten years—he was led up and into the Oval Office.

"Good evening, Mr. President," said SECDEF.

"Good evening, Mr. Secretary," said the President, who was seated behind his desk in shirtsleeves. "Please grab a seat."

SECDEF looked around at the others present—the national security advisor, the director of National Intelligence, the secretary of state. He noted that the guest of honor hadn't arrived yet and that none of the congressional leaders had been called in. It also occurred to him that the President should set the thermostat a little lower.

"While we're waiting for the ambassador to arrive, I'd like to get a better handle on what we can do to get these things back under control. I'm certain your Captain Chambers is correct that they're there, someplace. Especially since the Saudis haven't denied it. Can we do so in six thousand feet of water?"

"A number of years ago the CIA recovered a portion of a Soviet nuclear submarine from eighteen thousand feet in the Pacific."

"Are we equipped to do so now?"

"No. The Agency had to charter an oil drilling ship, totally restructure it and hire contractors to conduct the operation. Today we, the Department of Defense, have even less deep-recovery capability than we had back then. The navy no longer has any significant salvage capability. The whole operation will have to be conducted using remote operated vehicles. We'll have to hire contractors to do it."

"What about security?"

"As a rule, civilian contractors talk more than sailors. As for outside interference . . ."

"How long will this take?"

"Three to six months, if we're lucky. We have to open—or blow a hole in—hundreds of containers. Then, once we've found the ones with the missiles, we have to lift them to the surface."

"How much will it cost?"

"A great deal, sir."

A light on the President's desk blinked. "Here he is now," said the President as the door opened and the Saudi ambassador walked in.

"Good evening, Mr. President," said the ambassador.

"Mr. Ambassador," replied the President, his face showing no evidence of a smile. "I think you know everybody here."

"I do, sir."

"Then let's get right down to business. When I discussed this matter with the king, he said he knew nothing about it. Do you still stand by that position?"

"We do, sir, of course! We are firm believers in nonproliferation. There are far too many nuclear weapons around the world as it is. Even though he was not involved, the king finds this whole matter both disturbing and highly embarrassing. Our investigations have determined that one of the king's more powerful ministers, Prince Saeed, took it upon himself to launch the entire project. By way of background, the prince is a very devout Moslem. There has been some talk that in the past few years he has become too devout, shall we say. Unfortunately, again to our great embarrassment, we failed to act on these hints. Now, of course, he has been detained and is currently being examined to determine the identity of his coconspirators."

"It might be good if our people had a chance to talk to him."

"Of course, I'm sure it can be arranged, although I must warn you that the prince is an old man and not in the best of health."

"What about this Colonel bin-Sharif?"

"We have examined him and are convinced he believed the orders he was executing were lawful. He is a serving officer."

"You do understand that we require that the devices be recovered and destroyed."

"Yes. We will assume full responsibility and attend to it."

"I'm afraid we're going to have to insist on our supervising the operation. It'll be a very expensive one, however, and we will expect you to cover all costs."

"That goes without saying."

"Now, about what we'll say to the media. As you know, I believe in transparency at all times."

"Mr. President, the Kingdom and the United States have a very strong, mutually beneficial relationship. I think we all would hate to see it damaged by the insane stupidity of one man who, to use one of your terms, has proven to be out of control. Clearly, there are lessons to be learned, however."

"We must be totally forthright about this," said the secretary of state. "We must make clear to the world that there was a plot to arm Saudi Arabia with weapons of mass destruction. Weapons they could use against our friends. And ourselves."

"It does not appear that simple to me," replied the ambassador. "If the truth is revealed, then you will be compelled to demand that the United Nations invoke sanctions against us, and who knows where that will end?"

The secretary of state glowered, while the President looked worried.

"Mr. President," continued the ambassador, "this matter has become an affair of state, and the painful truth is that in such affairs you have many fewer options than you probably believed six months ago that you would. Rarely will you find it possible to do what you might very much wish to do."

"What do you suggest?" demanded the President, his anger obvious.

"Very few people know the true circumstances of the ship's sinking. Even fewer know exactly what the cargo was. I propose that the ship was carrying a cargo of spent uranium rods from a Russian reactor that were being sent to the United States for reprocessing, and along the way she was attacked and sunk by pirates. It's clear, it's simple and it's close to the truth."

"And the Russians?"

"They have no more desire than we do for the truth to come out."

The President found himself squirming in his chair. The Saudi ambassador's right, he thought. My options are more limited than I ever imagined.

* * *

"Thanks, Alan," said Mike into the teleconferencer aboard *Wake Island*.

"For what?"

"Following through on Ali. He just left for the hospital at Beaufort, and both Alex and I were impressed by that case officer you sent. She strikes us as a straight shooter and promised to stay with him until he got to that special State Department school."

"Everybody in my office is a straight shooter, Mike. And just remember that while I'm going along with what you say on this, I'm still not totally convinced about the kid. One wrong move and he's going to be facing some real questioning."

"Speaking about questioning, I hear Mandy somehow got her hands on Suleiman within twenty minutes of his arrival at LeMonier."

"The clan chief's son? Of course. I circulated that idea of yours about using him as a conduit to the clan chiefs, but nobody liked it."

"Who's nobody?"

"Nobody. Nobody who matters. Everybody feels that with some rigorous interrogation he's going to tell us a lot about Al Qaeda operations in the Horn of Africa. He knows a lot of movers and shakers through his father. He's going to be a gold mine."

"Who made the decision?"

"That's need to know."

"I think you're barking up the wrong tree."

"What you think doesn't matter. You're off the case now. SECDEF wants you and your crew back in Tampa ASAP. There are a couple new situations developing."

"Thanks."